C000173424

I Will Not Kill:

Whatever the Consequences

HJG Townesend

To Wendy
with love
Hugh

H J G. Townesend

RED CAP
Publishing

Published & Distributed
in Great Britain in 2015
by
RED CAP PUBLISHING
100 Marlborough Gardens, Faringdon, Oxfordshire, SN7 7DN
+44 (0) 7435456010
Email: info@redcappublishing.com

Copyright © HJG Townesend
The right of HJG Townesend to be identified as the author of
this work has been asserted by her in accordance with the
Copyright, Designs and Patents Act 1988.

Whilst this is a work of fiction and the characters, events and places are
either the product of the author's imagination or are used totally
fictitiously, much that happens is based on the contemporary writings of
real people and events. Apologies for any inaccuracies

The copyright holder assumes all liability for this book and indemnifies
the publisher against all claims arising from its publication. All aspects
of the work, including permission to use previously published material,
are solely the responsibility of the copyright holder.

A CIP catalogue record for this book is available
from the British Library.

ISBN 978-0-9931642-0-0

All rights reserved. No part of this publication may be reproduced,
stored in a retrieval system or transmitted in any form or by any
means (electronic, mechanical, photocopying, recording or otherwise)
without the prior written permission of the copyright holder.

Cover design by Jo MacDonald
Cover photograph of Richmond Castle by Mike Fenwick
Other photographs HJG Townesend

This book is Dedicated to the memory of my Friend
Henry Williams

also to all Conscientious Objectors who have suffered
for their cause.

Foreword

World War I was inflicting a terrible toll; by the end of 1915 it was clear that not enough men were volunteering to fight. The Military Service Act became law on March 2nd 1916. After that date all single men between the ages of 18 and 40 were deemed to be in the army, and were required to register. Later that year married men were also included.

Some men registered but refused to fight and were sent into the Non-Combatant Corps (NCC) as stretcher bearers, caterers etc. Other men refused even to register and were Absolutist Conscientious Objectors; sixteen of these men were, for a short while, imprisoned in the Norman Castle of Richmond in North Yorkshire; they became known as the Richmond Sixteen.

Chapter 1

Joseph

March 1916

Joseph sunk his head in his hands; he felt more lonely and alone than he had ever done in his whole life. 'How did I come to be here; miles from mi home, rejected by all except mi family and friends, an outcast, cast out, maybe a coward, only I know t'truth and I'm not sure even of that.'

He went to sit on the bank under a tree, to shelter from the keen March wind; the river Swale flowed near the railway station. He drank a little water and ate the bread and cheese Mother had given him for his snap, looking at Richmond castle nearby on the hill, its tall, square tower dominating the landscape, he thought over the events of the last few days.

He shut his eyes and remembered; he had stood back and admired his work. 'Grand, though I tells missen, 'tis grand; I hope I get it fettled in time.'

The village peeler had walked up the garden path of the cottage and round to the open door, removed his helmet and knocked.

'I've come to take Joseph, I'm afraid, Mrs Metcalf.'

'Eh up, Fred, come in, come in, we've been expecting a visit; we knew tha'ud be here soon enough, what with t'law coming into effect this week. Art thou keeping well, 'tis some while since we've seen thee.'

'I'm well, thank you missus; but I must fetch young Joseph, I have my orders.'

Florence called 'Joseph lad, 'tis time to go, Constable Harker has come for thee.'

'Now then, Mr Harker sir, can you just hang on a moment please? Th'art here sooner than I thought tha'd be; I didn't expect thee for a week or two. I'll get mi bag; I'm all ready to go.'

'Well lad, the new law has to be enforced and we have our orders, you haven't registered, nor, I expect do you intend to.'

Joseph gave a short laugh. 'Aye, th'art right there; and I knew tha'ud be here sooner or later.'

He had put away his tools, washed his face and hands at the pump and run his fingers through his thick, dark hair. He pulled himself up to his full height and turned to his young brother who had been watching from the yard.

'Now then, Jacob, I'm needing thee to look out for Ma and Hannah, th'art now Pa's right-hand man, I'm relying on thee.' He ruffled his hair. 'Tha'll have more room in t'bed now; and see if Pa will have time to help thee get this rocking horse polished in time for our Hannah's birthday.'

Florence gave Joseph a long hug and reached up to give him a kiss. 'Art tha sure about this son, really set on't?'

'Think on, Ma, think on, we have bin ower this time an' agin, and tha know'est that this is what I mun to do, and with the help o' t'good Lord and thy prayers I'm sure all will be well; th' know'est that.'

'I've put in a bit o' snap for thee, but I'm sure they'll see thee right tha'll not go hungry; but try to keep in touch; tell us where th'art, if tha can.'

'Oh Ma, you always do look after mi guts, t'family will never want for nowt while thou've aught to do wi'it. I love thee, thou know'st.'

Fred Harker was turning his helmet in his hands; he had known this family for years – God-fearing, law-abiding, hard-working, and in his heart he supported Joseph. He had seen the family out of many a scrape in the past and he had experienced the consequences of war when he fought the Boers, but the law was the law and Joseph hadn't registered.

'Where'st tha taking him, Fred?'

'Just to the local station to start with; I'm not really supposed to say but I did hear Pontefract Prison mentioned.'

Joseph plonked his cap on to his dark curls and hitched up the small bag he had put ready by the back door for this very occasion.

'I love thee Joe, I'll look after Ma tha' know'st, and help her wi' t'baking.' Little Hannah was nearly in tears.

'Aye lass, I know'st, and I love thee too, my little sister and thee my dear brother.' The words stuck in his throat.

'I'll not need to hand-cuff you, laddie, will I?'

'Nay, I'll not try to escape, tha know'st, but can we call in to t'bank, to tell Daniel that I'm off? He'll need to know for the cricket team; they'll start practice again soon, now snow's gone.'

'It's against the rules but it won't hurt as we are going past, anyway; I'll stay to one side.'

Joseph pushed open the heavy door of the imposing bank building; Daniel was at his usual place. As soon as he saw the two men, he guessed what had happened. Constable Harker turned away to talk to a friend while the two young men greeted each other.

'God's speed.' Joseph reached out his hand across the polished teak counter. 'Pray for me, for all of us, I'll pray for you, what ever you decide to do.'

'We need all the prayers anyone can say; may your God look after you. My papers came through yesterday.'

'What are you going to do?' asked Joseph.

'I'll register but ask to be an objector, see what happens from there.'

'Good luck, anyway; I hope to see you again sometime.'

At the police station the sergeant went through the routine paper work, filling in forms, making lists. He had no sympathy for Joseph's position. His sons had gone and he was proud of them; Joseph should go as well. Joseph answered all the questions politely, even though he knew that the sergeant knew most of the answers. He was left on his own in a cell, to think about his actions. Fred brought him a meal of soup and bread and a cup of water.

'Mrs Metcalf could bring you in more.'

'Thank you, but I've already talked with Ma about this and told her not to; no, I must take my chances, she has enough to deal with, helping Pa and looking after Hannah and Jacob.'

*

For the next few days, Joseph had had to share his cell with a succession of men who came for a night or two, before going to court for either imprisonment or release. Drunks, thieves, and disturbers of the peace; in this small town, they knew each other by sight, one or two had been to school with Joseph, some were interested in why he was there, others just couldn't understand it. He kept himself to himself and did little but read his Bible, pray and think.

8

Then came his time in court, to face a tribunal of old men, some from the military, some from the town council; most had served in previous wars. He had heard rumours about these courts from others who had been there before and was not expecting any sympathy or quarter. He tried to explain himself, to give the magistrates good cause not to jail him. But he was in breach of the Military Services Act and they all knew it, they had every good reason to send him to prison.

'Why haven't you registered?' The man barely glanced up at him.

'Sir, I am a Quaker. I cannot and will not take arms against my brothers; all men are my brothers in the sight of God. I cannot register and I am prevented from taking any part in the military system because of my religious beliefs. Therefore, I must not obey any military orders. My convictions are based on the teachings and example of our Lord Jesus Christ. I will take no oath of allegiance nor take any monies from the army. I will hold to this, whatever the consequences.'

'You could request to join the Non-Combatant Corps. Maybe you could do work of national importance, such as driving an ambulance, or in the mines, but I can't guarantee that such a request would be granted.' The man was tired and bored; wanted to be free of this difficult objector.

'It would still be helping the war, it would relieve another man to fight.'

'We'll have to see what we can do to make you change your mind,' he snapped. 'We have offered you the opportunity to avoid prison; this, you have refused. I can do nothing more for you, your destiny is in your hands and actions; it's prison for you, until you see sense or until another authority does something else with you. Dismiss, out, take him away, now!' He shouted at the guard.

'But...but.'

Joseph had hoped to have the chance to give his longer, prepared speech but was given no such opportunity; they had heard enough from other such men. However, he was aware that he was being treated with unusual courtesy and respect, and he appreciated that. He had heard tell of extremely rough and unfair judgement by the magistrates and the courts.

'We have no choice, it's jail until you change your mind or until the war is over. Go.'

*

At Pontefract Prison, the Governor was not pleased to see him; he was not used to courteous, law-abiding young men standing in his office, he could see that he should not be there; he didn't really know what to do with him.

'Put him in a single cell; keep him away from the others.'

Joseph was glad to be on his own; he always found the company of new people difficult, awkward to hold conversations with people he didn't know. The Governor was intrigued by the lad and made an opportunity to question him about his motives and beliefs; he tried to draw him out, they got on very well. The Governor knew he could trust the lad but Joseph did not generate the same feelings with the other prison staff; he received daily abuse, his food was spilled, his drinks spoiled, his cell turned over; the fact he didn't report it seemed to make them even angrier and rougher.

'Who do you think you are? With your 'Holier than thou' attitude, cosying up to the Governor, makes me sick. You should be sent out there, to see what it's all about.' The old men who had seen service resented being left behind for this conflict.

However, this situation couldn't last; within a week, the Governor received orders to send him to join other objectors.

'I can trust you, laddie, can't I? I don't need to send you with an escort, do I? You've got to go to Richmond Castle; I'll give you the paperwork you need. I truly wish you the best of luck.'

He was given a train time-table, a travel warrant and taken to the station in the prison cart.

'My lads have had to go; I don't see why you won't. I hope they give you hell,' screamed the driver. 'Why should you have an easy life when lads are out there fighting for our freedom?'

Joseph refused to respond to them. The rest of the journey continued in silence; he was roughly thrown out at the station, the guards spat at him before driving off, laughing and shouting abuse. His head ached and he felt sick. He found a water-pump, washed his face and hands and sat in the shelter of the station canopy, to wait for the train.

At York railway station, its beautiful curving roof of glass and steel made him stand and stare in wonder at the gracefulness of it, and that such a beautiful building was constructed just for people to change trains. At York, he changed to go on to Darlington; there he found the right platform and waited for the branch-line to Richmond. During the journey, he tried to keep himself to himself, sitting quietly in a corner smoking and reading, but he had to endure questions and comments.

'Why aren't you in uniform?' demanded one belligerent old woman.

'Where are you going?'

'Are you ill?'

'Where is your arm-band?' The questions kept coming.

Joseph gave up trying to answer. He found it difficult to respond in a way that they could understand; one very irate woman pinned a white feather to his jacket and spat at him. 'My lad died last week, why won't you go?'

'Madam, I am truly sorry to hear that your son has died, but it cannot make it right for me to go, to be a soldier. I hope you can find peace. I will pray for him and for you.'

He felt so sad for the woman, and knew that he would never be able to get her to understand his position.

*

He had pulled his jacket around his shoulders and dozed; the sounds of the River Swale gurgling as it ran under the bridge lulled him to sleep. When the church clock struck and woke him, Joseph was disoriented, couldn't work out where he was until he saw the castle again. He sat quietly in prayer for some time, maybe as long as half an hour. He prayed deep in his heart for the strength he thought would be needed to go through with what lay in the months, and maybe years, ahead. He stood up and gave himself a good shaking, pulled away from the riverbank, turned his back on the rushing water, brushed down his trousers and hitched up his bag and cap. The bag contained the little he thought he would be allowed where he was headed – pencils and paper, the Bible given to him by the Elders when he had been accepted into the Membership of the Quakers, a change of underwear, his washing and shaving things and, his tobacco tin.

11

'Come on, laddie, time to go,' he told himself.

He rolled a cigarette, glanced over his shoulder to make sure that he had left nothing behind, braced his shoulders and set off up the steep hill toward the castle.

The wide open space he crossed was planted round with trees; they had taken on the pinkish tinge that trees do before they burst into leaf, as they would in a few weeks time. He could see a group of boys shouting to each other as they kicked a football and heard some children as they played behind the bend in the river, beyond the trees. As he entered the market place, he could feel the cobbles under his feet; they seemed hard; he was more aware of them, or perhaps Richmond's cobbles were set differently from the ones at home. The curved Georgian façade, almost a horseshoe shape, with the curve at the top of the steep hill; the houses with their glinting windows seemed to him very elegant; he had never seen anything like it. They were tall and close together, appearing to make a continuous line; the cottages at home were mostly single-story and much older and all set in their own gardens. There were no gardens here to see; instead, all of the buildings had shops at street level.

So this was Richmond. How long would he be here? He was still so close to home near Masham, but felt so far away.

Chapter 2

Daniel

March 1916

The spider was oblivious to the turmoil in the world outside this small room. The world was at war, had been for over a year and now the day had come that Daniel had to take a stand. He didn't even dare admit it to himself – he was terrified, terrified of the idea of going to France, to the trenches, but more immediately of going before the tribunal, and today was that day, the day he had been summoned to meet the Board.

It was early. The light was trickling in through the little window, the sun just rising; the trees made patterns on the wall by his bed. Daniel thrust his mouth-organ under the pillow, 'I just can't get the tune to that new song,' he muttered to himself crossly; he hadn't been sleeping too well, worried about today. He scratched his head and pulled his ear as he paced up and down the tiny room, next to his bed. Looking up at the sloping ceiling where the paint was peeling, he watched a large spider weaving its web in the beams above his head; he idly thought of some king or other that he had heard about in history lessons, Alfred? Daniel? No, can't be Daniel; he would have remembered that name. 'Bloody useless, those damn history lessons, never told you anything helpful. I know that Daniel was something to do with lions in the Bible,' he mused to himself as he paused in front of the window.

'It was Robert and spiders.' Coming to a halt, he suddenly remembered, 'Daniel was in the lion's den, Alfred burnt cakes; Robert the Bruce had been in prison, watching spiders making their webs, but why, and what happened next? I can't remember. Lion's den, huh, that's what it feels like now; I suppose I am just a coward, but I just don't want to go, I can't admit I'm just terrified; how can I get out of it?'

He had told the manager of the bank where he worked that he had to have the day off, but he didn't tell him the whole truth as to why. Mr Fosdyke had lost two sons and a brother, and felt angry about the war. He hadn't gone himself because of the disability he had got in the previous war, against the Boers. He wore his medal ribbons on his suit, in or out of work; he made his point, no-one had any doubt that he had fought and been injured for his country, no-one would dare to give Mr Fosdyke the white feather.

Daniel pulled on his best trousers, letting the braces hang down either side of his body, put on the clean shirt Ma had left out for him, fished the mouth-organ from his bed and stuffed it into his pocket. He went downstairs, into the pokey scullery, to wash and shave. He took out his grandfather's worn razor and stropped it carefully; the rhythmic motion of steel on leather was second nature to him now. He poured hot water into the basin, from the kettle which stood on the stove. The face that stared back at him from the crazed mirror that hung over the sink was pale and frightened-looking, the eyes with dark rings beneath them.

'Are you ready for this?' He scowled back at his reflection. He flicked his fair hair from his eyes and shaved with greater care than usual, splashed his face with cold water and dried it carefully with the rough towel. He dressed in his Sunday-best suit, with the white shirt and his only tie, laced the boots that he had polished the night before and dragged a comb through his thick hair.

'Now then, Dan,' he addressed himself again, 'this is it; let's see if I can get away with it.'

His mother came from the kitchen and hugged him. He absently kissed the top of her head. 'Now then, Mam, why are you up so early?'

'Are you ready for your breakfast, Danny? I've boiled you a couple of eggs; couldn't have you setting off without something inside you. I always used to get up for your Pa, God rest his soul, before he went on shift.' She hated reminding herself of the night of the rock-fall at the pit; it killed four men, six years ago.

'Anyway,' she continued, 'Susie will be home for her day off. I need to do some baking before going to work. We'll all be here together this evening.'

'Oh yes, I forgot; Susie, how could I not remember? It's about a month since she was home, isn't it? She'll be getting quite grown up by now, won't she? I'll get home as soon as I can. Will Mrs Hill give you any time off work?'

'She said she would if we aren't busy. She's very understanding.'

'Mr Fosdyke has given me the day off, but he'll not pay me for

14

it; says the bank doesn't pay people not to work. I haven't told him why I am going before the Board, he wouldn't understand.' He tucked into his breakfast, porridge and the eggs with toast, drank his tea and wiped his mouth with his handkerchief.

'Ma, that was delicious, thank you.'

He picked up his snap-box that Ma had made up for him, a thick cheese sandwich and a withered apple, saved from last autumn's crop. He tucked it in his bag, with a bottle of water, a small book to read on the journey and the papers he had been sent.

'God go with you, my son.' She kissed him as he left and gave him a quick hug.

Elsie was very worried about her only son, but kept her thoughts to herself. As Daniel walked to the bus stop, pulling his coat close round him, he shivered in the sharp air of the March morning. He could see the remains of the snow that had fallen a day or two ago; most of it had melted but it still clung in the hedge-backs on the hills, where the sun didn't get. However, catkins were showing on the hazel trees and daffodils were through in the neighbours' gardens; spring was definitely on the way.

Daniel had been to Darlington only once before. He didn't like it; it was too big, too noisy. There were automobiles, and trolley buses, people on bicycles and too many folk rushing about in all directions, not looking, not taking any notice of this scared, lost lad in his country clothing. He glanced across the road, at two self-assured looking girls giggling and hurrying to work.

'Not my sort,' he told himself, 'I like a girl to be less giggly; give me a nice, quiet lass, but with a mind of her own, preferably slim and dark haired.'

He had to ask the way of an elderly policeman, the medal-ribbons prominent on his chest, the information given very reluctantly; the Bobby made it very clear that he had a very poor opinion of the lost lad; he knew why these young, fit men went to see the Board. He thought they were skivers, cowards, all of them.

*

'Daniel Braithwaite, 20,' he said in response to questions, 'I've been sent to appear in front of the Tribunal.' He handed in the papers.

He waited, self-consciously, with other young men who were smoking and joking between themselves; they all hoped, but didn't expect, to be absolved of the need to join up. One or two of them were clearly just cowardly – the brash way they were boasting about the mèthods they would use to convince the panel which would quiz them; they didn't really expect to get away with it but they were trying their luck, anyway. He listened eagerly, hoping to get some ideas to avoid the inevitable.

'I'm going to tell them about my poor, sick mother.'

'Is she sick? What's wrong with her, did you bring a doctor's note?'

'No, but they don't know that. What are you going to say?'

'I'll tell them I've got TB; might as well.'

'But they'll find out.'

'It'll buy me some time, anyway.'

But there were others there; members of various churches, Methodists, International Bible Students, Quakers, who had deep religious convictions against war, but Daniel's convictions came not just from fear but from an alternate belief. His membership of the Socialist Party of Great Britain had given him a different view on war, and this war in particular, but he still was scared, more scared than he could admit to himself, let alone anyone else, and he was determined not to fight.

'I'm going to volunteer to work in a hospital,' he boasted to the others.

'What? Safe away from the front line?' someone scoffed.

'But at least it will be away from the fighting,' Daniel said.

Behind the long table were seven elderly men and a woman. The Mayor wearing his chain of office, and his deputy, the Town Clerk looking very officious with his little pointed beard and dark suit; his deputy, a town councillor and the vicar looking self-conscious, all a bit unsure of themselves; a Major in full uniform, Sam-Browne gleaming across his tunic, swagger-stick and peaked cap on the table beside him, he glowered from under his bushy eyebrows; another soldier, maybe a corporal, appeared to be taking notes. Sitting next to the Major there was an elderly woman. None of them was introduced; they scarcely looked at him, kept referring to the papers on the table.

16

'Name?' The Town Mayor, chain of office glinting on his chest barked loudly, making Daniel jump.

'Age?' came from another. He found himself looking from one to the other to answer, 'Any disabilities?' 'Any brothers?' 'Where is your father?' The questions came thick and fast. 'What Church do you attend?'

Daniel tried to answer all these questions, but felt he wasn't being given time. '20, no, no, a sister; dead,' in answer. 'I don't attend church, except with my mother and sister at Christmas and Easter.' Daniel's pale skin was flushed; his eyes darted from face to face of the officious-looking people who ranged the other side of the long oak table; he tried to keep up with the inquisition.

'So. What are you doing here?' the Major snapped, half standing, at last looking at him; the gold braid adorning his collar and cuffs, cap badges gleaming, medals clinking.

'Sorry Sir. What do you mean?' Daniel stammered.

'Why are you here, in front of this Board?' The Major's eyebrows worked together.

'I can't go, I can't go and fight.' He ran his fingers through his hair.

The officials turned to look at him in unison, not a smile or a kind glance to be seen.

'What do you mean, boy?' the woman asked in a high thin voice. Her greying, faded hair under a grey hat set off with an unlikely red ribbon, the skirt of her matching grey suit swept the floor, the lace at her throat poorly disguised her scraggy neck. She testily repeated, 'What do you mean?'

Daniel remembered the words of the Party members and took courage from them. He cleared his throat noisily, took a deep breath and set back his shoulders. 'All men are my brothers; I cannot and will not fight them.' He could hardly believe he was saying these words.

'You one of those Quaker bods?' This unexpectedly aggressive tone came from the vicar of the local church, who appeared to wake up at the idea; his dusty black cassock with soup stains down the front had never inspired confidence.

'Certainly not, though my friend Joseph is, he has been very kind and helpful to me.'

17

The Mayor tipped his chair back, put his hands on the table, and stared him in the eye. 'So why won't you fight?'

'This war is none of the workers' business.'

The Major sat bolt upright in his chair. 'What do you mean by that?'

'I'm a member of the British Socialists' Party and very proud of it; we also believe that capitalism causes war and is therefore not a problem for people like me to sort out.'

'Where do you work? In a bank! Does your employer know about these dangerous views? And how do your views fit into the ethos of the bank?'

'I needed a job, I am good at it and I enjoy it. And no, I have not discussed it with the manager; I don't think he would understand.'

'I think you are right there.' The men laughed among themselves. 'You have given us no good reason why a fit young man like you can't fight for his country.'

'But I can't, won't go; it is against all my beliefs. I am a conscientious objector, like it says in the Military Service act.'

The Mayor spoke, 'You've not given us a good enough reason.'

'Do you have religious convictions against the war?' asked the vicar coming out of a doze.

'No, not as such; moral ones, there is a difference.'

They showed their disapproval clearly. 'We don't want any sissies or cowards; or are you a Nancy Boy?'

Daniel looked up at the accusation. 'Just because I have this belief doesn't make me one of those.'

The Major again half got to his feet, leaning forward, fists on the table. 'Didn't you hear? Report to your regiment, you will be sent your papers again. Dismiss.' He nearly shouted at him, his face red with rage. 'Now get out; report to your local regiment, I say.'

'But, but, I, I need time to explain.'

They would discuss it no longer, regarded him as being naïve, foolish and possibly dangerous. As he turned away, he heard the Major calling 'Next' and pitied the poor fellow that was to follow him.

18

He went back to the recruiting offices.

'I need appeal papers, please.'

'What for? What are you appealing against?'

'I applied to be a conscientious objector and they didn't even listen to what I had to say.'

'Here, this is what you need, but don't hold your breath. These appeal panels aren't letting many through, they are not sympathetic to you skivers. We need all the men we can get if we are going to beat the Hun.' The papers were shoved across the table to him; he stuck them in his pocket.

He went to a meeting of the Party and got his pal to help him fill in the forms, and took them back to the office.

'You'll be hearing from us, lad, but you'll be joining up, just mark my words or you'll finish up in prison.'

Daniel wasn't sure he had done a good enough job with the forms. While he waited for the appeal date, he tried to stay busy; he dug the garden, mended the chicken run, went to see Uncle Henry, helped his mother and he tried to keep out of Mr Fosdyke's way.

*

The date for his appeal soon came through, and within a week he was back in Darlington. He was worried and scared as he didn't know what more he could tell them; he didn't want to go to the Front, he didn't want to go to prison. As he stood outside the door of the enquiry room, running his fingers through his hair, pulling his ear, he recited the prepared speech to himself; all he could say was what he believed in. However, it was a different group of men this time; only three of them, and he felt the atmosphere was more sympathetic.

'So you are appealing against our judgement, are you? Why?'

Daniel drew himself up to his full six foot height; half closed his eyes and recited.

'The National Service League tells us that objections will be respected, it's in the Conscription Law, and The Socialist Party of Great Britain says that no interests at all justify the shedding of a single drop of working class blood and we enter our emphatic protest against the brutal and bloody butchery of our brothers in this and other lands. I read it in this paper I was given.' He produced a small magazine.

The officials looked unimpressed. 'Are you a Socialist?'

'Yes, I'm a member of the British Socialists' Party.'

'So you believe all this stuff?'

'Of course, that's why I am here.'

'So what will you do? Will you go into uniform, go in the army?'

'I'll not fight, I can't carry a gun, couldn't kill anyone. So what can I do? Sir, please could I do something different, I'm not a shirker or a coward, maybe I could work in a hospital, help injured men; you must need helpers, orderlies? I could help, and I have been taught some bandaging and have a certificate from the Boy Scouts.'

The attitude of the men in the room softened a little, and the Mayor hid a smile behind his hand. Maybe the lad wasn't trying to get out of it, he seemed to be genuine enough and could help; it was true, they did need first-aiders and stretcher-bearers.

'Hm. Now you're talking, we do need first-aiders; why didn't you say this at your Board?'

'I wasn't given a chance.'

The officials whispered among themselves.

'What about the Non-Combatant Corps, the NCC? You would be a soldier in every way but one; you won't have to carry a gun or fight. You could be a stretcher-bearer, a first-aider, even help out in a hospital.'

'What would that mean, Sir?'

'You would be sent to the Front, alongside our soldiers, render first-aid, carry the wounded back to the Field Dressing Station, maybe help in the hospitals; we would have to see where you would be most useful. You might even help out the Quakers if they will have you in their Ambulance Unit.'

'That would be fine, thank you very much, Sir, thank you. I look forward to it; but I would rather help out in a hospital, looking after the injured men, if that's alright.'

'Beggars can't be choosers; you can't choose what work you will do. Go home now and wait for your papers, they will be sent, in the next few days, to go to Richmond for training; you do know where Richmond is, don't you?'

20

'Yes Sir, of course and, again, thank you.'

He was given an arm-band with a red cross on it; he was to wear it so people would know that he was under orders.

*

The journey home on the bus was different. Daniel felt more relaxed, now that the ordeal was over and he had been taken seriously, but he was still terrified he would be sent to the Front, but at least he wouldn't have to shoot anyone, he had been listened to.

'Am I a coward?' he asked himself. 'Maybe.' It wasn't reassuring. He pondered what the future would hold for him, he wasn't sure he was up to it. At the same time, he felt excited, involved, wanting to be part of the action. He enjoyed being on the top deck of the bus, letting the wind ruffle his hair, watching the Dales come into view; lambs were playing and the gorse was coming out.

Daniel told Mr Fosdyke what had happened. He still wasn't all together happy but when Daniel explained that he would be going to the Front and helping out in a hospital, he became more understanding. But Daniel still couldn't tell him about his involvement with the British Socialist Party. Mr Fosdyke seemed pleased that Daniel was going, but concerned. He had become fond of the boy, even though he would hardly admit it even to himself.

'I'll miss you,' he said gruffly, 'we were just getting to know each other, I don't know what we will do without you, but one way or another, I knew you would have to go sooner or later.'

'Maybe you could take on some women?'

'Women! I'll not have women in my bank; I'm just getting you trained. Maybe you're right though, there is such a shortage of young men; maybe I'll be reduced to that. Mind you, I'll not take some fliberty-gibbits, all lipstick and cigarettes, and none of those girls that support those Pankhurst women. Maybe there'll be a job waiting for you when you get back, just maybe.'

Chapter 3

Annie

March 1916

'Annie Scott, what have you got there?'

Annie stood in the doorway of the small cottage, soaking wet; her coat clung to her ankles, water from her hat dripped into her eyes and wisps of her dark hair hung down like icicles. But clutched in her arms was a small, sodden, black and white bundle that was whimpering.

'I found him in the street Ma, his leg is broken.'

'Not another animal, Annie, you've only just given away Felix.'

'But this is different. I saw him being knocked down by a wagon. Please, Ma, I just can't leave him now, can I? He'll die!' She laid the bundle on her mother's lap. 'Please, hold him while I get ready.'

She hung her sodden coat and hat on a hook behind the door, went to her room, changed out of her uniform and put her boots in front of the fire. Her mother sighed and stroked the little animal. Annie found a box and lined it with sacking and a piece of old blanket; she gently rubbed the little dog dry with a bit of towel and laid him in the box in front of the range, to dry off and warm up. It was only a puppy really, could only have been about six months old, if that, and was of an indeterminate breed but attractively marked; it gave off that typical damp-dog smell.

'When he is warm and rested, I'll set his leg.'

Annie dried off her hair and tied it back in a long plait, took a hessian apron from the hook and bustled about collecting the bits and pieces that she thought she would need; she padded two pieces of stick with some calico and tore a few strips of Pa's old flannel shirt by way of a bandage.

Deftly, she wrapped the frightened animal in a towel, and while her mother held him, she gently straightened the broken limb, crooning to the animal as she worked; it seemed mesmerised, it didn't complain as she bandaged the splints to it.

'There, do you think that'll hold it?' She stood back to admire the handiwork.

Mother mixed up some bread and milk for Annie to feed to her new patient; she spooned some of the mixture into the animal's mouth.

'You should have been a vet instead of a nurse; if they would have a woman.'

'But I love nursing.'

'You are a natural Annie, The veterinary profession has lost out where nursing has gained.'

They lowered the little dog into its new bed, covered it with a bit of blanket, where it fell instantly asleep.

'I'll call him Rover.'

'A bit unimaginative I think,' called Ma over her shoulder, on her way to the scullery. 'But as you'll not be keeping him, I suppose it doesn't matter, so it'll do for the time being.'

*

Richard Scott came in and gave his wife and daughter a quick kiss. He took off his hat, shook out his coat and hung them behind the door, hefted his bag onto the table and, lowering himself carefully down into the chair, he rubbed his leg where it had been broken in an accident years ago. He put his head in his hands and took the cup of tea gratefully from his wife.

'You look exhausted, dear,' she said. 'What's the matter? Is your leg bothering you? Can you talk about it? I'll help if I can, you know that.'

'Yes, my leg aches terribly today, but it's not that. I don't know how to help them; the little children, they are so disturbed; they can't concentrate on their lessons. Their big brothers going off, some never coming back, others coming back so horribly mutilated that they are scarcely recognisable. The worst is when they are just missing. And with not knowing where Matthew is and Paul dead, I find it so difficult to know what to say to help. The other teachers are so good with them, but I can't seem to find the right words.'

Gladys set their tea down on the table. They ate their meal in silence, without really tasting the food, each of them wrapped in their own thoughts of the twin brothers who had gone off so cheerfully, to join up, do their bit, looking so smart and keen in their uniforms, just a few short months ago.

23

Annie cleared her throat. 'I need to talk to you both.' Annie pushed back her chair, stood up and looked at her parents. 'I've decided to go.'

'Go? Go? Go where?' Gladys lifted her head.

'I have been thinking about it for some time. Molly is going and I want to go with her.'

'You still haven't said where. Where are you going?'

'I'm going to volunteer to go to the Front, help out in a hospital. They have been asking for volunteers, and we both want to go. And who knows, I might even find out what has happened to Matthew.'

'Annie, you can't go, I just can't let you.' Tears started in Gladys' eyes. 'And, anyway, don't be silly, there are thousands of men out there; over hundreds of miles, you'll never find him, it won't be possible; please Annie, not you too.'

Richard stood in front of the fire, his back to the women. 'Well, I won't give my permission. I can't lose you too.'

'Oh Pa, I'll not be anywhere near any danger. I'll just be nursing in a hospital, like here but just there, in France and only injured men, no women, no children. I'm really sorry, Pa, but I don't need your permission; I'm over twenty one. But I really do want your blessings; both of you, please.' Annie wound her arms round her father's waist.

'Pa, you know what she's like. She'll go if she wants to, if she's made up her mind.' Ma wiped her eyes on her pinny.

'I have been thinking about it for some time; please give me your blessing.'

'I suppose there is nothing either of us can do about it; if you are determined, I suppose you have to. So go, look after yourself and come back safe. We do know that they need all the help they can get.'

'Oh thank you, thank you, you don't know how much that means to me. I promise I'll come back safe.'

'Have you seen Matron about it yet?'

'No. I plan to go tomorrow, Molly went yesterday.'

'She'll miss you both, won't she?'

'Many nurses are going; I don't know how she'll manage, but she will as there are so many who can't or won't go; I expect, some will have to do longer or double shifts. She'll work it out.'

They sat together round the kitchen table, each wrapped in their own memories, looking at the two empty chairs where the brothers should be. The only sounds that could be heard were the ticking of the clock, the quiet whimpering of the little dog, and the dripping of the rain on the roof.

Chapter 4

Joseph

Set back, behind the fairly new-looking market building, was the castle which Joseph approached with trepidation. Getting nearer, he felt the tower to be getting taller and taller. It seemed to loom over him; sounds of men, shouting, running, barked orders, came from the other side of the wall. Beneath the square tower was a huge metal-bound oak door; it was very strange, just to walk up to this door and knock on it, but there was nothing else to do. His knock felt very puny, but eventually a small door cut into the main one opened, revealing an old soldier who glowered at Joseph.

'Yes? Who are you? What do you want?'

'I've been told to report here, Sir.'

'Why?'

'I have told the magistrate that I will not fight, so I've been sent here.'

'One of those, eh? Where is your guard?'

'The Prison Governor at Pontefract said I didn't need one, so I came on my own.'

The soldier was very suspicious, looked up and down the street, grabbed Joseph by the arm as though he would run away, kicked shut the door, took an unwieldy key from his pocket and unlocked a small door to the left.

'I've got another one for you,' he shouted, pushing Joseph in and slamming the door; the sound of the key turning in the lock echoed along the corridor.

The smell of cold, damp, stale air struck him forcibly; such a contrast from the fresh air he had just left. There was a row of four iron-banded doors to his right. An old soldier clumped down the stairs from the upper floor. He wore several medals on his old, worn uniform and dragged his left leg.

'God help me,' Joseph silently and fervently prayed.

A soldier sitting at a desk at the end of the corridor looked him up and down. He took in the worn boots, the rough clothing, but mostly the look of determination in his face that barely masked the apprehension in his eyes.

'Good afternoon, Sir,' came from Joseph.

26

'Silence,' snapped the old man, his medals clinking against his chest, 'we have no talking here.'

'No Sir, sorry Sir, thank you Sir.'

'Silence! In there, take off all your clothes and change into these.' He was handed a bundle, hustled into a cell, the door swung shut with a sickening thud. The walls were stained with damp runnels; when he touched it, plaster smeared his hands, the ceiling was black with mould; the door, with a little spy-hole in it, looked strong enough to keep anyone either in or out. His practiced eye told him it was of best English oak. There was a high slit window with a permanently-open ventilation gap above it, through which whistled the keen March wind. He put his Bible on the hard pillow and his bag under the thin mattress and examined the clothing: long, woollen underwear, the khaki trousers, jacket and shirt of a soldier's uniform, socks and boots. He stripped off and put on the underwear and socks, the floor was cold and damp through the thin wool. Joseph felt sick at the sight of the khaki outfit; he just couldn't bring himself to wear it. He just sat on the bed, with his head in his hands. The soldier spied in through the little hole in the door, then opened it.

'Why haven't you dressed?'

'I can't wear this; it's a soldier's uniform, I am not a soldier.'

'You will wear it, anyway it is all there is. You are a soldier, that's the law; you are a private in the army now and you'll do as you are ordered.'

'Corporal!' the man shouted up the stairs. 'Bring a couple of fellows with you, we have another one here.'

Three more soldiers came in and pushed him back onto the bunk, one held him down and the others forced the trousers onto him; he decided not to resist but to go floppy, just relax. He remembered, with some shame, that this is what he used to do as a child, when Ma tried to get him into his uncomfortable Sunday best, the collar had scratched his neck and he had hated it. Eventually, the men got the trousers on to him and the buttons done up; they were far too big for his small frame. Up they pulled him, got a shirt on to him and the braces over his shoulders, followed by the jacket; his thumb caught in the folds of the sleeve, they pulled it back angrily, the pain brought tears to his eyes.

After what seemed to be over an hour, they left him standing dejectedly, the cap pulled down hard over his eyes. Joseph looked down his body, dismayed and unsure. The men crashed the door shut behind them.

He became aware of a tapping sound. He looked round and noticed a pipe going through the wall of his cell, under the window; the sound was coming from that, it was persistent, a gentle rhythm. The plaster round the pipe wasn't quite finished, leaving a gap, and from this gap there was a soft 'psssst'. He knelt down and looked through the hole; he could see a bright, sparkling blue eye.

'Hello,' said a voice from near the eye, 'I'm Norman. Welcome.'

'Joseph Metcalf, pleased to meet you, I've just arrived; they've put me in uniform.'

'If you want to, just take it off again, it keeps them busy for hours, trying to get you back into it again. It took eight men when I arrived, but they are getting better at it now. Just wear your underclothes, but you'll have to get used to the cold, it never gets any warmer than this.'

'I'll have to think about that.'

'I know it seems a little forward of me, but it would make it easier for me if you could tell me what you look like, then I can picture you,' said the voice.

'Well, I'm about five foot ten inches tall, with dark hair and brown eyes, and my hands are calloused from the work I do as a carpenter. How about you?'

'I am, of course, devastatingly handsome, have all the girls swooning at my feet; I am six foot six, with wavy fair hair and, as you have already seen, lovely blue eyes. My body is a temple.' There were noises outside 'Got to go, we'll talk some more soon.' With that, the eye was gone.

Joseph scrambled to his feet. The door was thrown open and a plate of none-too-clean boiled potatoes was put on the floor, with a cup of water.

'Enjoy your meal,' the soldier sneered.

He ate the potatoes hungrily. It had been a long while since he had eaten, and he was glad of the food. As he finished, he heard shouting and running feet outside. He stood on the bed and looked through the little slit window at the sunny area of grass below. He could see row upon row of huts set round a square. It was a strange sight. This was an army camp of many wood and tin buildings set inside these old walls; how old this castle was, he didn't know, but William the Conqueror came to mind; was it built by him or one of his lords? That would make it hundreds of years old; history was never his best subject. The castle appeared to be in bad shape now; crumbling, jagged walls and towers sticking into the air. The men outside, all in uniform, were forming a long, comradely, chattering queue, jostling each other for position. Joseph suddenly felt very lonely. He knelt on the floor and tapped the pipe; soon, the eye appeared.

'Now what happens?'

'Oh soon they'll serve caviar, champagne, roast duckling, to us all to celebrate your arrival.'

'What? What do you mean?'

'I mean that is it, that is all for tonight. Do whatever you need to do; say your prayers, read your Bible, but do it soon, soon it will be dark and there are no lights here, other than daylight. See you in the morning; sleep well, sweet dreams.' And the eye was gone.

Joseph curled up on his bunk in the slowly darkening cell; he felt very alone. He pulled the thin blankets round his shoulders; springtime it may be, but this place was very damp and very cold and smelt of mould and decay; the great, thick medieval walls maintained a constant low temperature. He was so grateful for Norman's presence next door, even if it was only one eye. It had been a very long day and he eventually slept, dreaming he was home in the little bedroom, in the bed he shared with his young brother, Jacob, under the eaves of his parent's house in Masham, not so very far away.

29

Chapter 5

Daniel

'What have I done?' Daniel asked himself. 'I didn't want to go at all and I'm scared stiff, now I am committed to going to the Front. I can't tell anyone how I feel.' He sat under the apple tree at the end of the garden, the buds of the tree that would be in blossom in a month or so were tight shut. He twisted his handkerchief in his hands till it was screwed up into a ball.

'This'll not do; come on, Dan.' He took his mouth-organ out of his pocket, wiped it on his trousers and played a few of the tunes that he had taught himself.

'Now then,' he told himself, 'things to do for Mam before I have to go. Come on, jump to it.'

During his last few days at home, he was rushed off his feet; he had such a short amount of time to do so much. And he had to help Mr Fosdyke train a new junior clerk; a clever young girl had been recommended by the local vicar and was picking it all up quickly. Even Mr Fosdyke was impressed. She was not a pretty lass, something Mr Fosdyke thought was an advantage; she was a quick learner and had a gift with numbers, however, and was compliant. Mr Fosdyke had to admit that he liked her.

Daniel's papers and orders came and with them lists of things to take and those he was not allowed. Elsie knitted socks for him which he added to the small pile of presents the family gave him: a photo of his parents with himself and Susie, a new razor and strop in a leather case from Uncle Henry, an old tobacco tin containing some sweets which Susie made for him; he would treasure the tiny prayer book from his mother, treasure it as the gift it was, even if he felt he didn't really need a prayer book. Aunt Ethel sewed him a dozen khaki handkerchiefs; no white handkerchiefs allowed, as they could be used to signal surrender. Of course, having sharpened the blade, he took his pen-knife. All these things joined the paper and pencils and a little book of short stories that he bought for himself.

To please Mam, he went to Chapel on Sunday and joined in the hymns and prayers and wondered how long it would be before he saw this little place again. He had been baptised and received into membership of the Chapel here, though since he had been adult, he had never really been a regular attender. He gazed out of the church windows at the familiar view, the Dales in all their spring glory. His apprehensions came bubbling to the surface of his mind again; he wondered what the future held for him. Daniel went quietly to see the Minister, to share his fears with him; they had known each other since Daniel was a child and he felt he could confide in him.

'I'm so afraid of going, afraid that I won't be up to the job. What if I just can't cope? I have asked to be a hospital orderly, to stay away from the Front. I know that seems cowardly but I have to realise I am frightened even though I hardly dare admit it even to myself.'

'You'll find the strength from inside and from the conviction that you are doing the best you can, as I know you are, and whether you like it or not, we will pray for you every day. You know I don't entirely hold with some of your views, but I do understand this one about not wanting to be a full soldier. I think you have made a good decision, a good compromise, and wish you all God's speed.'

'Hm, thank you for that, but I'm still scared. You won't tell Mam, will you?'

He was having difficulty sleeping, and when he did sleep, he woke in a cold sweat; he had heard so many stories about the terrible things that happened at the Front; the mud, the bombings, the cold, but had no idea if any of it was true.

'I do hope they'll let me just be a hospital orderly, away from the action.'

He went to speak to Socialist Party members but they just laughed, pounded him on the back and called him a stout fellow.

Once, a man who had been in the previous war, gave him some advice. 'Keep your head down, do as much, but no more than you are asked to do, don't stand out from the crowd. It's OK to be scared.'

*

Monday dawned, a beautiful spring morning. Daniel's small bag stood by the front door, his mouth-organ in his pocket. With these, his orders and travel warrant, coat over his arm, he said goodbye

31

to Susie and Mother; Susie had been given the morning off. She was crying. She pressed her special stone into his hand.

'You can't give me this. You've had it since you were tiny and found it in the stream. You love the smooth round shape of it, the colour; you said you would keep it for ever.'

'Whenever you want to remember us, or if you're frightened, just hold this and be strong. I want you to keep it; you can give it back to me when you come home.'

'You're a funny girl. Why should I be frightened?' But he took it anyway and kissed her on the top of her head.

'Please come back safe, Danny, please come back safe.' He hugged his mother. Elsie fought back the tears. 'Look after yourself, my son, and may God go with you.'

Daniel bit his lip; he couldn't break down now, not in front of Mother and Susie. 'If you need anything, ask Uncle Henry. Dad would have wanted him to look after you.'

He checked his pocket; he had the stone that Susie had given him, felt the smooth roundness from it tumbling in the water. It fitted into his hand, comforting.

He got on to the wagon going to Leyburn. 'I'll write as soon as I can, promise.'

The driver clicked his tongue and flicked the reins at the horse; he turned to wave but soon they were out of sight.

He had an hour to wait in Leyburn, for the bus, so he bought a post-card for Susie; it had a picture of the town on Market Day, all the stalls set out, animals in their pens; he wasn't sure what to write, so he drew a picture of a smiling cat on it. She would laugh at that, and he dropped it into the post box. The motor-bus arrived, he climbed the stairs to the upper deck so he could have the last of the smells and sights of his Dales, see the familiar country-side as the bus passed by. Penn Hill rose magnificent as usual behind him, the low spring sun making it stand out in silhouette; he turned in his seat to have a last look. The road climbed the hill between Wensleydale and Swaledale and skirted round the banks of the Swale. Gorse was out in profusion, covering the hills in patches of gold. 'Love in season,' he whispered to himself. Lambs were playing King-of-the-castle.

'Why do they do that?' he wondered. Two tiny newborns were

buffeting their mother for milk.

The bus pulled into the cobbled streets of Richmond and stopped by the market cross, near the church. Worries and questions crowded his thoughts. He went inside the church, to sit in the quiet for a while, but he found it impossible to be calm. He thought about reciting some psalms and the Lord's Prayer, but they had meant nothing to him for a while, and he couldn't expect them to suddenly have some effect. Outside, in the bright sunlight, he saw a pub and went in for a pint of beer and a cheese sandwich; as he downed the pint he pulled a copy of the Socialist Party Manifesto out of his coat pocket and re-read it, to try to reassure himself why he was doing this. The lady behind the bar saw his arm-band and asked him why he was in Richmond, out of uniform; he tried to explain.

'If you are a soldier, why won't you carry a gun? Seems daft to me!'

'I'll not kill a fellow comrade, a fellow worker, a brother. I'll be in uniform soon; I just haven't got into training yet, that's why I'm going to the castle. I'll get a uniform there, I suppose. I'm going into the Non-Combatant Corps.' He didn't think she was satisfied with his reply.

She seemed to know something of these NCC men but was puzzled by them. She hinted at other things going on at the castle.

'They say there are men locked in cells there; men, they say that have no clothes on.'

'Don't be silly, they'd not allow that, would they?' He dismissed this as the fanciful imaginings of a simple woman; she bustled off, other customers to attend to. Daniel brushed the crumbs off his trousers, finished his drink and left some coppers on the bar.

'I don't understand you, but good luck anyway. I hope you can do something useful,' the woman called out.

Daniel picked up his bag, made his way past a few fellow drinkers and ambled slowly up the hill to the castle; the cobbles felt hard under his feet and the curve of the tall Georgian houses round the sloping market place seemed to encircle him. He had been told to be there for one o'clock; the church bell was just striking as he arrived at the gate. Other young men arrived at

33

about the same time. They stood by the high walls of the castle, wondering what to do; the gates were firmly shut.

Eventually, as if by a magical hand, the doors swung open and the lads trooped inside, a raggle-taggle group of confused young men. Fear and excitement showed on nearly every face, though some swaggered as they passed under the tall square tower; they tried to show they were not afraid of anything. It didn't work.

Daniel found himself swept along with the others; one lad, about the same age as himself, tripped over on a cobble-stone in front of him. He leant forward to help him up.

'I'm Daniel,' sticking out his hand, 'Daniel Braithwaite.'

'Hubert, Hubert Cartwright,' taking and shaking it.

'He sounds a bit posh,' thought Daniel to himself, but said nothing; plenty of time to get to know him.

'Jump to it, soldiers! Stop gossiping like a lot of old women. You're in the army now, not a playground.' The Corporal, as they came to know him, shouted orders, trying to get them under some sort of control.

'Soldiers? Am I now a soldier?'

The strange mixed bunch of young men was lined up and marched off to a hut, one of many ranged within the huge triangular space of the castle keep. Theirs was set out with two rows of iron bedsteads crowded in close together, with a pile of bedding, sheets and rough, woollen blankets on each. Daniel and Hubert managed to get bunks next to each other. The thirty or so fellows were given fifteen minutes to make their beds and stow their bags. The lads helped each other; some had never made beds before, relying on mothers, sisters or even, in one case, a maid. Some had never had a bed of their own before, having to share with brothers.

More shouted orders and they were marched off to the Quartermaster's store where they were given their kit; everything from underclothes, trousers, jackets, shirts, boots, puttees and a canvas kit-bag, together with a plate, knife, fork and spoon and a tin mug; to top it all off, a great, heavy, waterproof cape. They were given half an hour to change into this new clothing and stow all the rest of it. It was very difficult; unfamiliar, stiff, woollen fabric, buttons that would not go into the button-holes; jackets that were too big, trousers too small, a cap that looked ridiculous and heavy boots that some had never worn the like of before. They needed all the time to get ready; they had been given brown paper and string, and were instructed to wrap all their civilian clothes, ready for posting back to their families. Their new property, along with their personal bits and pieces, had to be put away tidily; they found that they had also been issued with boot and metal polish and brushes. Outside again for inspection, they lined up in two ill-disciplined rows; however, this is where they found the more understanding side of the Corporal; he spoke to each of them in turn, adjusted their belts, asked about the fit of boots and repositioned their caps to a jaunty angle.

'You can't go to war in that lot, go and get something better fitting. You, you and you, jump to it.' Several of them were sent back to the Stores, to change jackets, trousers or boots.

'The rest of you, at the double!' They were sent to the barbers for a haircut. Daniel's was shorter than it had ever been.

'Oh well, it will be easier to keep tidy.'

At the medical officer, they had to strip to their underpants; teeth, chest, head, hair, bellies, feet and eyes – not a part went unexamined; several were found to be un-fit, they would soon get up to scratch with good, solid army food, exercise and discipline. One lad was sent home; he had cheated on his previous eye examination but was found out now.

'Good luck, lads, I'll be thinking of you all,' the officer called as he whistled away.

Daniel was angry by all this detailed examination; no-one had looked at him so intently before, no-one except nice Doctor Murgatroyd who had seen him through all his childhood illnesses.

'Get used to it, soldier,' was all the reassurance he got from this doctor.

'Soldier? What Soldier? Me?'

They got injections against typhoid, small-pox and some other diseases, Daniel couldn't remember what; the needles hurt his arms, blunt as they were from constant over-use.

After an exhausting time, they all managed to re-dress; it didn't seem so difficult the second time. They were marched off to the Mess Hut; huge mugs of strong sweet tea, a good beef stew with dumplings, followed by jam roly-poly with custard. Some of them had never eaten so well. Very soon, all the plates were empty and the lads hoped that what was left of the evening would be for themselves; no such luck. The Corporal reappeared and ordered them to spend the evening getting a shine on their boots and buttons and cleaning all the rest of their equipment. 'I'll see my face in it in the morning or I'll want to know the reason why,' he told them darkly.

They cleaned and polished until their arms ached and they felt they could do no more.

Nine o'clock, time to turn in and they were glad of it; it had been a long, confusing, tiring day. As Daniel lay on his bunk, he watched Hubert kneel by the side of his bed, to say his prayers as he had himself as a child; but his own thoughts were for his Mam and Susie and his own future.

'Where will I get the strength to face what is coming?' he asked himself, feeling envious of Hubert's faith. 'I really do hope I don't get sent to the trenches; I don't know how I'll cope.' He turned Susie's stone over and over in his hand.

In spite of the hardness of the beds, the unfamiliar surroundings and the presence of all those snoring strangers, soon all thirty exhausted men were fast asleep. Daniel's confusing dreams were of uniforms and chickens, high castle walls and jam roly-poly, boot-polish and motor-buses.

Chapter 6

Annie

Annie smoothed down her crisply starched apron, adjusted her stiff collar and cuffs, tucked her hair under her cap, knocked on the door and waited.

'Come in.'

Annie stood at attention, in front of the heavy mahogany desk, hands behind her back.

Matron as always looked daunting; dressed in her dark blue uniform with white collar and cuffs and frilly cap, but she raised her head and looked at Annie kindly as she entered. 'Yes, Staff Nurse Scott, what can I do for you?'

Annie twisted her hands together. Matron took off her spectacles, put down her pen and leaned back in the high leather chair.

'Are you unwell, child? You look bothered. Is everything all right at home? Have you heard about your brother yet?'

'No, Matron. No, we haven't heard yet, thank you, and no I'm quite well.'

What seemed like a good idea yesterday suddenly wasn't. 'I want to go... go with Molly, Staff Nurse Williams, she is going to France and I want to go, too; maybe I'll find Matthew.'

'Oh dear, I was afraid this would happen. You two are as thick as thieves. Staff Nurse Williams came to see me yesterday; I feared she might try to convince you as well. But France is a big place, so if you go, it must be to nurse and not to search; you do know you will be very lucky to find your brother.'

'Yes Matron, I know that, but I want to go, to help in some way, and if I find Matthew, it will be a bonus.'

'What do your parents think?'

'They don't want me to go, of course, but they are being really understanding about it. They've given me their blessing, reluctantly.'

'That helps. Well, I suppose I'll have to let you go. We will miss you of course, but if you are really sure that this is what you must do, then of course you must and you will be an asset there; they need good nurses like you. You go with my blessing as well;

37

our job will be waiting for you when you get back.'

'Thank you very much, Matron. I'll be back as soon as I can, as soon as the war is over; they say it will be soon.'

'Well, look after yourselves, won't you; you had better take the day off to get ready. When is Staff Nurse Williams leaving?'

'Next week, Matron. On Monday.'

'You had better go at the same time. Now go back to your ward, I'll speak to Sister, and I'll see you before you both go.'

Annie walked slowly out of the office, trembling from head to toe. She had done it now, committed herself. Behind the closed door, Matron put her head in her hands. All her best girls were going, they were needed out there but she needed them, too. Soon, all those that were left would have to be doing double shifts. She needed a meeting with her Sisters to discuss strategy. They would need some of these new VADs; they were keen but untrained, no replacement for the likes of Staff Nurses Scott and Williams.

*

Molly and Annie went down to the recruiting office to sign on, to be given instructions, orders and lists of things that Annie may need. Molly had already done this, but she went with Annie, to keep her company and give her courage; it made it much easier. When they were there, they made it clear that they were in it together and would serve together or not at all, not to be separated.

Annie stood in front of the recruiting officer, smoothing down her dress and fiddling with her hair. The officer looked stern. 'Why are you here?'

'I am a trained nurse, trained at York hospital; I am told you need nurses.'

'You do know it will be the hardest work you have ever done in your life; long shifts, non-stop, little time off?' The recruitment officer looked Annie up and down, taking in her trim figure, judging if she had the stamina needed.

'I am used to hard work.'

'Well, we have the reference from your Matron. She says you will be a loss to her and an asset to us, so I suppose we will take you on.'

'I thought you needed Staff Nurses like us.'

'Yes we do, but only those who understand the consequences;

it will be no holiday, you know.'

When all the paperwork had been completed, Annie looked at the lists. They were daunting; how was she going to afford all this?

'Oh Molly, what is all this? How am I going to get all this in the time?'

Over tea and some iced buns, the two girls chatted about the commitment they had made and what it might mean. They looked so different, sitting side by side; Annie slim with long, dark hair, pale skin, brown eyes and elegant hands. Molly had a very modern short bob to her fair curls which went with her pink and white complexion and bright blue eyes; she was what her father called nicely rounded, comfortable. They put their heads together, pouring over the lists, picking out bits they needed to buy and what they already had.

There were injections against typhoid, cholera and so on. 'The army do them if we go to the office in the morning; I've had mine – they make your arm sore.'

'Matron has said we may take our uniforms, which will make a big difference. But we need to buy ourselves another pair of boots each and the bits and pieces they have told us to take. But there are some things they have told us not to take.'

'I wonder how we get all our uniforms laundered.'

'Well, they have proper hospitals; which means getting sheets and bandages washed, so I expect we can use the hospital laundry. But it's a good point; we must take plenty of aprons.'

The door of the tea-room opened and in came two soldiers. One was leaning on his crutches, his right trouser-leg pinned up; he was wearing an eye-patch. The other had his sleeve flapping against his side, his head was bandaged.

The girls nudged each other. 'Those men are the sort who we will have to be looking after, soon; poor fellows, they look all in, so tired and thin.' They tried not to stare.

The men found a table in the corner and painfully lowered themselves into their chairs. The waitress came over. She looked old and worn, as though she had the world's worries on her shoulders. She pushed a stray lock of hair behind her cap and gave the two men a beaming smile which lit up her face.

'What are you boys having?' she said cheerfully, pulling out her pad and pencil, as though serving limbless soldiers in her tea-rooms was an every-day occurrence, maybe it was. 'House rules: all injured soldiers get their first tea and cakes on the house. Tell your friends,' she said. The men gave a tired smile and relaxed. 'Make yourselves at home. You are very welcome here.'

They ordered and got a big pot of tea and a plate of cakes. They winked at Molly and Annie, who blushed but smiled at them.

'We're nurses and we're going out to France next week.'

'Well, you are needed, but look after yourselves; pretty girls like you, the Bosch doesn't care.'

'I want to find my brother, he's missing.'

The two soldiers looked at each other. 'You do know that there are a lot of men out there? You may not come across him.'

'Yes, I know, and thank you, but it won't stop me looking.'

'Well, good luck. We hope you find him.'

'Time to go back on duty,' said Molly. They waved to the two men. 'Good luck to you too.'

At the hospital gates, they hugged. 'It will be alright; it will be fine and maybe you'll find Matthew. I'll see you in the morning.'

'Yes, maybe I'll find Matthew.' Annie looked sad and pensive as she hurried away.

When she came off duty, Annie pulled her nursing books off the shelf, the ones that had seen her through her examinations to become a Staff Nurse. Her favourite was one she chose to take with her: *'Notes on Nursing'* by Florence Nightingale. It had done her well. She also selected a book on trauma and orthopaedics as the most helpful. She would only take the two; they had been told to keep the weight down. What was the point in taking a book about nursing children or on gynaecology? She sat on her bed, smoothing the silkiness of her counterpane, looking out of the window, listening to the branches of the tree outside her bedroom window rustle in the breeze and watching the shadows chasing across her wall. She listened to the blackbirds singing to each other from the tops of the buildings; nesting and bringing up the babies would be underway soon.

'I'll miss all this,' she told herself, 'but it's too late to change my mind now.'

She went downstairs to tea, to tell her parents about her busy day.

Chapter 7

Joseph

Reveille sounded in the square outside. It woke Joseph; for a few moments, he wondered where he was. Where was Jacob? Then he remembered yesterday. He was freezing cold, it was difficult to move. He sat on the side of the bed, with the thin blanket pulled around his shoulders, wriggled his hands and feet to get the circulation going, stamped around the cell five paces in one direction, five in the other, up and down, up and down, banging his arms round his chest. He tried jumping up, trying to reach the ceiling with his fingers until, at length, the circulation returned. When he felt his brain and body were working together again, he sat on his bunk in prayerful meditation; he asked God for strength to help him in his determination to follow through whatever happened. He remembered the Meeting for Worship and the Friends who were supporting him with their prayers, all the people who were praying for him; he held them in his thoughts and prayed for them too.

He stood on the narrow bunk and, rubbing the dirt away with the corner of the blanket, looked out of the slit window.

'Well now, Joseph lad,' he told himself, 'this is it, tha's in for't now, let's see what t'day fetches.'

He heard a tapping on the pipe and knelt on the floor, to wish Norman's eye good morning.

'Sleep well? The butler will be around with hot water to shave you, and clean clothes; he will bring your breakfast of coddled eggs and toast.' Joseph found Norman's dry humour a great comfort.

'Well now, what really happens? Anyway, what does coddled mean?'

'Well, we do get water to wash and shave with and we do get breakfast after a fashion, then you might get a visit to help you to dress; that is up to you. We only get khaki and it is very cold if you don't wear it.' The door banged open. 'Slop out,' yelled the soldier.

'And a very good morning to you, Sir. I trust you slept as well as I did.'

'Silence! You have been told.'

'Yes, but it seems so rude not to wish you good morning.'

'Silence!' A purple vein pulsed in the man's temple.

Joseph picked up the bucket that had been provided by way of a toilet and took it, as instructed, to the drain at the end of the corridor. He was given a small bucket of tepid water to use for washing and shaving.

Breakfast was a bowl of porridge and a mug of cool tea. But no coddled eggs; he complained to Norman later.

Two warders came, ordered him to take the used water to the drain and put on his uniform.

'Give me some clothes I can wear and I'll gladly dress.'

'These are your clothes, Soldier. You are in the army now and don't you forget it.'

'I can't wear the khaki of a soldier, I'm very sorry.' He sat heavily on the bed.

'Well, we'll just have to help you, won't we?' They called for reinforcements.

Joseph decided not to resist but not to help, so he lay down and let his body go limp again. It took three of them twenty minutes to get him dressed.

'Now stay like that.'

It was very tempting; the thick woollen trousers and jacket were warm, but he thought he could compromise and have some fun. He took them off and put the jacket on his lower half, yanking the sleeves up his legs and buttoning it up over his belly, then he thrust his arms into the legs of the trousers. It made moving awkward, but he enjoyed the exercise, it warmed him up and it made him laugh. 'Ee Joseph lad, tha's a rig't silly beggar.'

A tapping on the pipe. 'What's the joke? What have you done, I could hear all the grunting.'

Joseph knelt down with difficulty. 'I don't think I can keep it up, but I've been trying on the jacket and trousers. I wish you could see me.'

As Joseph tried to explain what he had done, Norman roared with laughter. 'That's going to be interesting in a little while. It's drill next. We'll see what they make of that; I'm looking forward

43

to seeing you and the others.'

'How do you cope with that; with drill?'

'Well, of course it's up to you what you want to do, but two guards escort each of us onto the parade ground for exercises. It can be quite entertaining. But seriously, if you want to do as you are told, wear the uniform and so on, that is fine and your life will certainly be easier, but if you want to resist everything, that is also alright but we do try to be as peaceable as possible, and of course very polite; that really annoys them.'

The door was thrown open again. 'What the Hell...I suppose you think that's funny? Well, no time to do anything about it now. Out you go, on parade and drill.'

'Yes Sir, of course Sir, where would you like me to go?'

'None of your cheek, Soldier!'

'I apologise.'

'Silence!'

'Yes Sir, of course, I forgot, no talking.'

'Silence I said!' The man was apoplectic with anger.

'You really ought to calm down, Sir; this cannot be good for you.'

'Silence!!' He was nearly jumping up and down with rage.

Two warders frog-marched him out of the cell block and into the bright sunlight of a Yorkshire spring morning. Joseph held his hand up to his face; the sunlight was so bright, he felt temporarily blinded. He could hear a blackbird in the distance with its warning call, a cat must be near, and it would be in fear for its nest. He could feel the breeze on his face, fresh air in his lungs and could hear the sound of the river tumbling over the rocks below.

'What a beautiful day, isn't it, Sir?' He filled his lungs with the clean air.

'Silence! Don't you ever learn?' Joseph staggered as he was kicked in the back of his knees.

They pushed and pulled him into the centre of the parade ground. 'Don't move, stay exactly there.'

'Of course, Sir, certainly, Sir' He sat down on the grass, feeling the fresh dampness on his skin and waited.

The soldiers went back to get the rest of the men, sixteen in all, eight from the cells and eight from the room that they called the guard-room; it was the first time they had all seen each other. Some co-operated and some had to be dragged out, one or two were carried. Two were fully dressed in uniform, the rest in just their underwear, with a blanket pulled over their shoulders. No-one else had been as inventive as Joseph; they were helpless with laughter when they saw him.

'Silence! Silence!'

'Yes Sir,' they all chorused through their laughter.

'I'm Norman,' came a whisper from the corner of the mouth of the man next to him, 'pleased to see the rest of you; the effect is certainly eye-catching.' He was a very pleasant-looking man, but not as he had described himself; far from being six foot, six inches with fair wavy hair, Norman was about five foot seven with thinning hair, the eyes were a startling blue, though.

'You aren't exactly what I was expecting...girls will drop at your feet though, I am sure.'

'That's Bert, the really tall one; he is our unofficial spokesman and negotiator. For some reason, them upstairs seem to like him; went to a posh school in York,' Norman whispered and pointed out a distinguished-looking man with an air of quiet authority, older than the others. 'I believe he is a Quaker.'

'Oh good, so am I. And you?'

'No, I'm a Methodist, but I want to learn more about you lot. We can talk about it some more later. There are a variety here; men from the International Bible Students and Socialists, quite a few of them, all sorts of convictions, but we all have one thing in common, we will not fight,' said Norman.

The PE instructor came towards them. 'Silence! Drill, you 'orrible lot, we'll make soldiers of you yet.'

'Now for some fun,' whispered Norman, 'just watch, learn and copy if you want to.'

'Arms up, arms down, arms forward.' They were completely un-cooperative.

The instructor got angry, red in the face. 'I will not have insubordination in the ranks! You are in the army and you will do drill! Soldier, get me sixteen men, at the double.'

The sixteen young privates soon returned. 'Help this scurvy lot.'

45

A soldier stood behind every prisoner and, on command, moved the arms of the man in front of him, up and down, to the side, to the front. The sixteen prisoners laughed helplessly, until their arms were yanked painfully backwards.

The instructor soon yelled. 'Take them back to their cells, I've had enough.'

Most of the men dropped to the ground and lay on the grass; they listened to the sounds of the wind in the trees, the gurgling of the river, and just relaxed in the sun. Some were dragged to their cells by their arms. Joseph, remembering Norman's words about choices, stayed on his feet and allowed himself to be escorted; his arms were already sore from being pulled and pushed during the enforced exercises.

He lay on his bunk, thinking; this had been a strange day; the enormity of what he had let himself in for was beginning to dawn on him. He now knew that there were sixteen of the absolutist conscientious objectors at present in the castle, some in these cells in solitary confinement. Another group was in what had been the guard-room in a former life of the castle, when it was a Norman strong-hold; they were all in one room. Joseph didn't know why he had been selected for solitary, but he was rather glad, being in one room with several others all the time didn't really appeal to him. He also now knew that he and he alone, was responsible for his actions and he always had the option to obey orders or not, even change his mind and join up; but he could never do that. But whatever he did, he would not be judged by the others, it was between himself, his conscience and God.

Joseph rolled himself a very thin cigarette. He had no idea when he might get more tobacco. He looked at the spent match; its charcoal tip was black in his hand. He made a small mark on the wall; it made a good pencil. He started writing and drawing on the wall beside his bed; he began to make a diagram. Over the days, it built up into a series of triangles and lines leading from one random thought to another. He interspersed it with Biblical and other quotations that he had learned as a child. He signed his name and tried to remember the date. How many days had he been here? It was difficult; all days seemed to be the same.

Every night, his last thoughts before he fell asleep were prayers to be given the strength in mind and body for whatever lay ahead and for his family and members of his Quaker Meeting.

Chapter 8

Daniel

Daniel woke with a start, unsure of where he was, to see the laughing face of Hubert looking down at him from the next bed. 'Where? When? What? Who?' He scratched his head, feeling the shorn hair. He sat up and remembered; he was in the army. A bugle was sounding, loud, raucous, unfamiliar, outside the hut.

'Reveille, come on, get up washed and dressed.' Hubert stripped the blankets off Daniel's body.

'Ugh, if that is what you do to your new friends, heaven help the Bosch, he should be quaking in his boots.' He curled up in the cold morning air, clutching his feet.

'Come on, come on, rise and shine, don't let that Corporal catch you in bed. And, anyway, we have a delicious breakfast to look forward to; I expect we will have lightly poached eggs, kedgeree, steaming hot, fresh coffee, toast running with butter and honey.'

'What sort of breakfast do you think that is? I haven't had anything like that in my whole life? Kedgee-what? I don't even know what half that stuff is. Give me Ma's porridge.'

'Sorry, it is what we often have with Mater and Pater, but I was being ironic, I don't expect to have that sort of thing in the Army.'

'Ir...what? Mater and Pater?'' What sort of language is that? You and I haven't got much in common, have we? I look forward to finding out more about you. But push off for now, this miner's son needs to get up and dressed.'

Down the centre of the hut was a long bench with wash bowls and jugs. The men pulled blankets over their shoulders, and each taking a jug went outside to find water. A queue of scruffy, sleepy-looking men had formed by the taps. They filled their jugs and went in to find bowls; it was all too public for Daniel, but Hubert joshed him along,

'If you came from the same size family that I do and went to the sort of school I did, it wouldn't bother you, you'll have to get used to it. You're part of this family now.'

They struggled again into their new khaki, helping each-other with belts, caps and puttees; they made their beds and went out into the cold spring sunshine, to find breakfast in the Mess Hut. Big bowls of sticky porridge and mugs of sweet tea set them up for the day.

'This is more what I'm used to, but Ma's is much nicer than this, creamier.' Daniel scraped the bowl clean.

Hubert didn't seem to mind. 'It's what they gave us at boarding school.'

They didn't have long to enjoy it. The Corporal arrived, shouting instructions. 'I will be in your hut in ten minutes, heaven help you; you have that time to get ready.'

Chairs were shoved back as the men made a hasty rush for the door, in order to be ready for the dreaded visit.

*

Inspection; they had to stand by their beds while everything was examined minutely.

'You call that bed made? Looks like a tart's boudoir.' He yanked the blankets back. 'Your pyjamas will be under the pillow, folded, and just look at the state of this locker!' He pulled the contents out onto the floor, the owner standing by in embarrassment. 'And I told you to polish those boots; I want to see my face in them. What do I want to see?'

'Your face in our boots.'

'My face in your boots. Sir.'

'Yes, Sir, of course, Sir, your face, my boots, Sir.'

Each lad was subjected to the same degree of scorn, no-one was exempted; some for their bed-making skills, others for the tidiness of their belongings; some hadn't got the right amount of shine on their boots or buttons.

'Get this lot sorted out! You have half an hour and then out on parade. You, you and you, go back to the Quartermaster's Stores, to get a jacket that you can wear and trousers that fit; tell him I sent you; and you, you get a new cap. I thought I told you to get all this sorted out yesterday.'

'Yes, but...'

'No arguing, just do it.'

There was much grumbling from the boys as they set about, trying to satisfy the demands of the Corporal; half an hour later, most of them had assembled on what they guessed was the parade

49

ground; two were missing. They had lost their caps and didn't dare to appear without them.

'This is why we demand tidiness of you; how will you be able find anything in a hurry, under fire at the Front, if you have no idea where you have put things? Keep everything tidy and in the same place, that is not just advice, it is an order; what is it?'

'An order,' one or two of them replied.

'I asked a question. What is it?' the Corporal snapped.

All of the lads chorused. 'An order.'

'What is it?' Somehow, the Corporal had to make the lads jump at any command; that was his sole task, turn them into soldiers.

'An order. Sir.'

'That's more like it; whenever you are facing an officer, you will address him as "Sir", you have a lot to learn; now line up in two ranks.'

'You, boy, what are you doing, your hands in your pockets, playing with yourself, you some sort of weirdo?'

Daniel blushed to the roots of his hair, let go of Susie's stone and took his hands from his pockets. 'No, Sir, of course not, Sir. I was just…'

The long, hard task of moulding these young men into soldiers began. Over the next days and weeks, they learned how to obey an order without thinking, how to march in formation, how to keep going when they felt they would drop. They learned to keep their uniform tidy, their boots and buttons polished and their puttees clean. They did physical jerks, or PJ as they came to call it, twice a day, half an hour before breakfast and then more later in the day, wearing nothing but their long-johns, shivering in the cold. Some had never done exercises before and were out of condition, others had come from farm work and found PJ easy. One or two appeared to be fit from other exercise, such as smithing. There were no miners, any that had been called up had been sent to dig tunnels under the German lines.

'How come you are so fit, Hubert? I thought you were a real softie.'

'I could ask you the same question. You told me you work in a bank as a clerk. I played rugby, rowed for my school and was

50

training to represent it at some inter-school event; I only left at the end of last term, when Pater said I should do my bit for the country, join up and so on; he's furious with me for joining the NCC; will probably cut me off without a penny.'

'I am fit, as I play cricket and football when I can; and it is a two mile walk to work every day. Pa always encouraged me to take exercise, so I sometimes run to work. Mr Fosdyke, my boss, doesn't like that as I arrive all hot and bothered, but it keeps me warm in the winter. I don't suppose you know what work is,' Daniel teased.

'Don't you start; I get enough of that at home.' Hubert hared off round the parade ground, Daniel chasing after him.

The men walked, marched and then ran round the parade ground and later marched round the town, then made excursions into the woods for whole days' worth of exercises. It was relentless, they felt they could march in their sleep, they were given scant time off, they were at it from day-break to night-fall. By the end of the first day, they were tired; by the end of the first week, they were exhausted. But, at the end of the month, they were fit; muscles developed where they didn't know they had any. They became a unified force. All of them fell into their bunks at the end of each day and slept as soon as their heads were down. They developed voracious appetites and, whereas army food was nourishing and filling, it was not varied and became boring after a while, but none of them complained; they felt lucky to be so well fed: porridge every morning, stew and vegetables mid-day and bread and dripping in the evenings and, of course, tea with everything.

Twice a week, they were given the evening off. Most of them went to the cinema in town, to see the latest flicks; a welcome break for the grinding routine.

'I really liked that; that was good, very clever.' They had just come out from seeing one of the *Pimple* films, "*Pimple's Battle of Waterloo*".

'I laughed till my sides ached.' Daniel wiped his eyes. 'I've never seen anything like it, such fun. I hope we can see another *Pimple* film soon. I hear they are making a series of them.'

51

*

Every Sunday, they had compulsory church parade. Everyone was expected to attend, and all did, Methodists, Quakers, Socialists, IBA students; for whatever reason they were in the NCC, this church service gave them something in common, even the Quakers and non-believers joined in with gusto. The chaplain gave them pep-talks about God being on their side and Jesus being with them. They were told that good – England – will overcome evil – Germany. They weren't convinced; some of the men yawned openly but they sang the hymns, said the prayers, knelt and stood with everyone else.

'I suppose the Germans are given the same pep talk, but we'll be the bad guys,' Hubert pondered.

They were allowed Sunday afternoons off. Daniel and Hubert went out into the town, bought postcards which they sent to their families; Daniel to Susie and his Ma, Hubert to all his brothers and sisters. They took a bottle of water, bought cake, some apples and walked down to the river Swale, had a bit of a picnic, strolled along the bank, throwing stones into the water. The water was stained brown, toffee-coloured, tinged with the peat it had run through further up the Dale; it rushed past over the huge, flat stones, clattering and roaring, but other times it seemed to be just a trickle. They took off their boots and paddled. There were dippers and moorhens with their chicks, and they thought they saw an otter, but they couldn't be sure. This time was very precious, time to think and chat.

'You and I haven't much in common, have we?' asked Hubert.

'Why did you join the NCC? You said your Pater was furious with you.'

'Well, actually, I'm a Quaker; Pater wanted me to have a good education so sent me to the Quaker school in York, even though he and Mater are dyed in the wool Anglican. Of course, the school is run by Quakers and I met a lot there; there were very few of us that weren't. I learnt about it and asked to become a Member, about a year ago.'

'What does being a Quaker mean to you?' enquired Daniel. 'Of course, I have asked my friend Joseph, who is also a Quaker, but he doesn't say a lot.'

'Whew, what a difficult question. You know that in the Anglican Church there is a creed, something that says "I believe in...". Well, we don't say that, we have no creeds. We believe that Jesus came to us, to teach us a good way of life, but how we interpret that is up to us; we use the Bible, of course, but we also use all sorts of other books of inspiration.' Hubert struggled to put into words what he knew and believed.

'Like what?'

'Early Friends read and wrote a lot of papers and pamphlets, I don't know if I can get any here, but if I can I'll let you see them.'

'Thanks, I'd be interested to see some.' Daniel said.

'So most of us are Pacifists; our pacifist teaching is one of the most important.'

'What do you mean *most*? If that is one of the main teachings, why don't you all adhere to it? And why are you even here in the army.'

'We believe that everyone should make up their own mind and some believe in the concept of the 'Just War' and will support it by fighting in it. George Fox started it all when he refused to fight for neither Charles the Second nor Oliver Cromwell; he, with a group of other people who became known as Quakers, said "We utterly deny all outward wars and strife with outward weapons, for any end or any pretence whatsoever." I find it very challenging as, although there are the Elders who will always listen and guide, in the end I have to decide for myself. They said a lot more, but that is the most important bit to me. And as to being in the army, I wasn't given much choice; I had to be in the NCC or prison.

'Tell me more about this 'Just War' idea,' asked Daniel.

'Well, one thing is that, in order to be justified, a war has to meet most or all of seven criteria.'

'Hubert, you do use some long words; you make me feel ignorant.'

'Oh, I'm really sorry, it's that school I went to, they insisted we use this sort of language. Where was I? Yes, wars should meet several or all of seven standards. It should be legitimate, that is war should be declared; the cause should be just; it should have right intention, that is it should try to remedy an injustice; it should be a last resort; there should be a reasonable hope for success; the evil it causes should be less than the evil it prevents and there should be immunity for non-combatants.'

'Whew. I think I understand; I'll need to think about that, it's a lot to take in all at once.'

'Well, why are you here? Why did you decide to join the NCC and not the fighting army?'

'Well, I was brought up as a Methodist and used to go to chapel regularly. I lost my faith in all that when Pa was killed. People started talking about it being God's will, I couldn't believe that, I don't think a good God does that sort of thing, the props just gave way and he was in the wrong place at the wrong time; others escaped, it was all so random. So I'm a Socialist, a member of the British Socialist Party; I believe all men are my brothers and I cannot kill my brother.'

'We will get on famously, you and me, I couldn't have said it better myself.'

'Why don't you have a creed? I know Mam and Susie find it very helpful in church.'

'Well, early Friends wrote that "The letter killeth, but the Spirit giveth life", and I agree with that. We sit in silence at our Meetings for Worship, in expectation and hope, waiting to be guided by the Spirit; sometimes someone will speak if they are moved to, but I prefer completely silent meetings.'

'So you are guided by the Spirit to join the NCC in this war? I just hope I can do some good while it all goes on; sometimes, I feel that I'm a coward, but I will not kill.'

'Sounds a bit corny, but, yes I am guided to be of help to those at the Front who need us, but not to carry arms. Some Quakers will not join the NCC, will refuse to have anything to do with the war; as I said, they will land up in prison, or worse, I expect.'

'My friend Joseph is one of those, I think he might even be here, in Richmond. I heard a rumour that they are sending some of them here, while they decide what to do with them. I fear for him. I hope I can make some sort of contact with him, but I don't know how.'

*

Hubert asked for, and was given, a small room in which to hold a Quaker Meeting for Worship. Hubert asked Daniel if he would like to join them; in fact, they asked anyone who would be interested to be there for the hour on Sunday evenings. They set chairs in a circle round a small table; it held a Bible and one of their own books, *Christian Discipline*. Apart from the few Quakers, three or four others went. Daniel was very keen to join them; after his conversations with Hubert on their walks, he wanted to know more. As they all trooped in, Hubert, greeting them at the door, wondered if this was the first Meeting where all the participants were in army uniform. They sat in silence; some had their eyes closed and heads bowed, others looked around wide-eyed. They all had one thing in their minds: they were wondering what they had let themselves in for and how would they cope with what lay ahead. Hubert stood and read from the book. "Take heed, dear Friends, we entreat you, to the convictions of the Holy Spirit who leads through unfeigned repentance, and living faith in the Son of God, to reconciliation with our Heavenly Father, and to the blessed hope of eternal life, purchased for us by the one offering of our Lord and Saviour Jesus Christ."

Daniel was very moved and interested in this and repeated it over and over in his head. The silence seemed even more profound; it seemed that all minds had this one thought, as though they were all bound together somehow; he wondered about God, was He with them? He didn't really have a faith anymore, but these were interesting ideas to ponder; he had been to chapel on many occasions with Ma and Susie, but he had never really had this sort of experience before. After an hour, which seemed much shorter, Hubert shook hands with the men on either side of him, all the others did the same; it was the end of the meeting. They stood feeling refreshed, relaxed and strangely renewed as they went back to their huts.

As Daniel and Hubert crossed the parade ground one Sunday morning, on the way to Church Parade, they could hear singing; hymns being sung by what appeared to be a small number of men. Near the tower was a small block which they hadn't taken much notice of before. It had two rows of small windows and it was from here that the singing was coming. Hubert and Daniel stood beneath the windows and joined in quietly; they had no idea who was in there, singing with such gusto. When the singing stopped and they were turning to go, Daniel heard his name being shouted. He could just make out a face at the tiny, dirty window.

'It's me, Joseph. Daniel, what are you doing here?'

Daniel started round in surprise and shouted back, 'Joseph, my friend, how good to see you. I'm in the Non-Combatant Corps, training to go to France, to work in a hospital. I heard you might be here.' He wasn't sure he was heard.

'There are a dozen or so of us conchies locked in here for refusing to join up; we are expecting to be taken to France, as well. We expect to be shot. Good luck and may God go with you, dear Friend.'

'May your God go with you too.'

At this point there was a great shouting from inside and Joseph's face disappeared from the window. They saw their Corporal across the parade ground, glaring at them.

'Who was that?' enquired Hubert.

'The friend I was telling you about, my Quaker friend Joseph; doesn't sound good for them, does it?'

'I heard you say you were going to work in a hospital. You'll be lucky, I think we are all being trained to be stretcher-bearers and first-aiders, to work on the Front line.'

'I don't think I can take that. I can't stand loud noise, I don't want to be near bombs; loud noises hurt my ears and head. I do hope I don't get sent to the trenches.'

Daniel went back to his hut deep in thought. So, that is what had happened to Joseph. He must write and tell Ma who would tell Joseph's mother; she needed to know.

Daniel found his comrades busying about; many were trying to get the required shine on their boots or polishing their buttons, but a few had abandoned those activities and were reading, playing cards or writing letters; he shook his head. He wrote a short letter to his mother and Susie; all his news of the week including a little bit about Joseph. But he wanted some fresh air and exercise. 'Football anyone?' he called out. He took the heavy leather ball from the cupboard at the back of the hut and they tumbled out into the late sun. It was a very different game from that of the first week; they were fitter, more organised, knew each other's strengths and weaknesses and were able to sort themselves out

56

into teams quickly, to play a good, hard game. The Corporal passing by stopped for a while to watch; he saw a big difference in the men from when they arrived. He smiled to himself; they would make a good team, and he could see who would make leaders.

*

Every day followed the same pattern – up at 5.30 with Reveille, wash and shave at the tables down the middle of the hut; they were all losing their inhibitions now and wandered about in all sorts of dress and undress. Half an hour of drill, exercises led by the Corporal, then the usual breakfast of porridge, time to tidy the hut before standing at the foot of their beds for inspection. All the kit was laid out in a certain order; nearly always at least one of them would get bawled out for some misdemeanour, and woe betide anyone who had something missing. Everything was inspected and checked out; they had more items added to their packs: bandages, dressings, stretchers. Then out into the parade ground for more inspection by the commanding officer and more drill.

In the afternoons of most days there were lessons; they sat in rows in a school-room; they learned anatomy, what bits of a body went where. Some of them found this very difficult as they had had only a scant experience of school, others found it quite fascinating, never having really thought about their own bodies before, beyond what is visible, beyond their skins. Then there were the practical lessons; they worked in twos and threes, learning bandaging, they bandaged each other and applied dressings. They learnt what injuries they might encounter, how to deal with them, and carried each other for miles round and round the parade ground; they learned how to crawl on their bellies, dragging a stretcher with a man on it; none of it was easy.

Daniel was delighted to be chosen to learn to be an ambulance driver, but of course it wasn't just the driving, which he found fairly easy. He had to learn how to strip down and repair the engine, to change wheels, mend punctures, in fact everything needed to keep the vehicle road-worthy. Then he was also responsible for making sure his ambulance was properly kitted out; there were lists and lists of equipment that had to be stowed all in the right places, but he feared it meant he would have to go

57

to the trenches.

After four weeks, they were sent to the local hospitals to help in the out-patient clinics with the poor, the ill and the injured. Daniel saw people who had no money to pay for treatment and therefore had waited too long to seek it: men with farming or mining accidents, children who had got in the way of horses, carts or occasional automobiles or trains, women with injuries from the mills and factories. One man had lost a leg and a lot of blood; he waited stoically in line on a stretcher, waiting for the shattered limb to be redressed. He was starting to get septicaemia and would almost certainly die. And a child, with a terrible head injury from being run down by a cart, whose mother begged them to make him better. Daniel did what he could for the little lad, but he didn't hold out much hope for him. He was especially taken with a beautiful young woman called Ann. She had caught her hand in a machine at the mill. She had not come to them for a week, now it was an infected septic mess; she would lose her hand, maybe her arm or her life. She was flushed and delirious; her brother had brought her in a wagon. For all these and the rest, he did his best and learned how to care for a variety of injuries and illnesses. At the end of it, they all felt that they were actually doing something useful and gaining excellent experience.

*

The highlight of the week was Friday; Daniel's hut's turn for a bath. There were no facilities for this at Richmond Castle, so they were marched the mile and a half to the local army barracks; towel, soap, clean underwear and socks in kit bags. The huge wash-tubs were set out in two rows in narrow stalls; the low dividing wall gave a modicum of privacy. The tin baths were deep and long, and for the first in were filled with wonderful hot water. The men later on only had tepid water, but it was all welcome. The lads lay back and wallowed and sang songs. *"In Dublin's Fair City", "I'll take the High Road", "It's a long way to Tipperary"* and *"Pack up Your Troubles in Your Old Kit Bag"*; the sounds echoing along the building. It felt like heaven and they returned in high spirits.

However, the locals knew that they were in the NCC and that, although they were in uniform, they were not 'proper' soldiers.

Men, women and children gathered down the sides of the road and jeered and shouted, some women ran up to them with white feathers to pin on their clothes; children followed them all the way there with shouting and name calling. They waited outside, knowing that they could do the same on the way back; the taunts were difficult to bear. Daniel tried to befriend one or two of the little lads, but they weren't very receptive to his advances.

'Sweets might help, I'll get some next time we are in town,' he told Hubert.

Chapter 9

Joseph

The door crashed open. 'Breakfast!' the soldier yelled; a bowl of not very hot porridge and a mug of tea were dumped on the floor.

'Thank you so much.' And the man was gone.

A bucket of potatoes was flung down into the cell. 'Peel those.'

'Who are they for?'

'You lot, of course, who do you think? And that lot out there, the ones pretending to be soldiers, except that they refuse to do rifle drill or bayonet practice.'

'OK, but I'll need a knife.'

He enjoyed the task, one he had often done for his mother. He could imagine he was home again; it gave him something constructive to do, rather than just sitting, thinking. He was skilled and careful not to take off too much skin. The potatoes felt cool and heavy in his hand, he liked the feel of the mud. He took his time over it; the smell of the earth reminded him of his parents' garden.

'Good, well done! You've done a good job, they'll be pleased. I'll tell them it was you.' The old soldier took the bucket of potatoes and went away, whistling.

That evening, the potatoes that he was given to eat were not only not peeled, they were none too clean, either. He felt cheated; these were not the potatoes he had peeled that morning.

He was brought more potatoes to peel the next day.

'I'll not do those, I was lied to yesterday.'

'What do you mean?'

'I mean that the other soldier told me that the spuds were for us, but we had very dirty ones last night. I'll not do these for your officers, I'm sorry.'

'We all have to be fed.'

'Yes, I know, but I'll not do them.'

'It'll be bread and water for you, laddie, but that's your problem,' the soldier commented as he slammed the door.

'Tha'rt getting in deeper and deeper,' he warned himself.

Joseph was hungry. To take his mind off the pangs, he often stood on his bunk, looking at the activities below him; he watched

60

the men preparing for their part in the war. He thought hard about his commitment to absolute objection. He knew he was doing the right thing but doubts kept crowding into his mind. He hoped he would see Daniel again and thought he did see him once, but as the man didn't turn round, he couldn't be sure; everyone wearing uniform made it so difficult. They all looked the same, same clothing, same hair-cut.

Standing on his bed, he watched the sun set, the rays warming the stones opposite with a red glow, the castle sometimes looked very beautiful, in spite of the old, grey, high walls.

*

Joseph was at home, with Hannah, Jacob and his parents; helping with the hay at the near-by farm after his day at the workshop; he could smell the freshness of the newly mown hay, could feel the scythe in his hands, feel it cut through the grass; could hear the laughter of his friends, even taste the food his mother had made for them. A sound broke into his dream, an insistent tapping; reluctantly, so very reluctantly he opened his eyes to see the green and black stains on the wall, to smell the musty dampness of the air. He padded across the cold floor and knelt down by the pipe.

'I was dreaming of home.' He almost sobbed to Norman's eye.

'It's Sunday. I know you Quakers like to do your worshipping in silence, but we like a bit of a sing. Care to join us?'

'Why not? I'd really like to, so when do we start?'

'As soon as someone does.'

The eye disappeared and Joseph could just see Norman's ankle as he stood up. The hymns of Charles Wesley were soon echoing through the cells, every man there stood and sang at the top of his voice. The hymn *"Christ whose glory fills the skies, Christ, the true, the only light..."* seemed particularly appropriate for the occasion; they also sang the hymn of John Bunyan, *"He who would valiant be, 'gainst all disaster..."* The warders in the corridor outside stopped and listened, and some actually joined in; the passion of the singing was infectious. The sound leaked through the little ventilation holes at the tops of the slit windows, and men crossing the parade ground stopped and listened, a few joining in quietly under their breath. The last hymn they sang was sometimes called the Quaker hymn, *'Dear Lord and Father of*

61

mankind, forgive our foolish ways...' An NCC soldier called Daniel Braithwaite stopped on his way to the Mess Hut and stood with them in unity and joined them in singing, until a shouted order across the parade ground stopped him.

'What do you think you are doing, Soldier? Do you want to join them?'

'Yes,' Daniel replied, but *sotto voce*, 'but I don't have the strength. Oh Joseph, I am with you, do be careful.' He turned away to his breakfast.

Daniel heard his name; when he looked back, he could just make out a face in the tiny, dirty window.

'It's me, Joseph. Daniel, what are you doing here?'

Daniel started round in surprise and shouted back, 'Joseph, my friend, how good to see you. I'm in the Non-Combatant Corps, training to go to France, to work in a hospital. I heard you might be here.' He wasn't sure he was heard.

'There are a dozen or so of us conchies locked in here for refusing to join up; we are expecting to be taken to France as well, we will probably be shot, but for the moment we are well. Good luck and may God go with you, dear friend.'

'May your God go with you too.'

A voice shouted from within the cell, 'What do you think you are doing?' and Joseph climbed down from his bed.

*

The men started to relax, in spite of the locks and bars; they got on as well as they could with their warders. Corporal Jones was interested in their convictions, and when he was on the evening shift on his own would often visit one or other of the men for a chat and listen to their points of view. He was younger than the other warders, had lost a foot in an accident during training and couldn't be sent to the Front, but his experiences had made him doubt the rightness of wars and this one in particular. They discussed the concept of a 'just war' and its relevance to this one; does the end ever justify the means, especially when it does so much harm?

'A just war is based on the teachings of Saint Augustine,' explained Joseph. 'A war must be declared, be defensive and not aggressive, should try to bring justice, should hope to be successful and should not have use of excessive weapons. I think this one fails on several of those counts; I don't see this as a just war. But even if it were, I couldn't fight, as I can't kill.'

'Do you know exactly what Saint Augustine said?' asked Corporal Jones.

'I think it is "even in war, cherish the spirit of the peacemaker, so that even in conquering we may all be lead back to the advantages of peace". Something like that.'

They never did fully agree, but Joseph always enjoyed their talks, in fact the more they talked the more he was confirmed in his belief that he was doing the right thing. The soldier had joined up as there was no work available near his home and the army seemed to offer a good career. He had been able to stay in the army after the accident; it was a secure income for his family, but he didn't like this work as prison warder. They discussed the writings and drawings on the wall. Joseph tried to explain the triangles and lines of his complex diagram, which connected with biblical quotations. The Corporal himself was also artistic and, over many shifts, had drawn a picture of his home town of Yarm on the wall over the stairs that lead to the upper cells. He was pleased with it and showed it to Joseph, sneaking him out of his cell for a few moments.

'It reminds me of home, my childhood. I had to walk past it on my way to school every day,' explained the soldier.

'It's very good, you should do more drawing.'

'But I do, I've got some at home. I'll bring some in to show you.'

The next evening shift that Corporal Jones was on duty, he brought a folder of work; pictures of the farm buildings and cottages of villages near where he grew up, and ones of Richmond and the castle, beautiful pencil sketches, drawn with a sensitive eye and hand.

'I like this one.' A picture of the Tower.

'I'll get in touch when all this is over and I'll send it to you, a memento of our time here; no point in giving it to you now.'

They talked late into the night about the war, the terrible casualties. 'Thousands of men are coming home, horribly injured; they don't make much of it, they, the politicians, don't want to put people off joining up, but reading between the lines...'

'Are we better off here?' asked Joseph, troubled that he was taking the soft option. 'Should I go and help out? Join the NCC? Get involved?'

'No, stick to your decision. It won't do any good if you give in; don't tell anyone I said so.'

Chapter 10

Daniel

By the end of their training, the young NCC lads had put on
weight and muscle, stood tall and proud, their uniforms now fitted
in a way they didn't fit before; they had been turned into a unit of
men, of responsive soldiers and competent stretcher-bearers, they
felt ready for anything, but had no real idea what that 'anything'
might be. They were given a few days off, to go and see their
families.

Susie was waiting for Daniel at the bus-stop and threw her
arms around him. 'Oh Danny, you look so smart in that uniform;
come, Mother is waiting for you.'

'Now then, our Susie, don't pull my arm off.'

She caught his hand and dragged him home, skipping and
dancing in front of him, showing him off to her friends, she was
so proud of her big brother. 'Look at Danny, isn't he smart? He's
off to the Front soon.'

Elsie greeted him at the door of their little house. She hugged
him to her. 'My son, you look well, tired but well; come, come
you must be hungry.' She had made him his favourite meal, had
killed and roasted a chicken for him, cut some purple sprouting
and cooked baked potatoes and made a rhubarb pie.

'My, Ma, that was champion, I've had filling food in the camp,
but nothing as grand as that.' He sat back in his chair, happy and
relaxed. He rolled himself a cigarette and blew smoke rings up to
the ceiling.

For the first couple of days, he did nothing but sleep, but soon
he was very busy. Time passed so quickly; he dug the garden,
pulling weeds and sowing the seeds of beans and carrots; he
planted potatoes and raked the soil ready for the seeds his mother
or Susie would sow later. One evening, he and a school friend,
George, went into town to the flicks. George hadn't yet been
called up, as he was a farmer and was needed on the land. It was
quite an old film, made nearly ten years earlier; Daniel had seen it
before, in Richmond – *The Sorcerer's Scissors*. George hadn't
been to a moving picture show before and found it intriguing,
magical. The scissors came to life and performed tricks; they

really enjoyed it and laughed at the antics on the flickering screen.

Afterwards, walking home, they talked about the war. 'I'm fair mithered, I don't really know what to expect. We hear so many rumours, it's difficult to know where the truth is,' confided Daniel.

'Well, I'm glad I'll not be going; mind, I have never worked so hard in my life, most of the farm hands have been sent away, they only didn't send me because Dad died and left me and Mother to fend for ourselves; they make more and more demands on the farm. I don't know how I'll manage to keep up; I work from before dawn to after dark.'

'Well, I am also glad to be able to do something helpful, but I don't like the idea of fighting. It's not in my nature or beliefs. But, to be very honest, and you're not to tell anyone, I'm so afraid I'll be sent to the trenches, terrified, in fact; I'm hoping to get hospital work.'

'I'm lucky, I suppose, I don't have to go before a tribunal or anything. I just told them I'm a farmer and got no-one else to do the work and that was it. Someone did come and check I was telling the truth, though; I think he was surprised at how much I do. I quite understand about not wanting to go to the trenches; it's the last thing I'd want to do. But enough of the war, will you be coming to the dance in the village hall at the weekend?'

'Aye. Well, I will if I can, but I may have to go afore then.'

'It's been good to see you, Daniel. Look after yoursen.'

'You too, George. Give my regards to your mother, if I don't see you next weekend, I'll see you next time I'm back on leave. And keep the cricket team together.'

They shook hands, not knowing when or even if they would meet again.

*

Daniel went to visit his Uncle Henry.

'Now then, son, what have you been up to? You look well.'

'I am, Uncle, thank you. I've been training that hard, we've had exercises, drill, marching and learning about looking after injured men. I've also learnt how to drive an ambulance. I can strip down an engine and put it back together quicker than anyone else; maybe I'll be a mechanic when this is all over.'

'Maybe, lad, maybe. But are you still sure that this is right for you? There are those who say that you should be in the real army.'

'I am in the real army. I know that I'll be facing the same dangers as those you call real soldiers; the skills I have learned are essential, too many men get injured and will need my help.'

'I know that, lad; it's the others you'll have to convince.'

'Well, I haven't got time for that now; I'll have to rely on you. Now then, Uncle, please can I ask you a favour?'

'What is it, lad? You can ask anything, tell me what it is and I'll do what I can.'

'Well, you and I both know that I may not get out of this. I know better than some that causalities are very high, and I'll be in as much danger as anyone else. If I don't make it, please will you look after Ma and Susie? With Father gone, I worry about them.'

'Ee lad, you know you don't have to ask. I'll see them right, you know I will. I've already been to see your Ma and we've had a talk about young Susie. She's got all sorts of silly ideas in her head. I'll try to steady her.'

'She can be a bit of a scatter-brain, can't she? And a bit stubborn. Once she gets an idea in her head, she's hard to shift.'

'Your Ma and I will keep an eye on her, never you fret; you have other things to think about now.'

'I'm sorry I had to ask you, but it puts my mind at rest, knowing that I've heard you make that promise; thank you so much.'

The older man laughed, knocked out his pipe on the fender and tamped down a new wodge of tobacco. 'That's what family's for. Now then, will you have a cup of tea and a bit of cake; then we will have a walk and talk of happier times?' He drew on his pipe to re-light it.

*

Daniel went for long walks on his own, visiting the places of his childhood. Sitting under a tree, he took out his mouth-organ; he practiced a few tunes, thinking about what the future might hold for him. He met those of his friends that hadn't yet been called up; they played an early cricket match with the lads from the next village. After the game, they went to the club room, to talk over a pint or two of beer about the old days. Life would never be the same again. They talked about the friends who were away, called up and at the Front; he heard stories of missing men, injured, and of heroic deeds by some. There was no other subject of conversation; it wasn't a happy gathering.

Again he talked over his doubts with the Minister of his mother's Chapel. The old man reassured him and gave him his blessing. 'I know that, at the moment, you are not a regular chapel attender but God will look after you. May He bless you, my son, and watch over you until you return to us safe and sound.'

'Thank you, Minister. I've met a Quaker, and we find that we have a lot in common. I like the things he believes in. They are very like my own beliefs; he's an interesting man to talk to.'

'The Quakers are great pacifists; you can do a lot worse than team up with one of them.'

'I do really hope I'll be back when all this is over. I have spoken to Uncle Henry; you know, Pa's brother. He lives in the next village. He'll ride over regularly, to keep an eye on them. And if I don't make it, he'll look after the family.'

'Good on him. Young Susie will need some guidance, especially as she gets older and needs to consider her choice of husband, he'll guide her. And I'll also keep an eye out for them while you are gone; but come back soon and safe. We will pray for you, as we do for all of you young men.'

*

In the evenings, he sat up late, chatting with his mother. 'I have some good mates. We've been trained into a band of comrades; we look out for each other. I've thought about my decision some more, Ma. I know I am making life difficult for myself, and for you, but I have to do what I know in my heart is right. And, if I am honest with myself, and you, I am enjoying the discipline and the hard work, and the feeling that I might actually be useful. I don't even miss Mr Fosdyke, but don't tell him that.' He laughed.

'Bless you, son, you were always going to put yourself out on a limb, you always did. Now then, lad, do you know where you will be going to next?'

'Yes, we've finished our training; it is time for us to go out to France, to do what we can.'

'Do you know where in France?'

68

'No, and if I did, I wouldn't be allowed to tell you; no, they keep it secret as long as they can. I don't expect we'll know until we're there.'

'Oh my son, you will look after yourself, won't you? I worry about you. We don't get much news about what is going on out there, but we do get reports and see pictures in the Darlington and Stockton Times of lads when they have come home. We hear that some are terribly injured, some seem to lose their minds and too many don't come back at all.'

'It's those lads we are going out to help. I'll be alright, Ma. Now, tell me about Susie, how is she getting on?' He drew on his cigarette.

'She's grand, Danny lad, doing well. They have said that she will be made into a tweeny if she carries on as well as this. The owner is a kind man; he knows we need the money. But I'm beginning to worry that his motives aren't altogether as they should be; he seems to be taking advantage of the war situation, making too much money. Should Susie be working for a man like that?'

'I've always got on well with him, when he has come into the bank, but have a talk with Uncle Henry next time you·see him. He'll be able to advise you.'

'What does worry me now is that Susie has it in her head to work for the VAD, nursing on the land or even in the munitions factory. I'm doing my best to dissuade her, but you know what she is like.'

'She's much too young to be able to do any of those yet. Let's just see what happens and how things turn out; they say the war won't last much longer, anyway; they keep saying that it will be over by Christmas, but which Christmas, they don't say.' They both looked into the flames of the fire, thinking of the promises the politicians had made, which hadn't been kept.

'They said that this time last year and now look where we are – no nearer to the end than we were before, worse if anything.'

'I know, but the idea of Susie working in munitions really bothers me. They say that the girls who work there go yellow or green; it's the chemicals they have to handle.'

'I've heard that, too, but as I say let's just wait and see. Now,

I've seen Uncle Henry and the Pastor, and they will both look out for you both.'

'Thank you lad. Nearly everyone is being so kind. Henry has been across on his horse two or three times since you've been gone.'

Daniel stood up. 'I have to go to see Mr and Mrs Metcalf. I've seen Joseph in Richmond and have been able to have a very few words with him, through his bars in the castle.'

*

'Mrs Metcalf, Mr Metcalf, can I come in for a few moments? I have some news for you about Joseph.'

'Of course, lad, we are always pleased to see any friend of Joseph's. Do you know where he is, have you seen him?'

'Well, yes, I have seen him, very briefly'

'Where? When? How? We haven't heard from him for weeks and we are so worried.'

He told them of their brief conversation at the castle.

'Oh, Daniel, thank you so much, we are really grateful to you for coming to tell us, to know where he is and that he is alright. Did he say what is going to happen next?'

'No, I'm afraid not. I don't think he knows.'

'We were just going to mash some tea; you will join us, won't you?'

*

It was difficult to leave; Susie came along with them to the station very early in the morning. It was only just getting light.

'Danny, have you still got the stone?'

'I'm never without it. I hold it whenever I need to think of you and of Ma; it's a great comfort.'

'Let me see!'

He fished it out of his pocket. It had been rubbed so often that it had taken on a sheen. It nearly glowed.

'Good! Now, don't ever lose it.'

'I won't, it'll stay with me forever.'

She gave him an extra hug and a kiss. 'I love you, Danny.'

'I love you, my little Susie. Now you be a good girl and look after Ma for me, won't you. I'm relying on you. Ma, I'll write as soon as I can and tell you whatever I am allowed to say, but the

censor can be vicious with his blue pencil. Look after yourselves.'
Ma squeezed his hand. 'Look after yourself, my son, may God
go with you.'

Chapter 11
Annie

Annie clutched her Gladstone bag close to her; it contained three grey uniform dresses, ten aprons, two caps, two sets of collars and cuffs and her navy-blue hospital cape. She wished she could have more. She hoped that these would be adequate. Matron had been very generous but Annie couldn't afford to buy more. Of course, she had her two nursing books, along with her Bible and prayer book. She also had all the changes of underwear that she could squeeze in; several pairs of stockings were stuffed into a spare pair of black boots. She took her much-treasured, silver-backed hairbrush, a pair of scissors and the gold pocket watch given to her at the time of her Confirmation by her God-mother. Tucked in at the last minute were two photographs, one of her parents and one of her twin brothers, Matthew and Paul. In the pocket of her coat, she had the little box which Ma had given to her on the platform. It contained things that Mother said she might find useful, such as needles and thread, a card of buttons, a silver thimble, a tiny looking-glass, a pair of black boot laces. It was put together with a practical mind and all the love the reluctant parent could muster.

'Do look after yourself.' Her mother had tried not to cry as she had pressed the box into her hand. 'Come back safe; do, please.' Father was at work; they had said their goodbyes before he left.

Annie and her Ma hugged and kissed each other lightly on the cheeks. Mother gave her a little black velvet bag which she stuffed into her pocket. She carried her great-coat over her arm on this warm end-of-May day. Her hat was held firmly on her head by the beautiful hatpin her grandmother had given her; it was of green and blue enamel and sparkled in the light, and she loved it.

She and Molly held hands; they, and all the other young women, had unvoiced doubts about their mission but, having got this far, there was no going back. Annie and Molly got into the crowded carriage. The engine hissed loudly, the whistle sounded and the train pulled away. Annie, leaning out of the window, lost sight of her mother in a cloud of smoke and steam. It was a while before anyone spoke, wrapped as they were in their own thoughts and fears. Annie sat between Molly and a sweet-looking little lass with fair curls and a scared look on her face. She appeared to be far too young to be there. She was neatly dressed in a modern dress, with the shorter skirts that showed her ankles and made her look even younger; this fashion hadn't got as far as Yorkshire yet. The small case she held tightly in her hands had a crest with the initials 'FH' in flowing script embossed into the leather on its side; she looked nervous and ran her hands up and down the side of the case.

'Hello, I'm Annie and this is Molly. Who are you?'

'Florence, Florence Harrington. I'm called after Florence Nightingale, but you can call me Flo. Everybody does, except my parents. Mater always wanted me to be a nurse.' She had an accent that Annie had never heard before, clipped and hard.

'You've the same name as my grandmother, what a coincidence. Where did you train? I trained in York.' Annie suddenly felt awkward next to the girl, even though she was clearly very young.

'St Thomas's, of course, the Nightingale hospital, but I didn't like it.'

'So why did you volunteer for this?'

'To get away from my parents. I thought if I did this, they would let me alone; maybe let me get out of nursing, when it's all over.'

Annie laughed. 'I had to argue with my parents to let me be a nurse and then, to come out here, they didn't want me to. I had to point out that, as I am over twenty-one, they couldn't stop me. I was determined.'

'Why did you want to go against your parents? Mine couldn't wait to see me off.'

'They never really wanted me to go into nursing, said I should have been a vet. But it's very difficult for girls to get into the vet training schools. Mind, I love nursing, just seeing someone's face when you've made them comfortable in bed, I love that.'

'You must be a natural. I envy you. I don't mind looking after children, though, they don't complain like the adults sometime do. I would like to specialise in children's nursing, if I have to carry on.'

'I don't expect we'll see many child patients; well, I hope not. I hope all the children are out of the war. It'll be mostly men, I expect.'

'So, is that why your parents object?'

'No. One of my brothers, Paul, is dead; the other twin is missing, so they didn't want me to come; they're afraid they'll lose me as well. I am hoping I'll find Matthew while I'm here, but I know it is unlikely,' confided Annie.

The train journey was long, cramped and uncomfortable, the seats were hard, the air became stale and they had little to eat or drink; it took them into King's Cross. They had to change stations in London, crossing the city by army-truck to Waterloo where they had a long and tedious wait, but were given food and big mugs of tea. They arrived at Southampton after night-fall and were shepherded onto a boat. They were offered no facilities or places to sleep, so they just found space where they could. They curled up together in any corner they could find, pulled their cloaks over themselves and tried to sleep. The crossing was rough, not made easier by the zig-zagging of the boat as it dodged German submarines; several of the girls were ill. Annie found that she enjoyed the novelty of it, although she didn't really sleep. She had never been so far from home, nor indeed seen the sea before, so was disappointed that it was dark. As the moon glinted on the surface of the water, she could see the darkness of the waves as the boat rode up over them and slid down the other side; the phosphorescence gave a ghostly light.

*

In the morning, they disembarked in Le Havre. The woman in charge, who they were told was to be known as Matron, took the girls off to a truck. It was difficult maintaining decorum as they climbed up the two steep steps. Annie was afraid she was showing too much of her ankles as she hitched up her long skirts. They settled down, crammed up against each other on the hard benches. They were so tired that a few of them did manage to sleep a little, in spite of everything. Annie dozed against Molly's shoulder, her head bumping against the side of the truck. Flo snuggled into her like a small child.

As it got dark, they came to the outskirts of a town. The

headlights of the truck showed ornate gates as they pulled off the main road. The light swept round and picked out a series of army buildings set in what seemed to be the grounds of a big house. Matron hustled them off to the hut which was to serve as their dormitory and told them to make themselves tidy and to appear for a meal in fifteen minutes. There were two rows of sixteen iron bedsteads, each to be made up with the coarse sheets and rough, woollen army blankets that were folded and laid out at the end of each bed. Molly, Annie and Flo naturally took beds next to each other; the others accepted them as being inseparable. They hung their coats on the row of hooks by the door, tidied their hair and splashed water on their faces from the basins that were on tables at the far end of the hut. After making up their beds, they were soon ready to go and find their very late meal. They were given filling soup with thick chunks of bread and big mugs of sweet tea, but they hardly noticed they were so tired; little Flo almost fell asleep in her plate. They found their way back, slipped into their nighties and were asleep almost instantly.

*

'Are you awake? Annie, are you awake?' Annie slowly realised that Molly was calling her from her bed.

'What is it? I was asleep, it had better be important.' Annie hated being woken; her brothers would do it just to tease her.

'Shh, Shh,' came from another bed.

Molly crossed the couple of feet of rough boards between them and got into Annie's bed. 'I'm frightened. What have we let ourselves in for?' she whispered.

'So am I. We've been told so little, people don't say much about what to expect.'

'We've seen men coming home, brave men, missing arms, missing legs, blind; is that what we will have to cope with, to nurse?'

'Our Paul is dead, Matthew is missing, I just feel I must do something, and maybe I'll find Matthew,' Annie recited in her half sleep. 'We must try to get some sleep. It must still be early; it's not yet getting light.'

There was another loud 'Shh'.

The two girls curled up together, Molly fell soundly asleep, but

Annie's sleep was disturbed by thoughts of her brothers. She remembered how they played with her, turning the skipping rope as she jumped up and down, how they had helped her with her games of vets and nurses; they took turns in looking after first the soft toys and then the injured animals she kept bringing back into the house, even built her a little shed to keep them in while they recovered. When they had volunteered and went off to the war, they had had the photo of the two of them taken; she had brought it with her. They looked so happy to be going, to do their bit, as everyone kept saying. And, in no time, Paul was killed; he was buried out here in France, somewhere. Gladys and John had been sent all his possessions, his Bible all torn and stained with mud, his last letter to them hadn't even been finished. The letter that had come from his commanding officer, about bravery and that he hadn't suffered. Annie just prayed it was all true; it was just terrible to think about. But what was more difficult was that Matthew was missing, no trace or word of him had been found, so they carried on hoping and praying. Tears ran down her cheeks. 'Matthew, oh Matthew, where are you?' she whispered.

Molly's gentle, even breathing eventually lulled Annie off to a fitful sleep.

Chapter 12

Joseph

'Pssst.' A tap on the water pipe; there was Norman's eye again.

'Do you play chess? I've made a bit of a chess set, and if we enlarge this hole I think it'll go through.'

'A bit, not well, sorry, but I am willing to learn.'

'That will have to do, and practice will improve your game. Give it a go?'

'What have you made it of? It looks disgusting!' One of the strange shaped pieces was passed through.

'I made them out of bread. When it dries, it gets very hard. I've darkened the black pieces with mould off the walls, and of course the board is just a piece of wood I managed to smuggle in. I am quite proud of it.'

'Hm, well, very inventive, I suppose. Well done.'

So they each scrabbled away at the hole and managed to remove a stone and enlarge the gap until the make-shift set would go through without the pieces falling off. So started the first of many, very slow games, the tiny board passing to and fro, the minute pieces balanced precariously. It was cold and damp; sitting on the floor, both men had to take time between moves to jump up and down, to get the circulation back in their legs and warm up a little. The games went on until it was too dark to see; they hid the set in the gap in the wall and replaced the stones.

One day, instead of the usual chess pieces, there was a small lump of something possibly edible-looking. 'A present for you,' whispered Norman.

'What is it?'

'Bacon fat; I stole it and hid it under my belt.'

'I'll not ask how you got it ... thank you, anyway; what a treat.'

*

Over the days, they talked about themselves. Joseph told Norman about his home life; his brother Jacob who was doing so well at school and was keen to take up his apprenticeship as a plumber. Little Hannah, only twelve years old but mature for her age, who was such a quick learner; Mother wanted her to stay at school but Father might insist that she leave, to help Mother in the house. He told about his father's carpentry business where he was serving his own apprenticeship. Norman's father was a farmer, had Swaledale sheep and cattle. They used the milk, to make cheese to sell with eggs and vegetables; had some arable too, as well as hay meadows. Joseph told Norman about the Quaker Meeting and about when he decided to be an objector.

'I'm a Methodist, but tell me about the Meeting and about the Quakers, I'm interested.'

'Quakers don't have any formal service like you do; we sit in a circle, waiting on God, holding ourselves and everyone who is important to us in the Light. If we are moved by the Spirit, we can stand and speak; if not, we stay silent. There are some Meetings for Worship, when no-one says anything, other times several people are moved to speak. One morning, I was sitting with Ma, Pa and Jacob; Hannah had gone into her Children's Meeting upstairs. I looked round at everyone, some had their heads bowed, and some were sitting looking straight out. There was a paper on the table that had been sent to us some time ago and which I had read over and over, but suddenly it spoke to me. I know it by heart. I can still remember it, it is what keeps me going. "Christ demands of us that we adhere, without swerving, to the methods of love, and therefore, if a seeming conflict should arise between the claims of His service and those of the State, it is to Christ that our supreme loyalty must be given, whatever the consequences." I had received my papers the day before. So I stood and read the paper out loud to everyone, even though I knew that they had all read it. I asked them to pray for me, I told them that I intended to be an absolutist. At the end of the meeting, when we had all shaken hands, I felt supported and loved; a couple of the Elders spoke to me. 'We will be with you, whatever you do.'

'Hmm, "whatever the consequences", I like that but I do wonder what the consequences will be. Will we be shot or worse?'

'What's worse than being shot?' enquired Joseph.

'At least, it's over with quickly. Have you heard of Field Punishment Number One?'

'Well, there's a rumour; what exactly is it?'

'It is an official punishment sanctioned by the authorities, but I don't know who dreamt it up, some sadist; has to be. It is dished out to soldiers when they go AWOL, desert or something.'

'Is it as bad as I've heard?'

'It depends what you have heard, but it sounds pretty grim to me. But my understanding is that first, for us, it would mean we get taken to France, so we can be court-marshalled for refusing an order in the face of the enemy, assuming we do refuse,' explained Norman.

'Why do we have to go to France?'

'So that we are in the face of the enemy, as they call it. We have to refuse under those conditions in order to be court-marshalled.'

'So the rumours may be true; I suppose we'll go soon.'

'I understand that it'll be at the end of the month, in a few days' time. But to go on, when we are found guilty, which we will be, we will be imprisoned in huts, taken out and crucified every day.'

'Crucified? Crucified, what do you mean, nails and stuff like our Lord?' Joseph shuddered.

'No, rope; tied with rope by our arms against a post or wheel, and left leaning slightly forward so that the rope cuts in, and sometimes the feet don't quite touch the ground; left in the blazing sun or the pouring rain for an hour or so and then taken down. I have heard that sometimes they use barbed wire, but I'm not sure about that. That can happen in the morning and afternoon. Repeated every day, for up to three months, although I think you're supposed to have every fourth day off. This is an official punishment, officially sanctioned, dreamt up by the army; it was invented when they abolished flogging in the army in the last century. Jolly, eh? As I said, some sadist.'

'Ugh; sounds terrible, I don't like to think about it.'

'No, they really don't like us much. But they do it to serving soldiers for a whole variety of crimes; it is not just invented for us conchies.'

'Well, if our Lord can suffer it, I hope I can, with His help.'

'God help us all,' muttered Norman.

They fell silent, each with their own thoughts.

'Goodnight, Norman. I'm turning in, you've given me a lot to think about.'

79

'Morning!' The cheery voice of Norman was calling through the hole in the wall. 'Sleep well?'

'No, not really, I was thinking about what we were talking about last night, the Field Punishment, and asking myself how far I can go.'

'So? What did you decide?'

'Well, I've got this far, I'll go on and see where it takes me.'

Reveille sounded across the square. From his position on the bed, Joseph could see the NCC lads getting ready for the morning's activities. They were going to the Mess Hut and he sensed the camaraderie; in his mind, he could see Daniel sitting with his fellow soldiers, eating a hearty breakfast, inspection, drill; a sense of purpose. They were all doing something worthwhile, contributing to the war effort. What was he doing, just sitting in this cold, damp, smelly cell awaiting his fate? What use was that?

'Norman?' He tapped on the pipe. 'Can we talk? Don't you really want to join them?'

'Who?'

'Them, them outside, the NCC lads. I can hear them laughing together.'

Norman listened to his neighbour; such a young lad with such big decisions to make. 'If you do leave, no-one will hold anything against you. It has to be your decision, do you want to go?'

'No, not really, it's just, it's just ... oh Norman, I'm scared.'

'Not half as scared as I am. I'm terrified, but I pray for the strength to see me though. I know I can change my mind at any time. Read your Bible, it can help; the Lord said "Come unto me ye that are heavy laden and I will refresh you"; give yourself some time, and don't forget, we can change our minds if ever we feel we've had enough.'

One evening, a guard caught sight of the chess set when it hadn't been hidden carefully enough. He stamped on it, breaking every fragile piece and snapped the delicate little board. Joseph and Norman were devastated.

Chapter 13
Daniel

The train was packed with soldiers from every Northern Regiment. Daniel and other NCC men piled into one of the compartments. He slammed the door shut and lowered the window on its leather strap. The engine hissed, blew its whistle and slowly pulled out of the station. Daniel soon lost sight of his mother and Susie as they were enveloped in a cloud of smoke and steam. He leaned out of the window as far as he dared, hoping to catch a final glimpse, but they were gone. As he made his way into the compartment, he tried to avoid the regular soldiers. He knew that sometimes they weren't too friendly towards the non-combatant men, thought they were skivers. He heaved his bag onto the overhead luggage rack and squeezed in between two of his fellows. He rolled himself a cigarette and sat smoking and thought about the last few days at home, of Ma, Susie, Uncle Henry and his cricketing friends; he sighed a deep sigh. 'Poor Ma, she'll miss me.'

'When will you see them again, chum?'

He hadn't realised he had spoken out loud.

'Fancy a game of cards? Take your mind off it.'

He pulled a pack out of his kit-bag.

'Yes, but only if the stakes are these match-sticks. I've got no money.' He emptied a box out onto his lap.

'That's OK, neither have I; no money to spare that is, can't afford to lose it, eh? Let's make up a four; any of you lot want to play?' The regulars wouldn't have anything to do with them, but they found another couple of NCC men to play.

'Where have you been, bonny lad?' asked one in his distinctive Geordie accent.

'Home, to see my Ma and sister and my pals.'

'What, not your Pa?'

'I've got no Pa; he was killed in an accident in the mines, years ago. Ma's been managing on her own since. I've been doing what I can but now I've gone away she'll find it hard again.'

'Sorry to hear that. No other men in your family?'

'Yes, my father's brother, but he has his farm to run, can't help

Ma out much, but he does what he can. What about you?'

'I'm the middle one of five, a brother and a sister, both older and younger than me; I think Pa and Ma are glad to see me go, one less mouth to feed. My older brother went a year ago. He's out there somewhere I suppose, volunteered, I wouldn't have gone but now we have no option. Your turn to deal.'

When they got bored with cards, and Daniel had lost most of his matches, they sang songs, Daniel accompanying them on his mouth-organ. *"Pack up your troubles..."* and *"Goodbyee, goodbyee..."* seemed to be the right songs to sing, and when the regulars joined in, it brought them together on some sort of common ground. They sang all the rest of the way to London.

*

At Victoria Railway Station, Daniel was delighted to see Hubert; he had spent some of his leave at an aunt's house in London. Daniel felt that Hubert was very sophisticated, telling tales of the shows he had been to and the art galleries. All the way to Southampton they chatted, catching up.

'I am so envious of you. I have always wanted to go to London. This trip is the only time I've been, and Victoria Station is all I have seen. I'd like to see Nelson's Column and the lions, the mermaids in the fountains, the National Gallery. The most exciting thing I did on leave was playing cricket with some of the lads not yet called up.'

'I envy the peaceful time in your village. Pater doesn't understand why I won't be in the fighting force, be a proper soldier like he was and still considers himself to be, though he's now too old for this war, so he hardly speaks to me. Mater tries to keep the peace between us, but it's hard work, as we don't see eye to eye. That is why I came up to Town, to stay with Aunt Hilda. I take her to the theatre when I can, and she has shown me her favourites in the National Gallery. There's this picture of a Virgin and Child, which is so beautiful. She has such a serene expression on her face, makes me feel calm. Auntie's a brick, a bit of a suffragette but I don't tell Father; he'd have a fit. She's been demonstrating with the Pankhurst women out on the streets. I'm proud of her.'

'She sounds like a strong-willed woman, with a mind of her

own. Do you think women should have the vote?' asked Daniel.

Hubert laughed out loud. 'Yes, I do, but when it will happen, goodness knows; never, if my father has anything to do with it. Anyway, she is very supportive of my decision not to fight; I can talk about things with her. And she understands about being a Quaker.'

'I'd like to meet her.'

'Well, that's a treat that will have to wait until after this show is over; but I know you'll like her.'

*

At Southampton, they were allocated huts and bunks for what remained of the night. They had barely taken off their boots and belts before they were asleep. Reveille woke them; reality hit as they opened their eyes.

'Come on, Dan! This is it, up you get, get up you lazy cad.'

'Leave off, Hubert, give me a minute.'

'No, Corporal will be here soon and we had better be ready for him.'

The Corporal inspected his men with greater than usual thoroughness, finding fault wherever he could; beds were stripped back, boots and buttons had to be re-polished, kit checked and sorted. When all was eventually to his liking, he addressed them. 'We will be leaving for France tomorrow. You have this afternoon off, but behave yourselves. Curfew is at 9.00, be back by then or face the consequences.'

Daniel and Hubert walked into town, to do a little shopping; shaving soap, writing paper. Daniel found a little book of poems that he thought Susie would like.

'I find it so difficult to buy presents for her. She is growing up so quickly; what do you think of this?'

'Difficult for me to judge, old boy. Don't know her, do I? But from what you have told me about her, I would say it's just the ticket.'

They found tea rooms; they had an inkling that this might be the last opportunity for a long time where they could enjoy some quiet gentility. Daniel would have preferred a pint or two of beer, but Hubert said that he didn't drink alcohol. They were given a silver tea-pot, delicate decorated cups, and the waitress found them little, mouth-watering cakes with pink and white icing. They savoured it all. They didn't talk much, thinking about what they had let themselves in for, wondering.

*

Daniel stood away from the others on the deck of HMS Viper. He needed some time on his own. Hubert seemed to know somehow and left him to it. As the ship pulled away, he stared at England receding in the distance. To start with, there was shore on both sides of the ship as they passed through the Narrows around the Isle of Wight, but they soon left all that behind; the green trees, the white cliffs, the Needles; soon, there was nothing left to see of Blighty. He turned sea-ward; he had never seen the sea before.

'Hello Dan, old chap, you look a bit green round the gills.' Hubert was concerned.

'I don't like the look of this. I've never seen the sea before. I thought it would be blue, but this is grey and cold-looking, and it's so big. How far is it to France?'

'From here? About thirty or forty miles I think, not far.'

'Far enough; we've hardly started and this ship, the movement, my stomach, I feel ill.'

'Never mind, old boy, it won't be for long, just a few hours. Stay on deck, lie down and shut your eyes. Think of Susie, your Mater, anything to take your mind off it.'

'I really don't want to throw up, but that's what it feels like I am going to do.'

'Well, if you do, make sure it's over the side and the wind is at your back. You won't be the only one, good thing it's not rough.'

'Does it get worse than this?'

'Yes, this is nothing; wait till we have to cross in the winter.'

Daniel groaned, found a corner, wrapped his great-coat round his shoulders and tried to escape the feeling of nausea. He thrust his hand into his pocket and found Susie's stone. He smiled at the thought of the lass.

The ship was crowded with soldiers from many different regiments, some regulars and a few from different groups of NCC. Some, like Daniel, were feeling very unsettled, huddled into miserable corners, hoping it would end soon. Others were singing and larking about, smoking, playing cards, all without a care in the world, looking forward to the adventure. Daniel was envious, he would have liked to join them, play his mouth organ; but he felt too ill. He just stayed propped up in his corner.

As the sun began to set over the sea, Daniel saw a group of about sixteen men, separated from the others. They seemed quieter and withdrawn. They were too far away to see properly but Daniel was sure that one of them looked like his friend Joseph Metcalf. It could be him. He had heard that there was a rumour that those men were to be taken to France. He wished he felt well enough to go to see, but as soon as he tried to stand, his stomach turned over, so he just watched them. The man he thought was Joseph was leaning over the railing, watching the sun go down. He was deep in conversation with a tall, distinguished-looking man.

The light soon faded, the sounds of the men dwindled away. The only sound was the chugging of the ship's engines as it zig-zagged across the Channel. Daniel groaned, pulled his coat over his head and eventually fell into a fitful sleep.

Chapter 14

Joseph

Near the end of May, just as they were starting their Sunday service, singing a few hymns loud and confidently, the men were interrupted and ordered to dress in their uniforms and collect up their few belongings.

'Come on, get a move on! Haven't got all day. You're on your way. Out, out.'

The eight men from the cells soon stood shackled together under the great tower, waiting for the other C.O.s who had been incarcerated in the room that had been the original Norman guardroom. There was a deafening noise from within; furniture being dragged across the floor, men shouting, soldiers swearing.

'Let me go in and talk to them, I'll get them to quieten down.' Bert was the unofficial spokesman for the objectors; he had a presence about him, an air of authority which was most respected.

They reluctantly unshackled Bert and allowed him to speak to the men. Joseph could hear snippets of the exchange.

'Give no resistance ... don't make them use force ... the army knows all there is about force ... remember we are pacifists.'

Within a very short while, all of the eight had quietened down and, looking a bit sheepish, came out to join the others, straightening their jackets and tucking in their shirts.

They were all bundled into a truck and were on their way to an unknown fate. Bert got into conversation with one of the guards.

'Where are we going?'

'Not allowed to tell you, mate, but it's probably France.' The soldier turned away.

'What port will we be going from?'

'Southampton, but I'm not even supposed to tell you that.'

'So we're going to Le Havre? Then where? I've heard that there is a Punishment Block in Boulogne, is that it?' Joseph pressed him.

'Oh shut up. Yes, but you didn't hear it from me.'

'Of course not. Are we going to be given our postcards so we can tell our folks we are alright?'

As the trains trundled south, they were each given a pencil and the official army postcard; they had only to fill in the spaces or cross out phrases and add the recipients' addresses; they would be posted after the censor had had a look at them, they were told that they weren't allowed to write anything other than their names.

Bert took longer than all the others filling in his postcard, but the guards didn't seem to notice. They were collected up, with the promise that they would be posted as soon as they got to Southampton.

'We are going to France so that we can be given an order; when we refuse, we will be court-marshalled and could be shot for disobeying an order in the face of the enemy.' Bert was confident this was to be their fate; but they couldn't say that on the postcards, just among themselves.

Norman surreptitiously wrote a note with his pencil on a scrap of paper he found in the carriage, "To the No-Conscription Fellowship: sixteen C.O.s are being sent to Boulogne to be shot". As they went slowly through a station, he threw it out of the window. He didn't have much hope that it would be picked up by anyone sympathetic to them and sent on, but it was worth a try; anything to alert the Fellowship as to what was happening to them.

They continued their interrupted service, singing hymns at the tops of their voices all the way to Southampton; the rendition was interspersed with periods of Quaker silent worship. Joseph found this to be one of the most moving but unusual meetings for worship he had ever experienced; sixteen men, with their guard, in a railway carriage on their way to France and their certain deaths, in deep prayerful silence. Even the guard was affected by it.

It was a good opportunity for the eight men from the cells, to get to know the men from the 'guardroom'; they had only met before on the parade ground and had not had the opportunity to chat there. They found that, although they came from very different backgrounds, they all had a common purpose – not to lift a hand against their fellow man. They came from as far afield as Sunderland in the North to Doncaster in the South, though eight came from Leeds. They told the stories of their tribunals; they had had very different experiences of their Boards, though all with the same outcome; prison and France, all believed the war was wrong and that they would have no hand in it. None felt themselves to be skivers.

It was a long, tiring journey. They smoked, they sang hymns, and they dozed against each others' shoulders. The train stopped occasionally, which gave them the opportunity to look at the countryside; they never knew why or where they stopped. They were ordered out at a station somewhere in a small village and were given food, before piling in again onto the hard, wooden seats. The port was a hive of activity, troops coming and going, ships preparing for war, to go to all corners of the earth. A ship with a huge red cross on its side was unloading men into waiting ambulances; some were walking, some on stretchers, with nurse escorts. There was a line of men, one hand on the other's shoulder, bandages round their eyes, being led away in a long string; some were very quiet, others coughed incessantly – a bubbly, hacking cough. Joseph said a prayer for them all under his breath.

The prisoners were escorted onto a troop-ship, HMS Viper, and ordered to keep themselves to themselves; they were not allowed any contact with the Tommies on their way to the Front.

'Mind your own business and don't start anything,' warned their guard.

In the distance, there was a group with the armbands of the Non-Combatant Corps stretcher-bearers; was Daniel among them, Joseph wondered? He fancied he could see him but couldn't be sure, with the sun in his eyes.

It was a beautiful evening as the ship slipped out of the harbour on the late tide. Joseph, Norman and Bert lent against the railing, to marvel at the sunset. Joseph was moved almost to tears; he had never seen the sea before. It seemed vast and lovely. He had never imagined anything like it.

'It seems so big, as though it goes on for ever, strangely beautiful, but I did expect it to be blue; one hears of blue sea, not steel grey.'

'There are a few miles of it before we get to France. It will take us several hours. I suppose you don't know if you are a good sailor?'

'Good sailor? What does that mean? I've never even seen the

sea before, so how should I know?'

'When the ship moves on the waves, some people feel sick, some even throw up. But you won't know if you are one of those yet.'

'Sounds horrid, I feel alright so far; in fact, I am enjoying it. I expect I'll be tickety-boo.'

'Bert, I'm curious, why did you take so long filling in your postcard? It wasn't difficult.'

'I was being careful. I am really hoping for a busy censor,' Bert whispered.

'Why, what did you do?'

'It was something my brothers and I used to do to write secret messages to each other when we were children.' He laughed. 'I expect the parents worked it out for themselves, though. I underlined different letters and crossed out others. I'm sending it to my brother, Philip; he has friends in high places and he may be able to influence our outcome, but I'm not going to hold my breath.'

'What did you try to say?'

'Just that we were being sent to Boulogne; maybe he'll work it out from there.'

'Hm, I hope he does. I suppose, it all relies on the censor not noticing, the post getting through in time and your brother understanding your message. It's a remote possibility, I suppose, but worth the try. Well done.'

'And did you know that Norman threw a note out of the window as we went through a station? He addressed it to the No-Conscription Fellowship; let's hope it gets delivered.'

'Good for him; fingers crossed, eh?' Joseph was sceptical.

As it got dark, they lay down on the deck, made themselves as comfortable as they could, to sleep, rocked by the unaccustomed motion of the ship. They could hear chatting and coughing and quiet singing of the hundreds of men all around them; it all seemed unreal, unbelievable. Joseph slept well, in spite of the motion and the uncomfortable, hard surface of the deck.

*

The train went first to Amiens and then chuffed through the countryside, north to Boulogne. Joseph was fascinated; never having been out of Yorkshire before, he expected France to be very different. He was not disappointed. Whereas some of it did look the same, like the Yorkshire valley, the houses and roads were very different.

'It's so flat, and these roads are so straight,' he observed to Norman, 'just aiming across the countryside; the only straight road we have in my part of the world is the Great North Road built by the Romans. Did the Romans do that here too?'

'I think it was Napoleon. It's said he planted all those trees to provide shade for his marching troops.'

'How considerate of him.' Joseph was surprised.

'I don't think so. He didn't want them stopping in the middle of the day, when the sun was hot, just to keep on marching.'

'Typical. The arable is like ours, though; wheat and so on. I can't see any sheep, and will we see vineyards?'

'I don't think so. They are further south, but I'm not sure.'

Joseph stared out of the window, and he found himself longing for home and imagining what all the family was doing and how Pa was managing without his help. But the countryside was green and too peaceful-looking, the sun was shining and warm; it was difficult to imagine a war going on, not far away; men being killed and injured in trenches nearby.

After the many inevitable stops and starts, they travelled through Normandy and Picardy, eventually arriving in Boulogne. Late in the evening, they were herded into a camp not far from the sea at Henriville.

In their hut, the Sergeant Major addressed them. 'You are now regarded as being on active service, and you will obey orders or suffer the consequences, and you know what they are. You have twenty-four hours to do whatever you like, within reason. I suggest you use that time well, think about it. You'll see me tomorrow.' Contempt was written all over his face as he marched away, into the night.

Chapter 15

Daniel

At Le Havre, the terrible motion stopped and Daniel felt miraculously well and hungry, with none of the previous evening's sickness. He looked around to see if he could spot Joseph and saw a small group being marched off in irons. He still wasn't sure whether Joseph was among them or not, but he sent a prayer with them, anyway.

'Joseph, dear friend, wherever you are, may your God go with you and look after you, and may you find strength to do whatever you have to do.'

The men fell in as ordered and were marched off to a temporary camp, to recover from the crossing. Some men had been much sicker than Daniel had been on the boat, could hardly walk; they were dishevelled and had a green tinge to their skin. The Corporal had no sympathy for them, ignored their pleas for some time to get well again and had them out on parade and inspection. Daniel recovered quickly. Hubert's advice had been good, he too was soon tucking into a good meal. The next day, the men were on parade and marched to the railway station in good heart; they sang and whistled as they marched, Daniel accompanying many of the songs on his mouth-organ.

"It's a long way to Tipperary, it's a long way to go...", "Pack up your troubles..." At last, they were going to the Front.

But the day was hot and dusty. Daniel felt the sweat trickling down his neck, the coarse wool of his tunic irritated his skin, his kit-bag felt heavy on his back, and he tried to ignore it by playing more tunes. Some locals came out of their cottages to greet them; a young girl with long, dark hair and a shy smile ran out, gave Daniel a red rose. He tucked it into his cap badge and bent and kissed her quickly on the cheek.

'*Une rose pour vous, mon cher.*'

'Eh up lad, tha's got an admirer there.'

After some miles, the exhausted men waited on the railway platform for what seemed like hours. There was little shade; they squeezed into what there was. As the sun went down, the train arrived; and piling in, the men stowed kitbags and equipment where they could. They found seats and made themselves as comfortable as the crowded space would allow.

'I'm that disappointed. I had hoped we would travel by day. I want to see France. I've never been abroad before; we'll see nowt.'

'It's over-rated, mate, full of bloody Frogs,' said one cocky-looking fellow.

'Frogs? What do you mean *frogs*, small animals that live in ponds?'

'Nar. Frenchies, that's what they are called. Cor, you're wet behind the ears, ain't yer; where yer bin?'

'Doesn't sound very nice; I wonder what they call us?'

The last rays of sun glinted through the trees as the train pulled away. Daniel watched it set and thought of home, as he held the smooth little stone in his hand. The chatter stopped, the last cigarette was put out and the men slept leaning against each others' shoulders, as they were taken to the Front.

*

The camp they were marched to was a series of tents pitched in long rows; the Sergeant Major ordered parade in ten minutes.

'Tomorrow, we go out to do the job you 'orrible lot was trained to do. We'll march to the Front line and take our positions in the trenches; the men there need relieving. Any questions? Good, now get yourselves sorted out, we leave at 06.00 hours. Dismiss.'

'What did he mean, Front line and trenches? I've put in for hospital work. I don't want to go anywhere near the Front. I can't go there. I'm terrified by the idea.' Daniel was white and trembling.

'You know that we have to do as we are allocated. We have been trained to do stretcher-bearing, so I suppose that is what we will do, you and me together, like we've been practicing. And we make a good team, the same height and weight, we're good together. The two Musketeers; we'll look out for each other like we've promised. We'll be fine.'

'Have we made the right decision, Hubert?'

'What other decision was there, Dan? We could be firing at the Bosch, or locked up and been fired at by our own lads, like your friend. We are all in the army, whether we like it or not. We don't have any choice.'

'But the Bosch will be firing at us. We'll be sitting targets.'

'We're the lucky ones; at least, we can do some good and hopefully no harm.'

'I suppose you're right. And I thought I saw Joseph yesterday on the ship, and not knowing what will become of him worries me.'

'You've got other worries now, you can't be thinking about him.'

The Chaplain took over, gave a sermon about sacrifice and duty to which no-one listened; they had heard it all before. He said some prayers, and they finished off with a lusty rendition of *"Onward Christian Soldiers."*

It started raining, unrelenting stair-rods of rain. 'I hope this lets up by morning. I don't fancy marching in this lot.'

'Oh well, in a funny way I'll be glad to get there. We've been training for it long enough.'

Chapter 16
Annie

A beautiful spring morning dawned. Annie could hear the blackbirds singing from the top of their hut. When she opened her eyes and saw Molly beside her in the bed, she remembered where she was.

'Time to get up. We're here, in France. Time to go to work!' She shook her sleeping friend.

All the girls staggered out of their beds. They were still exhausted from their journey, but there could be no shirking. They washed in the cold water provided in the water jugs, helped each other into their assorted uniforms, brushed and pinned up their hair and fastened on the big, stiff caps. Annie didn't use the hatpin that her grandmother had given her to fix her cap; it was too precious. It had belonged to her great-grandmother before that. It had a talismanic quality; she kept it safe in its box, in her bag. They pulled on their starched cuffs and attached collars with studs, fastened their belts, laced up their boots and pulled their capes round their shoulders.

The young nurses crossed to the Mess Hut, looking like a flock of geese, chattering amongst themselves, sounding as excited as so many little sparrows. After a breakfast of porridge, with a spoonful of honey stirred into it, and a mug of steaming tea they were told to go back to their dormitory hut. There, Matron inspected them, their uniforms and their possessions, to ensure all was in order. They would work in the big house; it had been a Chateau in peace-time, but was requisitioned as a hospital, when the town's main hospital had been bombed. The Chateau was a beautiful, elegant building. Wide stone steps led up to the imposing front doors with stone dogs on either side. There were three or four floors; tall windows glinted in the morning sun. On what was left of the sweeping lawns, a few men in wheel chairs, blankets over their laps, and men with bandages round their heads were being led by nurses or orderlies. It looked organised, peaceful even. Matron allocated her new recruits to their wards. Annie, Molly and Flo went to ward Three; they were glad to be together.

Annie smoothed down her apron, adjusted her cuffs and lifted her head. The three pushed open the ward door. It wasn't like any ward they had ever seen before; ornate rococo plasterwork, little cherubs peeping out from foliage, busty half-dressed women. There were beautiful glass chandeliers, wall paintings of idyllic rural scenes, lords and ladies playing pipes and picking flowers, and some blank walls where tapestries had been removed. It contrasted sharply with the overwhelming noise and smell; it sounded like a cry from hell. Men groaning and crying out, the smell was a mixture of disinfectant, gas-gangrene and infection.

The girls looked at each other. Flo pressed her hand to her mouth and fled outside, to be very sick. Annie couldn't follow to look after her, as she was immediately seen by the Ward Sister.

She introduced herself. 'I'm Annie Scott, Staff Nurse Scott. We've just arrived from England, and this is Staff Nurse Williams.'

'Good, good, we need more hands. We are very, very busy. Come with me, I'll take you on a ward round.' Sister took them on a whirlwind tour of the patients and all the rooms – store rooms, dressing rooms, sluice room. Annie and Molly thought their heads would spin.

'I don't expect you to remember all their names right away. You will get to know the ones that stay for a while. Now, Nurse Scott, I will send you Mr O'Connor. He will be your orderly for the day, then start at that end and do all the dressings on that side of the ward. They are mostly amputees. Nurse Williams, come with me. By the way, I thought I was supposed to get three of you. What ever happened to the other girl?'

'She doesn't feel too well, I think, Sister.'

'Oh well, we will just have to manage without her, I suppose. You can check on her later.'

'Yes, Sister, of course. Do I *need* an orderly, Sister?'

'Yes, yes, you most certainly will. Many of these men take some handling.'

Sister looked at these young women, so new and shiny, so keen; would they stay? She had seen what happened to the other nurse; she expected her to be on the boat back soon. These nurses were volunteering; they didn't have to be here.

95

Annie stood on her own, in the middle of the ward; confused, bewildered, and keen to get on with it.

One of the men called out to her, 'Help me nurse, please, help me.'

He was answered by another. 'Aw, put a sock in it, will you, Jock! Can't you see, she's only just arrived? Take no notice, lass, that's my advice, you just do what Sister has told you.'

*

Annie found the battered-looking trolleys, all lined up against the wall; drums of dressings, which had been sent away to be sterilised in huge ovens and delivered back for use, on a shelf. The big, shiny boiler, with steam issuing from it, stood under the open window; this was where the instruments were sterilised by being boiled for ten minutes. She could see her reflection in its side; a neat nurse, trim with hair tidily tucked away, smart starched apron and shiny black boots. She hardly believed it was her. On shelves, there were trays of ready-rolled, clean bandages of various sizes, safety pins, bottles of hydrogen peroxide for cleaning wounds and, of course, iodine for dressings and a container of sphagnum moss for packing deep wounds. She felt daunted; everything was so unlike where she had trained. Here, it was make do.

She heaved a big sigh. 'Better get on with it, old girl; better make a start,' she told herself, removing her cuffs and rolling up her sleeves.

She found a box of masks and tied one on, picked up a bottle of disinfectant and, using the big forceps, swabbed down the nearest trolley and wondered what she would need. Sister had said she was to attend to the amputees, so she would need the hydrogen peroxide, swabs, dressings, maybe some sphagnum moss and bandages. As she opened the lid of the sterilizer, she was enveloped in a cloud of steam; when it cleared, she could see the rows of instruments. She picked up two pairs of the long-handled forceps from out of the jar of disinfectant solution and managed to get out the equipment she thought she would need and arranged them on the sterile sheet that she had draped over the trolley. She opened one of the drums and took out a selection. The door to the dressing room opened.

'Top o' the morning to you! You'll be Nurse Scott, won't you now? I'm Mr O'Connor, but you call me Seamus when Sister isn't around. I'll be being your orderly for the day. Sister Jackson sent me. I'm here to give you a hand.'

A happy-looking face appeared, it was cheerful and friendly-looking, and it was followed by a small, wiry man. Annie's spirits lifted. Seamus gave the impression of helpfulness and good humour; she felt she could trust and rely on him.

'I'm very new here, as you know, I only arrived today; I can do with all the help you can give me. I'm Annie, by the way.'

Seamus took an immediate liking to the girl. She looked like she would be able to cope. They would get on well together, he thought; a lass who knew when to ask for help. 'Good for you, my girl. The cocky ones, ones who never ask, don't last; just tell me whatever you need and I'll be doing my best for you. We'll make a good team; where do we start?'

'Well, Sister wants us to do all the amputees first. This is all very new to me. I'm used to nursing women. The only time I looked after men was in my training.'

'No women here, lass. The amputees are all down that side of the ward. I see you have made a good start with the trolley.' Seamus put on a mask. 'Well done, it's a good idea to do only the one trolley at a time. Some people pile on all the stuff they think they will need for the morning, then it gets muddled and they don't know what is what; it all gets into a mess. I'm sure in the end this way is quicker. Anyway, it is what Sister Jackson likes. Let's start with young Joe.'

Joe was sixteen or seventeen years old, had lied about his age to join up, go to the Front and to fight, he and his friend thought it would be a lark. His friend was dead and Joe had had both his right hand and left leg blown off. He was also badly shell-shocked. But he had been got to a dressing-station quickly. The operation to tidy up the bone-ends had gone well and he was thought to be healing satisfactorily. He was waiting for transport home, as were all the amputees. But Joe didn't seem to know where he was or understand what had happened to him. He cried all the time for his mother; he was really upsetting the other men.

Before Annie had left England, she and Molly had been practising bandaging for amputees. It was quite tricky; she never

97

felt that she had enough hands, but she felt confident that, with Seamus' help, she could manage Joe. But what she was not prepared for was the look on his face, the look of bewildered terror; he flinched away from her as she approached the bed.

'Now then, young man,' Seamus soothed, 'this nice young nurse just wants to have a look at your hand and leg.' Joe recognised Seamus and relaxed a little. 'Where's Ma? I want my Ma, is she here yet?'

'You'll see her soon, promise.'

Annie turned back the bed-clothes and began her work. She removed the bandages carefully and put them in a bag; they would be sent for washing and be re-rolled by the night-nurses or orderlies when they had a moment, for re-using. She cleaned the wounds carefully and gently and noted that they looked fairly healthy. She applied a fresh dressing and firm bandage to each limb as Seamus held it for her. They made Joe as comfortable as possible and reassured him that he would see his mother soon. Annie was pleased that this was the first and, as the morning wore on, it was clear that Joe was the easiest. Annie was very grateful to Seamus for leading her in so gently.

They worked their way down the row of men; they had lost arms and legs, feet and hands and were all what they called 'Blighties'. They would be sent home as soon as possible; their fighting days were over, they were relieved and quite cocky. Other men that were not so badly injured may be back to fight another day, when they were well enough.

'Come on, Nurse, what is your name? Scott? Well, Scotty, see what you can do here. I'm off to Blighty tomorrow.' Charlie didn't seem to realise the extent of his injuries. He would be lucky to make it home; the signs of septicaemia were apparent.

She and Seamus dressed all kinds of wounds; some were fairly clean and would heal well, but towards the door were the really ill ones. Some men had lain in the mud for hours, sometimes even days, before they were taken to the Dressing Station for first aid and their first operation. Their wounds were full of pus, green and yellow and some were black with gas-gangrene. These men were too ill to be moved; too ill to be sent home, they would surely die here. They were in terrible pain, crying out, given a small, too small a share of the meagre morphine that was available. They were delirious with septicaemia, and nothing could save them. More than once, Annie had to turn away for a breath of fresh air, more than once she had to fight to control the tears. But the men were to be kept clean and as comfortable as possible, until their time came.

Annie and Seamus worked side by side for six hours. 'Come on, we have done all the amputees. We deserve a break. Let's go and have ourselves some lunch. Sister, is it alright if we go off for half an hour, please?'

Seamus led Annie to the Mess Hut; she sat in front of her food and wept. Seamus just held her hand.

'It will get easier. Take some deep breaths. Here, drink some of your tea.' He placed the mug in front of her.

'How do you cope every day?'

'I try not to see their wounds, just their faces, their eyes. I know that every one is a mother's son, maybe a brother and that everyone is frightened and in pain. The cocky ones especially, it's a front; they are scared they won't make it home and many won't. They are scared that, if they get better, they will be sent back to the Front, and many will. That's the tragedy.'

Annie managed to eat a little. 'How long have you been here?'

'About twelve months, and in that time I've seen them all. In that time I've had seven days off.'

'Only seven days in a year?'

'Well, we've been a bit busy, but now you girls have come, maybe I'll get a few days together, maybe a week like I've been promised. I'd like to be getting home to see my parents. Come on time to go back.'

While Annie and Seamus had been busy doing the dressings on the amputees, Molly had been doing the other side of the ward, the body injuries, with Gordon. It had taken her a little longer, and she had taken her lunch later. When she got back, she and Annie were sent to sort out and tidy up the dressing room; they re-stocked the bandage tray, scrubbed the instruments and put them in the sterilizer to boil, re-packed drums with dressings, to be sent for sterilisation, sent dirty bandages for washing and cleaned down the trolleys. They also made a list of what they were running low on, for Sister to order more supplies.

Their conversation while they worked was whispered so as not to disturb the resting men.

'Have you heard what happened to Flo?'

'Poor girl, she's been sent home. I don't think she should ever have come out here. She thinks that the only thing she is good for is to get married to a nice, quiet husband so she can get away from her parents, and have one or two children. She could be right.'

'How did you get on?'

'It was terrible. These poor men, and one boy, Joe, so young, too young. He must have lied about his age; he shouldn't be here, either. He reminded me of your brother Harry. He is so frightened, I'm not sure he'll make it home, but if he does, what will he do? He has lost a hand and a leg and, I think, his mind.'

'Yes, I've had the same. I couldn't have managed without Gordon. The injuries some of the men have; I don't know how they stay alive. I've been doing body wounds; I've never seen anything like them.'

'Then there was Charlie. I'm not sure that he knows that he is dying. The infection is terrible.'

'I'm glad we've been practicing bandaging at home on each other. At least, I can do a decent tidy job of it.'

'I'm not sure which is worst,' said Molly as she handed Annie another packed drum, 'the chest wounds or the abdominal, they are all terrible.'

The two got on with the job on hand, glad to have some respite. Later, they had more dressings to do; not all of them, just the worst, the ones that were leaking and oozing. It was slightly easier, as Seamus had promised.

About 9.00 o'clock, the night staff came on duty. All the nurses, day and night, stood round Sister's desk, while she gave a report on each man. Some would need their dressings checked during the night. The nurses who had seen to the men during the day were sometimes asked questions about an individual; it was difficult remembering all their names.

All the staff, day and night, knelt together and recited the *Lord's Prayer* and the *Nunc Dimittis*; *"Now lettest thou thy servant depart in peace..."* Annie found this calming and

100

reassuring. She knew these old prayers by heart, she had been brought up on them, found them soothing and settling; they took away some of the stresses and strains of the hectic day.

The two girls went back to their quarters, holding hands as they crossed the wide lawns. They took deep breaths of fresh, clean air to clear their lungs of the smells of the wards. The blackbird was still sitting on top of the roof of the Chateau, singing. It felt like he was singing just for them. They could see him in silhouette against the darkening sky; there was an answering call from a near-by hut. Tears ran down Annie's face.

'I know, I know, it is just so beautiful among all this pain.' Molly hugged her friend. 'It won't be so bad tomorrow; we will know what to expect. It's the dreadful smell as much as anything, I'm not surprised Flo ran out, poor girl; I hope she'll be alright.'

'But what if our Matthew is a man like that, no memory, badly injured? How do I find him?'

'Annie, you won't find him. If he is here, he will find you. You should stop looking at every face, wondering.'

After supper, they unlaced their boots. 'Oh, my feet, my poor old feet. I thought it was bad in our hospital in York, but this is terrible.' They filled a basin with cool water and soaked their feet until they stopped throbbing. They changed into their nighties and dressing gowns and took it in turns to brush each other's hair. Molly's cracked with static electricity and stood away from her head like a halo which made the two girls giggle helplessly.

'Annie, when your Ma said goodbye to you on the railway station, did she give you something?'

'Molly, you're right, it was a little black bag, tiny. I just put it in my pocket, forgot all about it. There has been so much going on.'

Annie padded across to her coat and found the little bag deep in the pocket. When she opened it, she drew out a delicate gold chain with an exquisite locket hanging from it. She opened it up and revealed photos of her brothers. 'Oh, how beautiful,' Annie cried, 'do you know, I think this belonged to my grandmother, on my mother's side. I've seen Ma wearing it on special occasions; how very, very kind of her to give it to me. Look at the pictures of Paul and Matthew. And even the little velvet bag is lovely. I'm going to keep it under my pillow all the time.'

But bed time it was; they said their prayers side by side. Annie added little Joe to her list of people she prayed for. His haunted face was the last thing on her mind as she fell asleep, holding the black velvet bag with its precious contents in her hand.

Chapter 17

Joseph

They hadn't had a bath or even a proper wash in weeks, so it felt really good to be wet all over and to feel the sun on their bare skins. The men had gone down to the beach for a swim. Joseph and a few others had never had the opportunity to learn and, if he were honest with himself, he was a bit in awe of the waves, but he stripped off and ventured in, slowly. The coldness of the water took his breath away. He soon got used to it and joined in the games with the others. Naked, they ran up and down the beach, in the sun to dry off. Someone tied a bundle of shirts together and they played a great game of eight-a-side football. They felt strong and free, laughing, running and playing leap-frog.

Joseph suddenly felt very cut-off and far from home. There, across all that sea, was where he belonged. He felt tears prick his eyes. He pulled on his trousers and shirt, laced up his boots and called to Norman and Bert, 'What about a walk?'

They wandered away from the others; from a rise in the ground they could make out, far over the sea, the faint out-line of white cliffs.

'England,' pointed out Bert. 'Make the most of it; maybe the last time we will see her.'

'What do you mean, England?'

'Yes, see the White Cliffs of Dover, Kent or Sussex, the last thing, and the first thing, people see on either leaving or arriving there, as British as a cup of tea and fog. Feast your eyes.'

They wandered the short distance into town.

'Not seen any other conchies. They must have all given in,' observed Bert as they walked past the Punishment Block. 'Poor devils, I wonder where they are now. They can't be here or they'd never have sent us. Unless, of course, that's what they've got lined up for us.'

The three walked as apparently free men round the small town and into a tea-room where they enjoyed a tea and cakes that they could just manage to afford by pooling all the small change they had between them. Bert spoke a little French, had learnt it at school. The girl serving them was curious; they were, of necessity, wearing khaki but looked and behaved like no other English soldiers she had met before, no insignia or other badges, and they were so respectful.

'*Nous sommes ne pas allons a la guerre.*' Bert tried to explain but she seemed to be more puzzled.

'*Pourquoi?*'

'*Parsque nous sommes aimes tout le monde.*'

Joseph and Norman were baffled by this exchange and the girl left their table, shaking her head in incomprehension.

'Well, I tried to explain why we weren't going to war, but I don't think I did very well. I didn't get on with French in school.'

'Well, I'm impressed with it; we didn't do any languages in our school, but please would you explain to me why we are here? I'm not sure, either.'

The others laughed and thumped Joseph on the arm, 'Yes you do.'

*

Two days later, Joseph was wandering about the camp by himself, enjoying the sunshine and the peace, considering his decision.

He heard a man singing a hymn. Leaning against a fence, the man seemed to be standing with arms outstretched. He couldn't really see what he was doing and couldn't get closer. Joseph thought him daft to be standing there in the full sun, just singing, not moving. He called out, but the man didn't seem to hear him. He shrugged his shoulders and went on his way. He came to the hut where it was rumoured the prisoners undergoing Field Punishment number one had been housed.

'Over here.' A loud whisper.

He looked round. 'Where?'

'Over here, in the hut.'

He saw a face at a gap in the wall. 'Hello, who are you? Are you a C.O., too? We thought you had all given in, as we hadn't seen anything of you.'

'There are a couple of dozen of us in here. What punishment have you got?'

'We haven't been court marshalled yet. We expect that very soon. What about you lot?'

'We've got Number One, all of us. We take it in turns.'

104

'I've heard about it, but is it as bad as it sounds?'

'It depends what you have heard. We are taken out in small groups. Sometimes, we are handcuffed; arms behind our bodies, sometimes our arms are spread out. We are tied to beams or fences by our arms and ankles and left for two hours or more; no water, of course. That is the first day; the second day, we are turned around and tied facing the barbed wire, so we can't move our heads or else our faces would be cut by the wire. Most of the time, our feet don't quite touch the ground and usually we are leaning slightly forward, so that our weight causes the ropes to cut in. This happens every day, sometime twice in a day, but rules say that they have to give us every fourth or fifth day off; very considerate.'

'So that is what that man was doing, that I saw a few minutes ago. I just thought he was stupid, out in the sun like that. It sounds terrible. How do you stand it?'

'Some of us don't, some have given in and I don't blame them. It is the most inhumane thing I have ever had to endure; it goes on whatever the weather, rain or shine. Whoever thought this up must have been a sadist. And it's done to regular soldiers who step out of line, supposed to be more humane than flogging; but I wonder.'

'How long has this been going on?'

'Too long. I've lost count. Some of us are going mad; I know I sometimes feel I am.'

'Well, we may have that to look forward to.'

'Good luck, mate.'

'And you; if there is anything we can do for you, try to let us know. I'll pray for you, if it will help.'

*

The door of the hut slammed open. 'Up, up, up; the lot of you, out, at the double.'

'Now where are we going?' asked Joseph.

'Dunno, but it is too early to be getting up,' grumbled Norman, pulling on his clothes.

It was before dawn, just getting light. It wasn't just these sixteen men; the others from the Field Punishment Block were also turned out, about twenty of them.

'You lot, form a line down there, and you lot facing them, and

105

get a move on.' The Sergeant seemed to be more aggressive, more jittery than usual.

The two rows of prisoners lined up facing each other, across the parade ground.

Between them, a single post, about six feet high, had been knocked into the ground.

A squad of a dozen soldiers marched out, fully armed, and formed the third side of the square.

A single, very young soldier, a prisoner, stripped of all his insignia, was dragged to stand in the centre; he was weeping and shaking from head to toe.

Silence fell. The soldiers looked grim, stared into space, not looking anyone in the eye.

The realisation of what was about to happen dawned on the two rows of men.

'Dear God, I don't believe it,' someone whispered.

The Commanding Officer stepped forward and read, 'Having been found guilty by General Field Court Marshal of desertion in the face of the enemy, you are hereby sentenced to be shot.'

The lad fell to his knees.

The bored looking Chaplain, vestments flapping in the morning breeze, intoned a blessing, 'God be merciful unto you and bless you and show the light of his countenance upon you …and may God have mercy on your soul.'

A barked order. 'Proceed.'

The soldiers shifted from foot to foot.

The condemned man, a lad, hardly old enough to be shaving, was yanked to his feet, bound to the post, blindfolded, and a red cross pinned over his heart; he didn't resist, his sobs and cries for his poor mother were all that could be heard.

'Present arms – fire!'

A rattle of gun-fire and the boy slumped forward on his bindings.

Silence.

Joseph collapsed to the ground and vomited. His shoulders shook as he wept.

' 'e were no'but a bairn, no'but a bairn. Not old enough to be here. How could they do that, to one of their own? So young ...

deserter? He was probably just scared witless.'

Norman put his arm round Joseph's shaking shoulders. 'Come back to the hut, lad, come on.'

A silent Quaker meeting for worship started spontaneously. After a while, someone started singing, so soft, so low; it was difficult to hear, but soon they were all singing *"Abide with me, fast falls the even tide..."*

A blackbird sang its haunting song from the roof of one of the huts.

Chapter 18

Joseph

Each of the men was taken, one by one, to stand in front of the Commanding Officer; he asked them what they had decided.

'All the others have given in, why don't you?' He lied to them in turn.

'I will not go to war against another man. I can not kill.' Joseph felt he had recited this too many times.

One lad, the youngest, broke down under the pressure. 'I can't go on ... send me back ... I'll do anything they tell me ... don't let me be shot ... my poor mother!'

'All the best,' they said to him, 'we wish you luck, we don't think badly of you, we might do the same in a few days. It depends what they do to us and how long we can hold out. Look after yourself.' He was sent back to England, to plead his case and he hoped to be able to join the NCC.

*

'To the docks on the double.'

'Now what?' they asked each other.

'Nah then, you skiving lot. Unload them tins of bully-beef ready for the troops.' Not a man moved. 'Unload those bleedin' tins, an' jump to it!'

They stood resolutely together, staring at the stacks of tins that were waiting to be unloaded. The Corporal repeated the command. 'Didn't you 'ear what I said, you 'orrible wasters? Unload that lot!'

'Sorry, we can't do that, Sir.'

'Sorry? I'll give you bleedin' sorry; you know what this means, don't you? It means Court Marshal for the lot of you! Take the bleeders away.'

A rudimentary Field Court Marshal was duly arranged; the charge was read out.

'Did refuse an order in the face of the enemy. How do you plead?' came from the Officer Commanding.

They were each given the chance to say their piece. Joseph had rehearsed over and over in his mind and with Norman. He stood straight, hands behind his back.

'My refusal is consistent with my attitude since my arrest. This order is against me in France. I should never have been brought here. I should have been handed over to the civilian authorities in England, in accordance with Army Council Orders. I have consistently refused all military orders, both in England and in France, despite the threat of penalties of an extreme nature. I say again that I have taken no oath of allegiance and do not consider myself part of the military machine. Therefore, I am not guilty of this charge.'

'Not guilty? But I am told you refused to unload the bully-beef, refused an order?' By the time he had got to Joseph the man was tired and angry.

'I agree that I am guilty of refusing to unload the bully-beef destined for the Front, but not in the face of the enemy.'

'What the bloody hell do you mean by that? The enemy, Germans, are nearby, as you know.' The Major was getting exasperated.

'No man is my enemy, German or not, that is what I mean.' It all seemed so simple to him.

'I find you guilty. Have you heard of Field Punishment Number One? If you are not given that punishment, do you know that you will probably be shot, along with all the others? Sentence to be given next week. Dismiss.'

They all got the same, short shrift. But they had stood their ground. In their hut, they had a discussion.

'What are we going to do?'

'Pray and commend our souls to the keeping of God.'

'Do you want to give up?' they asked each other.

'No, we've come this far. Let them do their worst.'

'Their worst maybe pretty bad, you know.'

'Yes, but I'm not backing out now.'

In spite of the expected death sentence, they were allowed some time of freedom. A few of the soldiers guarding them respected their position; they trusted them all not to try to escape. They were allowed to go swimming, into town or for a walk; some stayed in the hut to read or write home.

'This all seems so unreal, Joseph. I can't believe it is really happening.'

109

'Norman, I really hope that we don't get the Field Punishment. At least, being shot will be quick, not like those others, in the hut over there that I told you about.'

Joseph went for a walk on the beach on his own; all these new sensations, he wanted to enjoy them – the smell of the sea, the sound of the waves breaking on the shore, the cry of the gulls screaming overhead. He could feel the crunching of the pebbles beneath his feet and the wind in his hair; he felt that he could walk for miles, to fly, just to be free. He sat on a rock and wrote a letter to his family.

"Dear Mam and Pa, Hannah and Jacob

We are here in France, I can't tell you exactly where. We have been Court Marshalled and we get our sentence tomorrow; we are expecting to be shot. Do not worry aBout it, I know that I have made the right decision and I will meet God with a clear conscience.

At the moment, I am sitting on a beach, I never expected to see the sea, the waves are breaking softly on the shore, the breeze is ruffling my hair, I can hear gulls crying and the sun is warm on my skin; I feel content and at peace.

I love you all, and may God go with you.

Thy loving Son and Brother,

Joseph."

Back at the hut, the men asked for, and were given, assurance that, in the event that they would be shot, the letters would be posted. They gathered together; Christians of all denominations and atheists, softly someone started singing *"Lead Kindly Light amid the encircling gloom..."* They said the Lord's Prayer and, after a long period of silence, Joseph stood and again sang the Quaker hymn *"Dear Lord and Father of Mankind, forgive our foolish ways..."* They all joined in.

Chapter 19

Daniel

Daniel and the other men were allocated billets in barns and farm-houses, they eventually settled into a routine. The shelling would go on for hours and hours, while the stretcher-bearers just waited behind the lines, helping those they could help. When it stopped, they would turn out, and parties would go into No-Man's Land, crawling over and under the barbed wire; or make their way down the zig-zagging trenches to collect the dead and wounded, dragging them back as best they could. They would assess the injuries, carry or escort the wounded to advanced Dressing Stations for first aid treatment. Some would then be taken to the waiting ambulances, be piled in and driven to the hospital. The dead and body parts were stacked up; they were to be buried at night, if possible.

'Hubert, I don't think I can take much more of this, day after day, night after night.'

'Yes, Dan, yes you can! You, we, have to, it's what we are here for.'

'But all that pain, injury, limbs missing, bodies torn apart, and we just have to go out there into No-Man's Land and scoop them up.'

'Every time I go out, I think it will be my last, and the noise of those shells, the smell of cordite, it terrifies me,' admitted Hubert.

'You frightened, as well? I thought it was just me.'

'No, I'm just scared out of my wits most of the time, or bored; depends what is happening. It seems to be nothing else, boredom or fear.'

'It's the ones that get gassed. I hate that smell; bloody fools most of them, either taking too long to put on their masks or else they've left them behind. Coughing their guts out, spewing all over the place and we have to clear up after them, patch them up. Take what is left of them to the Dressing Station, then to hospital, if they are still alive. Bury the ones that aren't. I've had it.' Daniel was nearly in tears.

'How many times have we been to the hospital? I've lost count. And how many men have we taken in?'

112

'Dunno. The grey-yellow mud; why did they have to hold their bloody war here? Couldn't they have chosen somewhere nice, without mud? It sticks to everything. I saw two men sucked right into that stinking mess yesterday. I couldn't help them, they had fallen off the duck boards, got sucked in by the weight of their packs. I couldn't reach them, they just slowly disappeared; I'll never forget the look of abject terror and fear on their faces. The last thing I saw was their hands.'

They were silent, troubled, quiet, thinking. 'We do so much waiting: waiting for the shelling to start and then to stop; waiting to take people to hospital; waiting for orders; it's that boredom as much as all the rest that gets me down.' Daniel put his hand into his pocket and turned Susie's stone over and over in his hand.

'What have you got there, old chum?'

'This? It's a stone little Susie gave me as a talisman before I left. I laughed at it at the time, but strangely, I find it comforting to hold it when things are getting too much for me. Don't tell anyone, will you.'

'Don't be embarrassed. I've got a lucky rabbit's foot; a bit gruesome but I've had it since I was sent away to boarding school when I was eight. I seem to remember it was a swap, for sweets I expect, but I've had it ever since. I found it comforting then, and I do now.'

*

One quiet evening, they were sitting in the dug-out, again waiting, and watching a pack of dogs scavenging among the debris. 'Dan, you've been to ward three, haven't you? Did you notice a pretty blond nurse, blue eyes, peaches and cream, well covered? I really like the look of her. Can you find out her name next time you are there? Do you know the one I mean? I'd like to ask her out.'

'Now you are talking. I think she's called Molly, but I rather fancy the dark-haired one, lovely slim figure, Annie Scott I think they call her. We've had words over the stretchers. I was going to ask her out. Maybe we could make a foursome.'

'We don't see enough of ordinary life, do we? Girls, going out, dances?'

The men fell silent, smoking cigarettes. Then the scream of the shells overhead and the flashes of the bombs as they exploded and the flare of the Very Lights.

'We'll be busy tonight,' observed Hubert.

'Hm, yes, what were you saying?'

'I was saying we will be busy tonight. Where were you? You looked like you were miles away.'

'At home. I was thinking of Susie. She has written, says she wants to work in a munitions factory, but she's not old enough yet, thank goodness. As we have no Pa, Ma has said she must ask me.' Daniel was worried. 'I'll have to tell her no, but to talk to Uncle Henry.'

After what seemed like hours, cooped up in the dug-out, dozing and smoking or huddling in a corner, with their fingers in their ears, the shelling stopped, the rifle fire quietened, a narrow moon came out.

'Time to go! Collect up those poor sods out there, the ones that are still alive.'

The team gathered up their stretchers and first aid equipment, opened the gas-curtain and, leaving the dug-out, set off as quietly and stealthily as they could. They picked their way into the trenches, over the duck-boards, barely noticing the bits of bodies that made up some of the embankments and underfoot. The sounds of moaning and crying directed them towards their goal.

They found some, crawling towards them, got them onto stretchers and carried them away.

'There is another one of them out there. I can hear him; last one, I expect,' said the Corporal.

Hubert and Daniel again inched up the fire-steps and on their bellies, into No-Man's Land, dragging their stretcher behind them. By crawling under the wire, they found the young lad, what was left of him. He was only about 50 yards away. They rolled him on to the stretcher, dragged him back. He was screaming all the way; the whole operation took about an hour and a half. Back in the trench, they found that most of the wounded had already been taken away, so they had this young Tommy, another stretcher case and three other men who were bleeding but able to walk; they bandaged them up as best they could. One had face wounds and was probably blinded.

'Put one hand on my shoulder while we carry this one,' Daniel told him.

Keeping their heads down, the party picked their way back to the waiting ambulance. The trench floor was covered in inches of mud; the stench of death was overpowering. The journey was long, too long for the lad who cried for his mother the whole way.

'Two stretchers, three walking, I think that is all for now.'

Daniel took over the driving. 'I've got room for only one bearer. Which one is it to be? Okay, Hubert, you come, you might see your blond nurse.'

In the back, Hubert watched over the injured men and tended them as well as he could. The road to the hospital was pitted and cratered with shell holes. No puddle could be trusted, as Daniel never knew whether it would be two inches or two feet deep. As the ambulance swerved and rattled, the patients groaned and cried out at each bump. In the cold moonlight, the countryside that Daniel drove through was bleak; dead stumps of blackened trees, water-filled craters and the ruined remains of farmhouses and barns. No apparent signs of life. It was a truly depressing sight. But Daniel didn't have time to think about it, he had his ambulance to drive and the men to consider; the two on stretchers rolled to and fro. Hubert tried to steady them; the sitting-wounded just had to hang on where they could.

The contrast between the ruins they had just past and the relatively unscathed Chateau that was the hospital struck him again, as it did every time he went there. It was so elegant, such a beautiful façade, tall windows, little turrets. He parked at the foot of the wide, sweeping stone steps to the huge front door. He took the steps, two at a time, to find an orderly to help them with the stretchers, while Hubert took the walking-wounded inside.

Between them, Daniel and the orderly carried the two men into the ward. Each man was greeted by a nurse who did her best to get him into bed and assessed as to the urgency for examination by a doctor.

'Why are you here? Why didn't you go to a Dressing Station first?' asked the Ward Sister crossly.

'Orders. The Dressing Station was full to overflowing, so we were told to come straight here.'

Sister pursed her lips, but she had to accept the filthy men.

115

Two nurses took charge of the patients by the door and asked questions of Daniel. 'Do you know his name? What injuries do you think he has? How long ago was he injured? How long was he lying unattended?' They were so concentrated on what they were doing that they hardly noticed the two stretcher-bearers.

Daniel and Hubert were exhausted. After they had finished their work, Sister sat them in the corridor. 'Nurses Scott and Williams, will you take these two to the Mess Hut on your way to your break. Make sure they eat. They look like they need food and rest, before going back.'

'Have we been introduced?' asked Daniel. 'We've seen you on the ward, of course, but not really to speak to. I'm Daniel Braithwaite, and this here is Hubert Cartwright; stretcher-bearers, drivers, first-aiders, musicians, general dogs-bodies at your service.' And he gave a deep bow.

The two girls laughed. 'I'm Annie Scott, and this is Molly Williams, pleased to meet you, I'm sure.' They dropped elegant curtsies.

'By, it's good to have proper food that is hot and doesn't taste of mud and smell of petrol.'

The four fell into easy conversation; in between mouthfuls they chatted about their accommodation, the hours they had to work and the problems they had. The minutes passed, and soon it was time for the men to go back to their billets.

'I saw a poster on the way in to the Mess Hut, about a staff dance,' said Hubert. 'Would the two of you like to go with us? If you are off together.'

Annie looked at Molly and grinned. 'We would really like that. We were planning to go, but it will be so much better to have partners. It doesn't start until just after we get off duty, so we will have a few minutes to tidy up.'

'It all depends on Fritz, of course; if we are very busy, we won't make it.'

'If we are very busy at the hospital, it will be cancelled.'

'Well, see you on Saturday. We look forward to it.'

Whistling, the men drove off in their ambulance and the two girls returned to work, chatting excitedly about their dates.

116

Saturday couldn't come quickly enough. That evening, the Ward Sister noticed an air of anticipation so didn't keep the nurses longer than necessary at the end of their shift; they had little enough entertainment and relaxation, they had worked very hard.

Everyone went to the dance in uniform; few people had anything else to wear. Annie took off her apron and cap and changed into a clean dress. She straightened her collar and cuffs and fastened her gold locket on its chain around her neck. She took the pins out of her hair. As she brushed it, it fell in a dark chestnut cascade down her back to her waist. When Molly took off her cap, her hair sprung out from her head like a halo. She never could control it properly.

They pulled their navy cloaks round their shoulders and hurried to the Recreation Hut. Hubert and Daniel were waiting by the door, smoking. Their uniforms brushed and buttons and boots as clean as they could make them, caps tucked under their epaulettes. They crushed their cigarettes under foot as the girls approached.

'Hello, good to see you.'

'I hope we didn't keep you waiting too long. We've only just got off duty.'

'No,' said Daniel, 'we've only just arrived ourselves.'

'Come on, let's go in. I think they've started.'

The band was playing as they entered the hut; they found a table and sat down. 'Would you like a drink?' asked Hubert.

'Yes, please, but just a soft drink. I don't drink alcohol. Squash or tea.'

'I'll have a beer, if they've got it,' said Daniel. 'See what they've got.'

Hubert returned with four glasses of squash. 'Sorry, no beer.'

Daniel sat next to Annie. 'I'm not a good dancer, I'm afraid,' he admitted. 'But I do enjoy it.'

'I've not had much opportunity to learn,' replied Annie, 'I've always been too busy, but I do like dances; the music, the movement and, until the war, looking at the clothes people wear. So elegant.'

'Not much chance of seeing lovely clothing here; everyone is

117

in uniform of one sort or another.'

'Yes, but you look so smart in yours. I think uniform really suits you.'

'I find it embarrassing, as I don't really like being a soldier, but what else could I do?'

'Let's not talk about it now. I want to enjoy myself.'

'I hope you don't mind my saying this, but you have the most beautiful hair. I didn't realise, with you keeping it all covered up under your cap.'

Annie blushed at the compliment as Daniel stood up. 'Let's try dancing; I really like these country dances.' They joined in the set and found that they both knew the Strip-the-Willow. With the others, they linked hands, danced back and forwards, up and down the set and into the grand-chain which, as usual, ended in chaos. They were all laughing as someone got their left and right hands muddled.

'Why does someone always do that? It creates mayhem, but at least it makes everyone laugh.'

'That's why I like country dances, it brings people together,' said Annie.

They did a Valetta, a Military Two-Step, the Gay Gordons and a Dashing White Sergeant. There were also quick-steps, and a ladies excuse-me. A light supper was served and the evening finished with a final waltz. It was time to go; Daniel and Hubert escorted Annie and Molly back to their quarters, before driving off to their billet.

'Molly is a beauty, a real English rose,' Hubert enthused.

'Give me Annie's looks any day; she's a stunner and she's quiet and thoughtful, just my sort. I'm going to ask her out next time she and I are off duty at the same time; I want to get to know her better.'

Chapter 20
Joseph

Joseph was convinced now, more than ever, that he was doing the right thing. In the first sun for days, he was sitting outside the hut, on an upturned bucket, reading his well-thumbed Bible. The sun was warm on his skin and he felt relaxed. He had just finished writing a letter home, with little hope of it being delivered but it helped him clear his mind, to write down all he was feeling. Two men strolled toward him, deep in conversation. They both were tall and distinguished-looking; so alike that they could be brothers. As they got closer, Joseph realised that one was Bert, but the other was dressed in the uniform of a Major. The soldier looked tired and drawn but animated as he talked, waving his hand and swagger-stick. The officer had clearly tried to have his uniform spruced up but it was worn and shabby; however, his boots and Sam-Browne belt were polished and the pips on his shoulders and cap-badge gleamed and caught the sun; his bat-man had done a good job.

'Joseph, good to see you. Where are the others?' Bert asked.

'They are about somewhere, playing football or swimming, no doubt. I needed some time to myself.'

'I would like you to meet my brother Philip. Don't look so startled. We brothers took different paths in this war; Philip volunteered and, having been to the right school, got a commission; we agree to disagree, but we support each other. Philip, this is Joseph Metcalf, a fellow Quaker.'

'Good to meet you, Friend.' The men shook hands. 'How did you know where to find us?' Joseph asked. 'Bert has never said anything about a brother; he's kept you well hidden.'

'I wouldn't have said anything, never expected a visit,' admitted Bert.

'Remember that postcard Bert filled in on the train? Dashed clever of him. We used to send messages to each other like that when we were children so Mater, Pater and Nurse wouldn't know what we were plotting; they probably worked it out for themselves, though.' The two brothers laughed with the shared memories.

'Pip, that card only said we were going to Boulogne, we had no other information.'

'Yes, but the only place that they can send you C.O.s in France, where there is a Field Punishment Block is at Henriville, so I guessed you would likely be here.'

'We're waiting for our sentence, after the Field Court Marshall.'

'What have you done?'

'It's what we haven't done that's the problem, that's why we were brought here. We have refused an order in the face of the enemy. It's a foregone conclusion, we'll be shot or get Number One; we are all resigned to it.'

'And then there are the others. Didn't Bert tell you about them?'

'No, we've been catching up on family; Mater isn't well, worries about us all. What others?'

'The fellows in the Field Punishment Block; there are about two dozen of them.'

As they walked outside and round the end of the hut, Philip caught sight of a long, low hut set away from them. 'What is that building over there?'

'It's the Punishment Block. They, or at least some of them, get Number One regularly; we've been expecting it ourselves. Horrible business, that; who in the military dreams these things up? We never see them, except the other day, at the terrible execution.' He shuddered with the memory.

'I've heard about Number One, of course. I'm never going to inflict it on anyone myself. I couldn't, it sounds really cruel. There is enough cruelty going on out here, without adding to it. If I can do anything for you, and I can't promise, I will try to get them seen to as well.'

'Come and have a look at our palatial accommodation.'

Joseph pushed open the door to their hut. Philip took in the cramped conditions, the holes in the wooden walls, the narrow iron bedsteads, thin mattresses and meagre blankets. He could see that the men had tried to clean it up. It was tidy, to an almost military level; folded bedclothes, lined-up wash bowls, and the worst holes had been stuffed with bits of paper. It reminded him

120

of his dormitory at boarding school. However, he remembered his and Bert's home, the big rooms, carpets, cosy comfortable beds, live-in servants, warm clean clothing. Neither of them were having any comfort in this war, suffering the same flea infestations which recognise no rank.

'Bert, are you sure about all this? I'm glad Mater can't see you, and I'll not tell her.'

'Pip, you know I am, and I know it's not grand but I'll bet it's better than the accommodation you get at the Front, but we're all in this together no favouritism, except I'm the only one to get a visitor.'

Philip's eyes twinkled. 'I don't often get to pull rank, away from the field. I don't have to, these pips do it for me. But to see the expression on your Captain's face, when I said I wanted to see my brother was a sight to see. I'm on my way to Blighty, for a bit of R and R. I thought I could call in, it was nearly on our way.'

'"Our"? Who else is with you?'

'Just my driver. One of the perks.'

'As a family, we have a few friends in high places, and if you have strings you might as well pull them, so I will if I can. For you and those other blighters,' said Philip.

'Well, I hope you can do something for us. I would really rather not be shot or get number one.'

'Now then, Joseph, can I get a message to your parents for you?'

'Yes please.' He pulled the letter he had just finished out of his pocket and wrote the address on it. 'Just tell them that I am well and in good spirits in the hands of God. Thank you so much.'

'Of course, of course; I'll do what I can. And please, say nothing about this to the others; no point in getting their hopes up.'

The two brothers shook hands and embraced. 'Give my love to the parents and Nurse. I never asked how she is.'

Joseph moved away and watched the two make their farewells.

Bert stood for a long time, after his brother had got into his vehicle and was driven away. He knocked out his pipe, tamped down the tobacco and, puffing to get it lit, he walked round the back of the hut, deep in thought.

121

London

'Get me Asquith on the phone, will you, Jessica?'

'Asquith, this is Mayhew, Albert Mayhew MP for...'

'Yes, yes. Good to hear from you, old boy. How's the family?'

'Fine, fine, thanks for asking. But it's not the family I'm ringing about, but it is a personal problem and one I think you should know about.'

'I'm curious, tell all.'

'It's that family Hewitson, good friends of mine; one of the sons, Major Philip Hewitson – got a bit of a problem with the brother. I'm wondering if you can help.'

'If I can, dear boy, if I can. What's up?'

'It's that younger brother; they all call him Bert.'

'What's he been up to? Is he that 'conchie' brother, there are two or three of them, aren't there?'

'Yes, that's the one. Bert managed to get a message to him, though how it got through the censors, I'm blowed if I know; must have been asleep on the job. Anyway, he said that they were being sent to Boulogne. The only reason Philip could think of for them to be sent there is so that he and the others from Richmond Castle can defy orders in the face of the enemy and be shot. He went to Henriville on his way home and he was right; they are all waiting for the sentence, to be shot, no doubt, having been court marshalled. And he tells me that there are another couple of dozen enduring Field Punishment Number One; been there some weeks.'

'Dashed annoying that, I can see, and worrying. So you are telling me we have about forty men being punished out in France? Don't want that – we have enough martyrs, don't we? I'll see what I can do. Kitchener was keen to make an example of them, so is Haig, but with Kitchener drowning in the Orkneys...' He paused. 'Terrible tragedy, that; I don't know how we'll manage without him. Anyway, I'll have a word with Haig. I know Parliament doesn't want martyrs; I'll talk to you soon. Must meet up sometime for a

122

snifter or two. I'll get on to it.'

'Jessica; get me Field Marshal General Haig on the blower, will you, old girl?'

'Haig, Asquith; we've got a problem, those 'conchies', some of them have been sent to Boulogne and then to Henriville, presumably so that they can be shot. And I've heard that some are getting Number One.'

'How do you know that, Sir? If you don't mind me asking.'

'Never mind that. Sorry can't say. Now then, I know that you and Kitchener were keen, make an example and so on, but Parliament isn't happy, doesn't want martyrs. What can we do?'

'Dashed if I know. As you said, I am keen to make an example of them, show the others this 'conchie' lark isn't worth it,' said Haig.

'We think it would be bad for morale to shoot them, so I think we must just bring them home quietly, and tuck them away somewhere obscure, say Scotland; make them break rocks for the duration.'

'Very well, if that is what you and the Government want, I will have to go along with it. I'll send a signal, leave it to me.'

'Thanks, old chap, we'll talk soon.'

*

TO HENRIVILLE BARRACKS JUNE 20 1916

COMMUTE COs DEATH AND NUMBER ONES STOP TEN YEARS HARD STOP

SEND TO DYCE SCOTLAND SOONEST STOP

HAIG

Chapter 21
Joseph

The men knew that this would be a definitive day. They were woken early and ordered to dress; they shaved, washed and dressed carefully. Breakfast was a quiet affair; the usual porridge and mugs of sweet, strong tea being consumed in near silence. The soldiers guarding them seemed more subdued than usual, none of the banter from the friendly ones; even those who were normally offensive and surly didn't seem to have the heart to be as rude or as contemptible as usual.

All the men from Richmond, as well as those from the Field Punishment Block, were escorted out onto the parade ground in the bright, chilly morning. A skylark rose in the air. They could hear its call high above them. Round the perimeter, the trees were in full leaf, and wild flowers were at their best, on this day of early summer sun. Joseph took great gulps of the fresh, balmy air.

Soldiers were drawn up on three sides of the square, including a few from the Non Combatant Corps. Joseph shielded his eyes, trying to see if Daniel was among them; he didn't really expect him to be. The prisoners, nearly forty of them, made up the fourth side of the square. The Major marched to the centre and, taking a paper from a Corporal, slowly and deliberately read the names of all of the men, one after the other, relishing his task.

'Private soldiers Barrett, Beavis, Bonner, Brewster, Brocklesby, Cartwright, Cryer, Evans, Foster, Gaudie, Hall C, Hall S, Hewitson, Hicks, Jackson, Jordan, Law HG, Law WE, Lawn, Marten, Marlew, Martlowe, Metcalf, Muffin, Mayers, Priestly, Renton, Ricketts, Ring, Routledge, Senior, Scullard, Spencer, Stanton, Taylor, and Walling.'

A bugle sounded. Not a man moved.

'Having been found guilty by Field Court Marshal of disobeying an order in the face of the enemy and disobedience while undergoing Field Punishment, you are all hereby sentenced to death by firing squad. Sentence confirmed by General Sir Douglas Haig.'

A long silence

'So that's it, that's what it's come to.'

124

'Well, we expected it, didn't we?'

'The visit from Philip made no difference then.'

'I had hoped he could have used his influence. Maybe he didn't get home in time.'

The whispered words were directed to no-one in particular.

'Silence! No talking in the ranks.'

Someone giggled nervously. 'What's the punishment for talking?'

The Officer took another breath and looked dejectedly at the paper in his hand, then took a deep sigh of disappointment. 'Sentences commuted to ten years penal servitude with hard labour. Dismiss.'

'What? What did he just say?' There was a collective murmur from all the prisoners and soldiers alike.

They were marched back to their huts, grins all over every face.

'Collect your things, you are moving. We don't want you here, getting in the way,' ordered the Corporal.

*

The men from the Field Punishment Block were shipped out by train over night to an unknown destination; the fifteen 'Richmond' men were moved into the block that they vacated. They were locked together into one cell.

'You'll be here until we have other orders. Make yourselves at home,' sneered the soldier, 'none of the comforts you have been used to now; hard means hard.'

The men looked round the cramped cell. One small, high window gave a minimum of light and ventilation, one bucket in the corner provided for the use of all the men for their bodily functions; one plank cot, no mattress, no bedding. Loaves of stale bread and mugs of water were given to them as night fell.

'Please, I wonder if you know, if you can tell us, how long will we be here?' They were still polite to their guards.

'No idea; you'll have to make the best of it. Days, weeks, years, who knows? Sleep well.' The door slammed behind the guard.

By dint of fitting themselves together like spoons in a cutlery drawer, two men managed to fit onto the 'bunk', the rest did the same on the floor; there was just room enough for them all to lie down. One unfortunate had to sleep next to the, now over-flowing, slop bucket.

Daylight creeping in through the window brought welcome relief from the sleepless night.

'Much as I love you, chaps; I do hope we don't have to stay here long.'

'We are in t'same position as before, just not knowing. I hate it; I don't know how I'll cope.' Joseph looked haggard. He looked more frightened than he had done at any other time. He constantly ran his fingers through his hair.

'Steady on, old boy, we'll all look after each other. We've come so far, they can't break us now. Can they?' Norman put his arm round his shoulders.

'A few hymns will lift our spirits, something cheerful.'

'I like *"All Things Bright and Beautiful, all creatures great and small..."* It reminds me of home. I know it is usually sung at harvest time, but it's a good song, uplifting; so long as we don't sing that verse about the rich man and his castle and the poor man at his gate. I've had enough of castles.'

'Off we go then.'

The door crashed open. They didn't stop singing.

'Come to join in, Friend?'

'No, and you are to stop.'

'You cannot stop us praising the Lord.'

At the end of the hymn, the soldier was still there. 'Slop out! One of you – you, take the bucket down the corridor and empty it.'

'Do you think we could possibly have the luxury of another bucket or two, or maybe just empty this one more frequently?'

'What do you take this for, the Dorchester?'

'Well, no harm in asking, mate. May I ask when do you serve breakfast?'

The soldier turned on his heel.

'I'll take that as a 'no', shall I? As a 'not-going-to-get-any', shall I?'

The men took it in turns to stand up, to move as much as possible, to lie down, and to doze. At night times, they took it in

126

turns to sleep next to the malodorous, constantly overflowing bucket. Days and nights turned into a week and then another. Food and drink was limited to once-a-day bread and water. The men were getting ill; they didn't wash, shave, clean their teeth or change their clothes. The lice multiplied; rats scuttled over their bodies at night. The smell of unwashed bodies and the bucket was overpowering. As the daytime warmed up, the temperature was stifling. Tempers were breaking. The pressure of living in such a confined space was telling on them all. Some of them were saying things they later regretted.

'I can't stand your "holier than thou" attitude. Who do you think you are?'

'You with your posh accent, I hate the way you are always falling back on your supposed deprived education as an excuse; you're no more deprived than the King of England himself.'

'Can't you give me any more room? You always take too much space when you sit down, with your sharp elbows sticking out.'

'Peace, friends, peace. Remember what we are here for.'

'And you can just stop that. Bleeding peace. What's that, I've forgotten?'

'Now then, Friends and comrades. We must stop this arguing – it's getting us nowhere.'

'Yes, I know, but I can't take this any more.' The man burst into tears.

'Well, I hate to remind you all that we do each have a solution, but none of us wants to quit now, do we?'

Joseph hardly said a thing to anyone, just sat in a corner with his arms round his legs, rocking, always rocking; he didn't speak even to Norman who was getting worried about him. 'Come on, Friend, buck up, there's a good chap. Look, if you stand over here; you can just see the sun coming up.'

They did their best to maintain courtesy to their guards who were not to blame for the situation. One or two even showed some kindness and respect for them, but none stayed to chat; in that stinking hole, no-one wanted to.

'Up, up, up, you lazy cowards, you are on your way. Outside, you lot!'

'Now where? Wherever it is, it can't be as bad as this, can it?'

'Kind Corporal, do you by any chance know where we are going? I only ask out of curiosity.'

'No, and if I did, I wouldn't tell you. Now get a move on.' A foot landed on his shin.

The men were bundled out into the cool morning of a July day. They staggered as they could hardly walk; such was their lack of exercise during the previous two weeks. The light made them wince with its unaccustomed brightness, the rain was soft on their skins, and they took in great gulps of fresh air. Trees and grass had never looked so green, dandelions looked like gold coins, and the grey sea in the far distance seemed to sparkle as with diamonds in a stray shaft of sunlight.

'I can't stand this, all this brightness. I'd like to do a cartwheel.'

'I shouldn't if I were you, you're too weak. You'll fall and you'll get no sympathy from anyone.'

'Smell the birds, hear the air, it's deafening. The daisies and dandelions are so bright, they are dazzling and beautiful.' He laughed at the mix in his words. Even Joseph cheered up and looked reinvigorated and managed a smile.

*

The train took them back to Amiens and then to Rouen. They watched the countryside as they passed by, the crops ripening, people going about their every day activities.

'Is there really a war going on here, just a few miles away?'

'Gi' away! Do you see the workers in the fields? Old men, young boys and women, there are no men of our age; they are all fighting or dead.'

'Crops have to be harvested, animals tended, people fed, regardless of war; more important because of the war.'

'It's all so beautiful, relaxed even; timeless, seeing the horses pulling the wagons, the hay being turned, the activities of normal life. How long will it last?'

At Rouen, their guards took them first to the wrong prison, the civilian one, where they were unceremoniously turned away.

'Non, non, non, espèce d'idiot. Allez, allez vous en! Celui-ci est une prison civile, non militaire. Allez.'

'Désolé camarade, alors, ou devrons-nous aller?'

'Anyone here speak Frog?' Their British guard couldn't understand a word.

'I think he is saying that we have been brought to the wrong prison,' offered Bert. 'That's French authority for you.'

'Allez, allez tout suit. La prison militaire est la bas, la prochaine rue.'

'Merci, comarade, Je suis vraiment désolé.'

Allez, partez, partez maintenant.'

They were directed to the Military prison in the next street; the guards were given a good dressing down for taking their prisoners to the civilian prison. The men were allocated three to a cell, seeming luxury after the hell-hole of their accommodation at Henriville. The Governor visited them and was overcome by the stench of unwashed men and slop buckets; he ordered water, clean clothes, and regular slop-outs to be provided. They were also given proper food – porridge for breakfast and a bit of meat, some potatoes and vegetables once a day; it seemed like heaven.

'It's Sunday, time to wake up and get up, time to sing some hymns and have some prayerful silence!' Norman called out.

They broke into a few verses of *"Onward Christian Soldiers, marching as to war..."*, laughing at the irony of the words, but it was a good, rousing tune.

But they were soon interrupted. 'Work-party – here, take this spade. You are to dig holes there and there, to use as latrines.'

'Sorry, can't do that.'

'Why, for Pete's sake?'

'It's Sunday, a day for rest and prayer. Anyway, if we wouldn't work at Henriville, why should we here? We have the same principles now as we did then.'

'Back to your cells! Three days bread and water for you lot!'

'Oh well, it was good while it lasted.'

But they didn't get the full three days. Manacled together, they

129

were on their way to the docks. They stood waiting to be escorted onto the troop ship that was to take the injured home for treatment. The locals wanted to know who they were and why they were shackled as criminals but in uniform. They mistrusted them and clearly were eager to throw them into the dock.

'Qui êtes-vous? Pourquoi vous-êtes en uniforme mais sans des insignes, sans signes d'indentification?'

'Ils sont les tires-au-flancs, les grévistes. Ils refusent à combattre; ils n'aideront pas nous ni vous. Refusent de se bagarrer.'

'Allons-nous eux jeter dans le dock, laiseent eux noyer pour leurs lâchetés.'

Bert was doing his best to explain to the people, *'S'il vous plait, nous sommes suivre le Maitre, connais vous le Maitre? Nous ne pas mauvais, nous sommes désire la Paix.* Oh bother, how do you say it? My French is so rusty.'

'You are doing fine, keep going.'

'Nous sommes désire à un example de le paix. Nous prier do vous montez compassion. Pour le Maitre, tout pour le Maitre' Bert held his hands together to indicate praying.

The French men and women stood around talking about what they had heard. Some had difficulty trying to understand his terrible school-boy French; one of the men broke away; it seemed that he had understood.

'Oiu, nous croyons que nous avons bien compris, vous êtes courageux.'

A woman ran forward and kissed Joseph on the cheek. *'Nous avons quelques cadeaux pour vous, du pain, des pommes. Dieu vous bénisse et pouvons-nous vivre en paix bientôt, nous prières pour vous.'* She pressed a basket of bread and apples into Joseph's hand.

'What was that all about?'

'I think they wanted to know why we weren't wearing proper uniform, wanted to throw us in the dock because some of them saw us as cowards. I tried in my best School Certificate French to explain, but I couldn't remember the French for God. It seems that they got the gist of it, though, judging by those presents.'

The men were herded onto the ship, past the lines of stretchers

130

with their attendant nurses. One of them, a dark-haired, slim lass, was smiling at them. Joseph couldn't resist speaking to her.

'Now then lass, what's your name?'

'Annie Scott, but I'm busy. Who are you?'

'We are C.O.s being taken back to England for a ten year prison sentence.'

'Nurse, nurse, here please.'

'I can't stop, got to get back to the hospital when these are safely on board; but nice to meet you. Good luck, wherever you go.'

'Thank you, goodbye, and good luck to you too.'

The maimed, gassed and blinded were loaded onto the ship, white-faced, some clearly in terrible pain, but most apparently cheerful looking.

'Why so many? What has been happening?' Joseph asked an orderly.

'Don't you know? Where've you been, chum? We've been fighting and winning and loosing a few yards near the river Somme. It was a hard battle, lost quite a few men. This lot all have Blighties, they are going home to recover.'

'What then? What will happen to them then?'

'If they are well enough, they go back to the Front, don't you know nothing? Some men go back two or three times.'

'What happens if they are not ever well enough?'

'Well, I suppose their families have to look after them, those that survive.' The orderly seemed disinterested.

'What do you mean? Why won't they survive if they are getting good treatment?'

'Infection, mate. Cor, you really are a higorant one, aren't you? Infection, gas-gangrene, there is only so much we can do. Most of the ones with wounds are infected and once it gets into the blood stream…'

'God help them…'

'You're right there; God is the only one that can help some of these beggars. Some of them just have shell-shock; not actually injured, they've just lost their minds. We send them to the loony-bins, maybe they can help them there. Sorry mate, I'd love to chat all day, but I have work to do. So long.' The man went about his business, helping the nurses.

The ship cast off and sailed down the river Seine, toward the sea. The prisoners were in the care of an understanding Corporal; in exchange for a promise not to try to escape, they were allowed to stay on deck, unshackled, to watch the beautiful river-scene as they passed by. As the sun set behind the trees, they were quiet and pensive, thinking of the wounded men below that they were travelling with, the death sentence that they had just avoided, wondering what ten years of hard labour would involve.

Somewhere towards midnight, Joseph lit a cigarette.

An order shouted out, 'Put out that light! No smoking! Do you want the subs to see us?'

'So you are still awake.'

'Yes Norman, and you?'

'I'm glad to leave all that behind, but I do wonder what they are plotting for us now.'

'I can feel the ship moving differently. I think we must be at sea.'

'I wonder if I'll ever get to France again. It's not been a good experience, has it?'

'Goodnight, Norman, sleep well. Let's pray for the future.'

The ship zig-zagged its way across the Channel, dodging the submarines until it reached the safety of port.

Chapter 22

Annie and Daniel

Daniel was standing at the door of the hospital, twisting his cap in his hands; his eyes brightened as he saw Annie.

'I'm sorry, I hope I'm not late. Sister kept me back. That John Smith you brought in yesterday is, was, Robert Wilson; he died and I had to do all the paperwork and packing of his belongings.'

'No, no, don't worry. I'm early. But I hardly recognised you in ordinary clothes. I've only seen you in uniform.' Annie was wearing a long, dark coat over her one non-uniform dress, with a demure hat pinned on with her Grandmother's hat-pin; her gold locket caught the sun.

'Well, I've only got this, so it will have to do. We spend so much of our time in uniform; it feels strange not to be wearing it.'

'Well, I'm afraid uniform is all I've got. Anyway, if I didn't wear it, I would just get taunts from the local people; they would think I am a skiver.'

'Well, it suits you.'

'Let's not talk about work and the war. Let's just enjoy ourselves.' Daniel took her elbow. 'Come on, there's a bus in a few minutes.'

They climbed to the upper deck, to enjoy the fresh air and the sun on their faces.

'I can't get used to the French driving on the other side of the road. I've nearly been run down a few times, by looking in the wrong direction; lucky they make enough noise,' said Annie.

'The countryside always looks different from here, doesn't it, don't you think? But it is beautiful; difficult to remember there is a war going on just round the corner. I like to see things from up here, looking over hedges and walls, seeing all the crops ripening and the animals in the fields.'

Annie was suddenly shy, in the company of this handsome young man. 'Yes, it's lovely.'

'How long have you been a nurse? Where did you train? Do you enjoy it?'

'Three years, York, yes. Why are you a stretcher bearer? Did you ask to be?'

'I only joined up because of the Military Service Act. I'm a conscientious objector but I want to do my bit, which is why I joined the Non Combatant Corps and became a stretcher bearer,' he prattled on. 'Got any family? I've got Ma, and Susie is my little sister. But Pa died in a mining accident. I've got no brothers; always thought it would have been nice to have brothers. Have you got any family?'

Annie burst into tears.

'I'm so sorry, here's me jabbering on, being insensitive. Please forgive me. Here, take my handkerchief.'

'No, you weren't to know. It was you talking about brothers; our Paul is dead and Matthew, his twin, is missing. One of the reasons I came out here was the hope I could find him; maybe you could help?' She took the offered handkerchief and blew her nose.

'Oh Annie, I'm so sorry, of course I'll help if I can, but I don't know what I can do. The chances are very slim; there's an awful lot of men out here. Now, dry your eyes, please. Let's try to forget this beastly war for a few hours. But when you are ready, I'd like to know about your brothers. I feel that I eat, sleep and dream the war; it's beginning to get me down. But I can't say anything to anyone.'

'Hard to forget it, with you in your khaki,' she smiled.

'Sorry, it's all I have, nothing else.'

'Don't keep saying sorry, you don't have to.'

'Sorry.' They laughed together.

The bus delivered them to the town centre. Annie undid the buttons on her coat; the sun was quite strong.

'Can we go into the church? I'd like say a prayer and light a candle for Matthew and Paul.'

'Of course, we can say a prayer together for this war to be soon over, though I'm not very good in churches.'

It was cool and dark in the old, ornate Catholic church. The icons looked sad and neglected. They sat down near the front and whispered to each other; their voices seemed to echo in the space.

'I find Roman Catholic churches so over decorated and no-one ever seems to dust all these statues. Give me my mother's chapel any day. It is peaceful and I can find some calm there. This is too busy but sad looking, but I quite like the smell, I don't know why,

134

but it's such a contrast from the trenches.'

'I quite agree, Daniel. I go to the Church of England, it's fairly simple. We have a Catholic church in the town. I went to a service there once but it was all in Latin. I couldn't understand a word. I didn't go again. I think the smell is a mixture of candles and incense. It always reminds me of something, but I can never think what. I wonder if they have anything other than Catholic churches here; I doubt it.'

'Well, I don't go to chapel any more, except on Christmas and Easter, to keep Ma and Susie company, but I used to go regularly when I was little; I do admit, I miss the singing.'

'Why don't you go?'

'It all seems irrelevant in this war. If we are all Christians and therefore followers of Jesus and lovers of peace, why are we fighting? I think, most Germans are Christian, aren't they? I've joined the British Socialist Party. We object to the war, as we believe that all men, and women, are brothers and sisters and we shouldn't fight.'

'Sounds like very Christian beliefs to me; yes, Jesus said we should love our neighbours as ourselves. Wars don't make any sense to me. All wars are ended by people talking, unless everyone is killed, so why not start that way?'

They chatted about their childhood experiences of church and chapel going and found that they had much in common, same hymns, some of the same words in the services.

'My favourite hymn is *"All Things Bright and Beautiful"*, the way it celebrates the seasons, and nature. I think it's a pity we only sing it at Harvest Festival,' said Annie.

'I love the Christmas carols, everything from *"Away in a Manger"*, which Susie and I used to sing together, to *"Good King Wenceslas"*. Before my voice broke, Pa and I used to sing it together, taking the parts of the King and Page.'

'At home, I met a couple of Quakers. I don't know much about them, but I think they don't sing hymns. I wonder if they miss them.'

'Not if they've never had them, I suppose. I have a friend, Joseph; we were at school together, he's a Quaker. I think he's out here somewhere. I'm sure I saw him and more than a dozen others, on the boat coming over here. They were all in irons; it really bothered me.'

'Why ever in irons?'

'He's an absolutist conscientious objector, won't register or have any part of the war. He's been in prison and I think he has been brought to France so he can be shot.'

'That's terrible! Why? How?'

'It's the penalty for refusing to obey an order in the face of the enemy; that's why he and the others were brought here, to be in the face of the enemy. I'm going to light a candle for them, Joseph especially.'

'Do all Quakers take this stand?'

'No, some of them are in the NCC with me and I understand that there are men other than Quakers with him; Methodists, International Bible Students and some of us Socialists.'

'How do you know all this?'

'When I was training at Richmond Castle, there was a group of them, including Joseph, locked up in the cells there, and you know how folks talk.'

'Sounds horrible; were the cells the dreadful underground dungeons that they have in some Medieval castles?'

'No, it was just a small block beside the great tower; there was a group in the guardroom as well. They called it the guardroom, but it was only that when the castle was first built, in Norman times; of course, there was a new one that we used. Anyway, we could hear them singing hymns, used to really annoy their guards and our Sergeant Major; I joined in with them sometimes.'

'Let's change the subject. Can we go back out into the sunshine again? I'm getting quite chilly.'

'Let's go and find a tea-room. I think it is very strange that, with a war going on so close to here, we can hope to find a tea room that will, if we are lucky, have some of those delicious French pastries. Come on!'

Annie tucked her arm into Daniel's. She was starting to feel at ease with him now, more relaxed.

'Here, this looks nice.'

They went in and, between their French and the waitresses' English, managed to order tea and the pastries that they had been looking forward to.

Over tea, Annie told Daniel all about her beloved twin brothers, her father's teaching job and the injury that stopped him being called up for this war. Her eyes shone as she told of her home, of her brothers who had been so close to her. And all about her childhood passion for looking after sick and injured animals, that had lead her into her vocation as a nurse.

'I really feel called. It's as if there is someone, or something, guiding me, watching over me. I can't really explain properly.'

Daniel told Annie about how his father had been killed in the mines, how his mother was managing, about little Susie in service and how well she was doing.

'I've had a letter from her. She wants to do her bit toward the war effort. She's thinking about the VAD and working in a munitions factory when she is old enough. I hope she doesn't, it's a hard, dangerous job and poisonous work, and they call the girls canaries as it turns their skin yellow. I've asked Uncle Henry to keep an eye on her.'

They went for a walk round the town, looking in shop windows, and caught the bus back.

'Can we meet again, please?' pleaded Daniel.

They had got back to the hospital and Annie's hut.

'I would like that, but we will have to wait until our off-duties coincide. We'll see each other at the hospital, won't we?'

'Over a romantic meal in the Mess Hut,' laughed Daniel.

Chapter 23

Joseph

There were many stops and starts on the train journey from Southampton to the north. They were getting bored and very uncomfortable on the hard, wooden seats but relieved at being back in England again, concerned about their futures.

'Norman, I've been thinking. Have we all been offered the Home Office Scheme?' asked Joseph.

'Yes, I think so and I don't know what to make of it. I've been told that we could go to a work camp and do work of national importance, but I wonder what that would be.'

'I think I'll sign up for it and see what happens, at least we can then get letters and visits and not wear army uniform; it's very appealing.'

'I don't expect it will be easy, though. We were sentenced to ten years *hard* – and I expect that means hard.'

'Surely, anything is better than prison. I don't think I could take that any more; and if it's national importance but not military, maybe it will be worth doing.'

As the train pulled in at York, Joseph became aware that the train journey would be going very near his home. 'If we stop anywhere near Masham, I'm going to make a jump for it.'

'You'll be caught.'

'I'm not going to escape, just tell the family that we're alright. I'll ask them to write to all our families if you give me their addresses.'

'You're barmy, but we'll cover for you if we can.'

In the evening, the train stopped in a siding just outside Ripon. The Corporal said that they had to stop for the night, to take on more coal and water for the engine and they would be there until morning.

'Make yourselves comfortable and I'll see what can be done about food. And behave yourselves.'

'Yes, Corporal, you can trust us.'

'Decent chap, that Corporal, not like the other one.'

The men were allowed down onto the track, to get some air and stretch their legs. Joseph ran off to a local farm.

'Ey up; thou art t'Metcalf lad, aren't 'ee? I thought tha were in t'France.' The farmer was astonished to see Joseph.

'I've run away, just for a few hours while t' train was in t' siding. I've a big favour to ask o' thee – could I borrow thy trap so I can tak missen t'Masham to see mi parents, just to comfort them? I'll bring it back t'night.'

'Aye, come in lad, I'll do better than that. Thou must be famished and nithered. The missus will get thee some snap while I get t' trap and t' horse out and I'll fetch thee there missen; you don't know t' roads well enough, things have changed a bit round here while th'st been gone, and it's nigh on dark. Missus,' he called to his wife, 'tak a look who's here.'

Joseph warmed himself by the crackling fire while the farmer's wife ladled soup into a bowl; he tore hungrily at the fresh-baked bread. He had just finished when the farmer announced that the trap was ready.

*

'Now then, Mam.'

'Joseph, mi son! I'll go to t'foot o' our stairs; what art th' doing here? My heavens, th'art so thin, so poorly-looking. Come in, come in.' She threw her arms round him as she burst into tears. 'Jacob, run and tell thy father, tell him to mek haste.'

The farmer left the reunion, shaking his head at the stories that Joseph had told him on the short journey.

'Ma, Pa, I'm only here for a couple o' hours, t' others are looking out f' me and in return they have asked me to ask thee to let their families know that they are all graidley and safe in England. One or two have been badly but that's all ower.'

'Happen we can do that f' thy friends; art thou sure tha be fettled?'

He gave them the addresses and tried to explain what they had all been through, without causing too much alarm. He told them of the understanding and compassion of some of their guards, but made light of the hatred and contempt of others. He made no mention of the conditions which they had had to endure at Henriville, but told of the camaraderie and companionship of the other absolutists.

'It was a bit touch and go for a wee while. I were fair frit at

139

times, as well as frozz, but we are all champion now. One of our number, Bert, his family has posh friends in high places, his brother came to see us and mun have pulled some strings because here we are. I think we're off t'Scotland, we have been given a sentence of hard labour. That won't bother me, I am fitter than most. But how about thissen?'

'But I'm flummoxed, tha doesn't look fit my son, tha is't ill thriven, thy clouts fit where they touch, an' tha looks right jiggered.'

'Gi' ower, Ma, we haven't been enjoying good scran lately 'tis bin a tad tacky, but that'll change they cann't expect us to work not properly fed.'

'Can'st thou let us know where th'art going to int' Scotland?'

'I don't know; dinna fret if thou doesna' hear; they never tell us what is up wi' us.'

The few hours were soon up. 'And now, Pa, I'm afraid I am going to have to ask thee to fetch me back to t'station at Ripon. I don't want t'others to cop f' me as I've bin gone. I'll not see thee again f' a while; look out f' thissen Ma. Jacob an' Hannah, be good and help thy Ma an' Pa.'

'Oh my son, thank thee so much for coming to see us, I've been fair mithered about thee. I hope tha doesn't get into bother having come.' She kissed and hugged her lad and stood with Hannah, waving goodbye.

With his pockets full of bread, hard-boiled eggs and cheese to share with the others, his father drove him back to the train in their little trap, young Jacob at his side.

*

The train rumbled on through the next day and into the night; when they stopped, they could see, by the light of the gas lamp, that the sign on the railway platform said 'Dyce'.

'Where on Earth is Dyce?'

'Blowed if I know.'

'Corporal, kind Sir, could you please tell us where we are.'

'Sign says Dyce, cunnit? Can't chou read?'

'Yes, of course. Silly of us, but us ignorant Northerners are not entirely clear as to where that is. It is a long way from Southampton and, by the size of the station, I would guess that it is not a big place,' enquired Bert.

'Dyce is, you higorant lot, Dyce is in Scotland, I suppose you 'ave 'eard of Scotland, snow, whiskey, bagpipes and haggis? Eh? And I'll be glad to get back to the Smoke, it's flippin' cold up 'ere.'

'Yes, we guessed it was Scotland, by the amount of time it has taken us to get here, but Scotland is a big place. What is the nearest big town?'

'Blowed if I know or care, I'm back dar'n sarff tomorrow and good riddance to the lot of you, I say.'

'Goodbye to you too, and have a safe journey.'

They were lined up and marched off; a road sign said "Aberdeen 5 miles".

'No chance of any visitors then,' said Joseph, 'they'll not be able to get this far, in spite of their promises.'

*

The men joined the over 200 other conscientious objectors who had been sent to the quarry. They were allocated tents, tents that looked like they had seen better days, and were issued with picks, shovels, hammers and wheelbarrows.

'Aye, hard means hard, and I'll show you what hard means, you lazy Sassenachs.'

'Not a happy Scotsman then, that Mr McBride,' observed Joseph, 'you have to feel sorry for him, I suppose, stuck away with us when he would far rather be enjoying himself with his family; eating Scotch pancakes and eating Scotch Broth and drinking Scotch whiskey, I suppose.'

'So it's quarrying for us. Well, hard work won't kill us, I hope.'

Each day, they were woken in the dark and by daybreak, after a meagre breakfast, they were at work. A few men were detailed off, to learn how to drill holes in the rock face and pack them full of gunpowder. The resulting explosion reverberated round the deep quarry and sent tons of stone crashing down in a cloud of dust and noise. Silence. Crows screamed into the sky, the nests of small birds were destroyed; rabbits, badgers and all kinds of other creatures were made homeless. The men cleared the stone and broke it into gravel with hammers, shovelled it into waiting carts, to be pulled away for road building. The work was hard but, to start with, they enjoyed the change of activity, the fresh Scottish air and the beauty of Scotland; the hills were just getting their autumn colours. The war and their terrible time in France seemed a distant memory.

'I am beginning to enjoy this, Norman. I am used to hard work, and the beauty of the countryside almost makes up for the cold. And the smell of autumn, fallen leaves and peat, I really like it.'

'I wonder what it will be like when it gets really cold. We are only just into autumn now.'

But the food was insufficient and the tents kept out none of the keen, cold air as it whistled round the camp site or the icy rain; it was very cold, wet and windy. They had to plodge through muddy puddles, to get to and from the rock face and their footwear didn't keep out the water.

'Sergeant McBride, these tents leak, and don't give me the 'Dorchester' line, we've had that one before.'

'It's all the army could supply you with, ye ken, they dinna want them.'

'How ironic that we have to use army tents. Why didn't they want them?'

'They said they weren't good enough for their men. Yee'll just have to make the best of it.'

'If we carry on like this, some of us will get ill. You don't want that, do you?'

'It makes no difference to me. I'm here to make sure you work; and work hard. "Ten years penal servitude" you got, and I'll make sure you get it.' He marched off to his warm hut.

They were constantly soaked, ill with colds, bronchitis and other chest complaints. Their clothes were always damp, their boots sodden. Their feet were blistered and rubbed, sore with trench-foot, there was scant medical attention.

'Sergeant McBride, Sir, we need a doctor. Roberts is very ill.'

'Tell the lazy Sassenach to pull himself together. I'll give him the rest of the day off, that'll fix him.'

'But ...'

'No buts, just get back to work. Maybe I'll have a look at him if I get time.'

'Harry, I've asked McBride to send for the doctor, but he's not taking it seriously, I'm afraid.'

'Thanks. I'll be fine. A day's rest will see me alright. I'll be fettled soon enough.'

He was ill, feverish, hot and shivery in his leaking, cold tent. The doctor came eventually and diagnosed a severe chill.

'The man's just a chancer,' the doctor said to McBride. 'Give me a nip before I go back to surgery. This cold is getting to me.'

*

'Will you write a letter for me, please? I need to write to Mother, and I'm not sure I'm up to it, I am feeling very weak,' Harry asked Joseph.

> *"Dearest Mother*
> *The doctor says I have a severe chill, but the fellows here are very kind and are looking after me,*
> *I'll be strong in a day or two.*
>
> *Your loving son, Harry."*

Two days later, Harry was dead of pneumonia.

*

'We can't go on working here, can we, Norman, Bert? What are we going to do?'

'No, not only is Harry dead, but I've just found out that this stone is not being used for civilian roads, but for the barracks away in the east.'

'I say we go on strike, refuse to work, if it's military work; we've done it before.'

'I'll see the Officer.'

'I need to have a talk with you, McBride,' said Bert as he approached the officers. 'We are not going to work anymore; Harry is dead, the conditions are terrible, we have no proper shelter or food, we will all be dead soon. And we have found that the rocks we are breaking are for military roads. So, as from now, we are on strike.'

'Get back to work, I tell you. We'll get you a bit more food;

143

will that satisfy you?'

'No, we won't break rocks for military roads. And you need to stop any more of us dying; you'll not get away with it, you know. When they hear in London, there'll be hell to pay.'

*

'What are we going to do now?' the Corporal asked the Sergeant. 'I suppose, we will have to tell them at the office; we can't have any more of them dying off.'

'I'm not surprised at it. We know that the conditions we have had to put them in are terrible. They were very unfit when they arrived here, but we had to make do with what we were given.'

'I'll send a cable, see what they say. I don't want to be blamed for this.'

16TH OCTOBER1916 TO HOME OFFICE

ONE CO DEAD STOP

ALL ILL STOP

AWAIT FURTHER ORDERS STOP

DYCE WORK CAMP

17th OCTOBER 1916 TO DYCE WORK CAMP

ALL COS TO BE SENT SOUTH TO PRISONS STOP

ARRANGEMENTS BEING MADE STOP

HOME OFFICE

Bert found an old newspaper dated 19th October. 'Here, listen to this. It says that Ramsay McDonald was furious to hear about our conditions. "In a speech to The House, he defended the men", that's us, "recognising that the conscientious objectors want to put something in, to which they feel they can put their hearts and regard, and which they feel is work that is really useful to the State." He's right there. I wonder what difference it'll make to us. We can't go on here, they'll kill us all.'

'How old's that paper?'

'Only a few days.'

'Well, I do know that they are worried. I've seen them looking at us, and just when I expected bread and water again, our food is a little better and we've been given a bit of meat.'

'What shall we do, Norman?'

'I don't trust them anymore. They said we were making gravel for civilian roads, but we found out that it's for the military. I'm not going to do the Scheme any more, come what may.'

'It means prison again. I'm not sure I can take it.'

'You have to do what is right for you, Joseph, you know that.'

'I suppose, I can go back into the Scheme later if I get the opportunity, can't I?'

'So what have you decided?'

'I'll go to prison with you and Bert, the three musketeers, eh?'

'Good on you, lad, you had better tell the Sergeant before you get sent to Dartmoor.'

Chapter 24
Annie

Annie couldn't sleep properly. The thin curtains did little to keep out the daylight, they were too short. She hadn't any dark fabric to pin to the bottom. At least it wasn't hot. The autumn had brought not only some refreshingly cool weather, but also dreaded rain. She knew what rain did; she had seen the men caked in thick, yellow-grey slimes of slippery, clayey mud. She had been moved to the night-nurses' hut, so she and the others wouldn't be disturbed by comings and goings of the day staff. Some of them managed to sleep all day. She heard their regular breathing; one or two even snored in a most unladylike way. Annie only fell into a proper sleep about five o'clock, when it started to get dark. It was about that time that the blackbirds started their evening chorus, but that didn't disturb her. She actually found it comforting; a sweet lullaby.

Eight o'clock, time to get up. She washed her face and hands in the icy cold water and dampened her hair before pulling it back and pinning it up expertly into a neat bun. She dressed routinely in her grey dress, white collars and cuffs and crisp clean apron. She was always surprised at how the laundry managed to take her stained, rumpled uniform and transform it back, or nearly back, to its original condition. She fastened on her big, starched cap, which covered most of her hair, and stared out of the window. She could see what had once been beautiful lawns, clipped topiary, herbaceous beds; but now, no-one had mowed what was left of the lawns, and the beds were in need of weeding and having all the old growth cut down. When she had some time free, she liked walking through what had been the gardens; the smell of the fallen leaves under-foot reminded her of home. The flowers had been beautiful during the summer, in spite of the terrible weather, but that was over and now it was just dead stalks and damp, withered leaves. What puzzled her was the topiary; it was in good condition. The little she knew of the subject told her that it needed constant attention to keep tidy, and it was tidy.

'I suppose, someone comes from the village, but I've never seen anyone,' she mused to herself. 'I am so glad they do. Maybe

146

it's that old man I've seen wandering about the place occasionally. He never speaks to anyone '

Row upon row of buildings had gone up on the lawns; on the right, accommodation for her and the other nurses; day-nurses' huts and, at this far end, those for the night-nurses. Down the middle were the Mess and Recreation Huts and, of course, the kitchens where the unexciting but satisfying food for the staff and patients was prepared. Seamus, the other orderlies and some doctors slept in the left-hand row. Close to the hospital were the buildings used for stores, where she had had to go on many occasions, to fetch bandages and other supplies. At the far end of one of these, there was what looked like a locked cage where the drugs were kept; morphine and anaesthetics, there never seemed to be enough of these to go around. Supplies of everything kept running out; shipments didn't get through, lost from the ships in the Channel, sunk by the submarines, from bombed trains or just bogged down in the mud.

This had been home for months; was it only months? She could hardly remember her old life; it felt like it belonged to someone else. Did she really grow up in that little cottage, in her village so far away? Did she really go to York, to learn to be a nurse? Here and now was her reality; constant tiredness, sore hands and arms, swollen feet, no time to think. She had even stopped looking at every face, hoping it would be Matthew. But then, there was the stretcher bearer Daniel. Thoughts of him kept her going. She really liked him; they had seen a lot of each other, on and off duty.

She turned away from the window, pulled her cloak around her and, joining her fellows, crossed what had been the lawns into the Mess Hut. They didn't serve breakfast in the evening, and she really didn't want stew and dumplings; being on night-duty did unsettling things to her digestion.

'I just want some scrambled eggs, neither breakfast nor tea, just something soothing to my stomach.'

She made herself a jam sandwich, not really nourishing but it managed to assuage her strange hunger. 'No wonder I'm getting thinner.'

By Sister's desk, Annie tried to listen to the litany of admissions, discharges and deaths, orders for dressings to be renewed, tasks to be done. It seemed that the day staff thought that the night-nurses had plenty of time to spare, but they didn't. The patients were just as demanding and there were only ever two staff on duty at right. Prayers were said; the *Nunc Dimittis,* as usual. She wondered how many of these servants would depart that night and would it be in peace.

'Staff Nurse Scott!' Sister's voice cut against her musings. 'Are you with us, Nurse? Here, take the keys. I hope you have a quiet night; I've left a list, in case you have some time. I'll see you in the morning.'

The day-nurses trooped off, chattering to each other, ready to go to bed. Annie was glad that Seamus was also working the night shift; she had had to work a few without him and hadn't liked his replacement; found him lazy, aggressive and unhelpful.

'We can settle down the easy ones first, down at the far end, and then tackle the dressings. Are there any beds empty that we need to make up, in case we get any admissions?'

'All the empty beds are ready, the day-nurses seem to have left the place ship-shape, Sister Jackson will have seen to that.'

Several of the men were very cheery, in spite of their injuries, and were making good progress after their operations. Some knew that they would be on their way home tomorrow.

'I'll be sorry, in a funny sort of way, to see some of these go. I've got quite attached to them, even though they are here for such a short time, young Charlie for instance.'

'Come on, Annie, you know we mustn't have favourites.'

'Yes, I know, but why do we call Charlie 'young'? He must be the oldest here. He served in the previous war; you'd have thought he could be exempted from this one.'

'Hello there, Charlie. Ready to go back tomorrow?'

'Yes Nurse, can't wait, see the missus again.' He coughed painfully, holding his chest with his remaining arm. 'Though I'm not sure she'll be glad to see me in this state.'

'Have you told her about your injuries?'

'Not really; didn't want to worry her.'

'Well, she'll see you in hospital first; you'll not be ready to go home until this wound has healed up and your cough is better. You got some gas, didn't you?'

'Yes, just a whiff of it; it's vicious stuff; damn Bosch.'

Seamus and Annie worked their way down the ward, giving out morphine as necessary, checking and renewing dressings and bandages.

About midnight, Annie pulled out the list that Sister had left for them. 'Why do they always think that night-nurses have time on their hands?' she sighed. 'Seamus, please will you sit with Freddie and roll this bag of washed bandages while I check and sort the syringes and needles.'

Annie shut the dressing room door behind her and looked at the tray of assorted glass syringes, the barrels and pistons all mixed up in the disinfectant. Each part had a number printed on it in very small print. Each barrel had to be married up with a piston with the same number; if she got it wrong, it wouldn't fit, would be too big or too small. She gave a big groan, pulled up a stool and, with forceps, started to pair them all up; the more she did the quicker she was, fewer left to use.

'Why are there always a few odd ones left? I suppose, there have been some breakages, or else I've got one or two wrong.'

She checked them again to make sure; it all took so much time and it made her eyes ache, looking for the tiny numbers in the poor light. Then there was a container of used needles; all had to be checked for burrs, which blunted them, by dragging them over a piece of cotton wool; then they had to be cleaned out by passing a thin wire through them. The ones that were acceptable had to be carefully lined up in a shallow tray of disinfectant and covered with a cloth. Her back ached, her eyes ached, and her feet always ached.

'Why am I here?' she asked herself, and then suddenly thought of Matthew. 'I wonder where he is and whether I will ever find him.' She found tears pricking her eyes.

Seamus stuck his head round the door. 'Time you had a break, young lady; you nearly finished?'

'Yes, just; have you made tea?'

'I made some for Freddie, he isn't sleeping.'

They sat companionably in the centre of the ward, a dim light over their heads, the men snoring and groaning all round them.

'Have you heard from Matthew yet?'

'No, I've just been thinking about him and wondering.'

'It must be terrible, all that waiting and not knowing.'

149

'I'm just going to check on Charlie again.' Annie got to her feet hurriedly.

'Why? He's alright, isn't he?'

'I've just got a feeling ...' Annie took a light and passed down the ward. She stood over Charlie's bed. He looked so peaceful, not a sign of pain on his face and years younger. After waiting a few moments, she took the little mirror out of her pocket and held it to his mouth; not a breath misted it. She drew the sheet over his face.

'He'll not be going home tomorrow. Help me move his bed, will you?'

The two of them pushed his bed out into the empty corridor; they washed him, laid him out, tied a label onto his toe, wrapped him in a sheet and lifted him on to a trolley, ready for the orderlies to take to the mortuary. They made up his empty bed, ready for the next soldier to need their care.

'His poor wife; she's seen him through the Boer War, two Blighties from this one. I wonder how she'll cope.'

They sat down again to continue their tasks. 'Did you manage to roll all those bandages?'

'Yes, it is so much easier with one of those bandage roller machines, just have to turn a handle and guide them in.'

'Now we have to make gauze squares and a drum full of cotton wool balls.'

Seamus took out a pair of sharp shears, unrolled the gauze along the desk and cut it into lengths. He and Annie folded them in threes one way and then fours the other and packed them into the autoclave drums for sterilising. Before sending the drums off, they moved the sliding metal plates that circled them, exposing the holes that let in the sterilising steam; when they were taken out of the ovens, the plate would be moved back over the holes.

'Have you been seeing that young man of yours? Daniel, isn't it?'

'He is hardly *my* young man but, yes, we manage to see each other nearly every week; we are lucky to be working so close together.'

'So, when will you be wed?'

Annie felt the blush creeping up from under her collar and into the roots of her hair. 'He hasn't asked me, and I don't know what I would say if he did.'

'Well, you love him, don't you? I've seen you together.'

'What a question. But, yes, I think so. Mind you, I've only known him here. War has brought us together. What happens afterwards? Will we be the same?'

'Hm, you're right there, just wait and see. But maybe you should think about what you would say if he did ask, just in case.'

'I know you are right. I am just so confused.'

'Just enjoy what you have. Who knows where we will all be, or what we will feel after this is over, and it has to be over some time.'

When they had filled two drums, they made cotton wool balls by tearing off small pieces from a huge roll and rolling them in the palms of their hands. They packed these in more drums.

'I hate this job, it makes my nose itch.' Annie sneezed three times. 'But it's on our list. I'm going to do a ward round, check up on everyone. Will you come with me?'

There were dressings to do, more morphine to inject, the dressings room to be tidied, the instruments to boil up. Seamus sorted out the sluice room and cleaned all the used bedpans and bottles. The work seemed to be unending. And Charlie wasn't the only one to die that night; there were three more empty beds to make up before morning, waiting for more injured men.

The two of them felt they hadn't stopped, but they had at last completed Sister's list. Annie collapsed into bed exhausted; she tossed and turned all day, until it got dark again and the blackbird started singing.

Chapter 25

Daniel

The shadow from the aircraft fell across Daniel's face. 'It'll be a bombers' night tonight,' he muttered to himself, 'not a cloud in the sky'. He was lying on his back at the edge of the field, mud and shell holes all round him, waiting. In spite of the bitter cold, he grabbed this moment of solitude gratefully. He hated being cooped up day and night, with men who he would otherwise not have a pint of beer with; having to share his most intimate times with strangers who had now become firm friends regardless of background, who he knew would take all sorts of risks to protect him as he would them.

'God, I'm bored, bored, bored. Is this what war is all about, being bored and terrified? In between bouts of boredom, we have spurts of terrifying activity, being rushed off our feet, no stopping, no rest, being gassed, shelled and shot at, until the next lot of boredom.'

He know this happened only rarely, but he had found a few moments on his own, quiet, no noise, no shouting, no guns, no-one telling him what to do. He sat up and rolled himself a cigarette and lighting it, inhaled deeply, letting the smoke fill his lungs. He laughed ironically to himself. 'Jerry is always wanting to fill our lungs, but not with cigarettes.' He shuddered at the memory of those who had been gassed and who he had tried vainly to help; they all died, drowning in their own lungs. He pulled a piece of paper and a pencil from his tunic pocket and began to write a letter.

"My dear little Susie.
I need to tell you how it is here; firstly of the terrible noise, of broken bodies, constant gun-fire, the pain, the death, the fleas and huge rats; the terrible smells, cordite, unwashed bodies, rotting flesh, the gas that hangs over us; and the mud, oh the mud, nasty, clinging, yellow-grey mud that gets into everything, coats all I have with the slime. But also strangely of the beauty here; the occasional flowers, in the summer the poppies were so beautiful, the trees that try against all

152

odds to stay alive; birds, especially skylarks and blackbirds, their song fills the air. But most importantly is the camaraderie between the men. We all look out for each other. Barriers of languages between French and English and Belgians seem to disappear and even when we capture a German, we seem to understand each other.

We are in it together, doing our masters' bidding, whether we like it or not. They, the Germans, are just as frightened of us as we are of them, more so as when they are captured, they expect to be tortured as they have been told that we are monsters. Just like us they want it all to finish as soon as possible. And they look just like us, mostly blue eyes and blond hair, just a different uniform.

Dear Susie, my little sister, I miss you and Ma so much and I don't know how I'll stick it out. But we have to, until we are wounded or dead, or someone ends this dreadful war. I still have your stone. I keep it with me always, it is a great comfort.

Look after yourself,

Your loving brother ... Dan".

'Braithwaite? Braithwaite? Where the hell are you?'

Daniel sighed, stubbed out his cigarette and got to his feet. 'Here, Serge, just coming.' Daniel knew he would never send the letter, but he felt calmed for having written it all down. It made Susie and his home seem closer and this terrible place go away for just a very short time. He stuffed the letter into his pocket and pulled his greatcoat round him, to keep out the chill wind.

Unexpectedly, a shell whistled overhead, missing him by several yards. It was the start of a bombardment which seemed to go on for ever. Daniel and the other stretcher-bearers could do little but crouch in the trench until it finished, waiting. Men were falling all around them; when they could, they would crawl toward an injured man, to render what ever first aid they could after dragging him to the dug-out or the Advance Dressing Station. There, they tried to stop any bleeding, apply a tourniquet or bandage. The injured couldn't be moved far, while the shelling continued. As suddenly as it started, it stopped. Daniel and his companions waited, just to make sure, before setting off across No-Man's Land with their stretchers. Above the sound of the wind, in the remains of the trees, were the cries of dozens of men. In the distance he could see German bearers doing the same. There seemed to be a sort of gentleman's agreement that men collecting the injured should be left to it, not shot at. It took hours to collect all the men and then the dead. Daniel was detailed off to drive the ambulance to the Dressing Station, to leave the worst of the casualties to the ministrations of the surgeons there; it took many journeys before he was done. When the last of the living had been driven or escorted by foot, he found that some of the Tommies had buried the dead just behind the line. He was grateful for that; it was a job he hated more than any other, and digging through the frozen earth was very difficult.

All was overcome with a surreal quiet. As night fell, the moon rose; a silver half, giving a ghostly look to the country side. The bare stripped tree-stumps were silhouetted hard and black, night animals were out on the scavenge, strange rustlings could be heard as the men tried to find some comfort in the wet trenches. The smell of mud and decay pervaded everywhere but they were so tired they just didn't notice.

*

Daniel was on watch when the next bombardment started.

'Damn, that was close. Look out for the other two or three.' He dropped as fast as he could for the cover of the trench.

Another shell thumped into the mud in front of him, scattering freezing earth, mud and stones in all directions, leaving a great crater.

'Bosch is getting better.' He heard one man call out. 'Take whatever cover you can.'

The third shell was right on target; it landed in the trench, a few feet away from Daniel, blowing him off his feet. He lay still for several minutes, expecting a fourth shell, but no more came. He tried moving but found that he was covered from the waist down with mud and wood from the duck boarding. He was held fast, his legs hurt.

'Hubert, Bill, anyone there?' he called. But there was nothing but deathly silence.

'I'll have to help myself,' he muttered. He found that by scraping he could clear some of the earth; soon, he could sit and take stock. He looked up; a great hole had been blown in the side of the trench. Still it was silent. Next to him was Bill. He recognised him by the bandana that he always wore round his neck, but there was little else left of Bill, or of Bill's closest mate, Fred. 'At least, they went together.'

He tried calling again, but no sound came from his mouth. 'Hubert,' he tried again. 'Hubert, my old mucker, give me a hand. Bloody Hell! Has he gone, as well?' He felt near to tears when, over the top of the heap of earth, he saw Hubert. He was making faces at him but not saying a thing.

'Why doesn't the old bastard say something? Hey, Hubert, here, over here.' Again, no sound came from his mouth. But Hubert turned towards him, moving his mouth. Then Daniel realised what had happened. He had seen it before, the shock waves had deafened him. Only time would tell if it was temporary or permanent.

'I can't hear you, Hubert,' he hoped he said, 'you'll have to write it down.'

Hubert slithered down the slope to Daniel and started scraping the mud and pulling the boards off his legs. As he was doing it, Daniel's ears popped, one after another and cleared. 'Thank God for that, I couldn't manage deaf. What's the damage, Hubert?'

'As you can see, Bill and Fred both copped it, on the whole I think the unit has been lucky, but we haven't assessed all the injuries yet, including yours.'

'I don't think I'm injured, just stuck. Help get this lot off me, will you.' He tried to pull himself out. 'Ouch, that hurts.'

'Just be patient, will you. Yes, it seems that you've been protected by the duck-boards, but I can see some blood. Let's have a look.'

Daniel rolled his trouser-leg up. 'It's nothing but a scrape; I reckon I've been lucky. Just give me a dressing to stop this bit of bleeding, will you.'

'I want you to get it properly seen to, Dan. It looks deep and nasty.'

'Now, stop fussing, will you. Just stick a bandage round it. I'll get it looked at in the morning. You all need help. Now my ears are nearly clear, I can hear that we've several who need seeing to.'

The two men set to; they collected the injured from No-Man's Land, tended their injuries and got them to the Advanced Dressing Station. When they had been seen to there, the men that needed urgent hospital care were loaded on the ambulance and, with Hubert in attendance, Daniel drove them over the shell-pocked tracks; all in their days' and nights' work.

As they drove their load away, they saw a ragged line of local people; old men, women, children, pushing barrows, carts, bicycles, donkeys and a pony all loaded with whatever possessions they had been able to rescue as they fled. Two young girls stood looking despairingly at their cart with its broken wheel.

'We ought to stop and help.'

'We can't, you know that. We've got this lot to get to hospital.'

Chapter 26

Annie

Now back on day-duty, Annie heard Sister calling her.

'Staff Nurse Scott, come into my office in ten minutes, will you, please?'

The colour drained out of Annie's face. What had she done wrong? She tried to think. She put on her cuffs, tucked her hair neatly into her cap, smoothed down her apron and knocked on the door of Sister Jackson's office.

'You wanted to see me, Sister?' She twisted her hands behind her back.

Sister Jackson looked up, smiled and lent back in her chair. 'Don't look so worried, Staff Nurse; we have a problem and I am wondering if you will be able to help us out.'

'I'll help if I can, Sister.' She felt her shoulders relax.

'Matron has asked me to ask you; the Dressing Station that we get most of our casualties from is short-staffed; we wondered if you would be willing to go out there for a while? It's much harder work, but I feel you are up to it. Your work here has been excellent. I've been watching you. Unfortunately, I have to ask you to make a quick decision.'

'Would I go on my own, Sister?'

'No, you and Mr O'Connor will go together. You seem to make a good team. I'll ask for him to be sent, too.'

'What if he doesn't want to go?'

'He's in the RAMC, so in the army. He'll have to do as he's ordered. But before you answer I have to warn you; it is much more dangerous work, near to the Front Line, and a lot more responsibility.'

'Can I think about it, please?'

'Yes, but I'm afraid I need to know this morning.'

Annie closed the door behind her and leant against it, excited and anxious, proud that Sister had chosen her.

'Seamus, will you go with me to the Dressing Station at the Front if I go?' They were in the Mess Hut.

'Of course I will, if I can. If I'm sent, I get little say in what I do; has Sister been asking you if you'll go?'

'Yes, and I don't know what to say. I feel I ought to say yes.'

'I've been wanting to get nearer to the action. I would like to get stuck in, get really into it; also, it will be good experience.' Seamus looked enthusiastic.

'But, oh dear, I'm just beginning to get to know Daniel.'

'Oh, come on, Annie, you can't be letting that rule you; not here, not now. If it is to be, somehow it will happen and, who knows, you will probably see him there; he goes to the Dressing Stations as well as here, as you know. And it won't be for more than a week or two, will it?'

'It will be such good experience; more responsibility, but very dangerous.'

'If you were afraid of danger, you would have stayed at home, working in that little local hospital of yours, delivering babies, making tea and not volunteered to come out here. You want to do your bit, serve your country and all that.'

Annie nodded, took a deep breath and went back to Sister's office.

'I've decided, I'll go, but only if Mr O'Connor goes, too. How long will it be for?'

'Thank you so much, Nurse. I'll let Matron know. It will only be for a week or two, a month at most. I want you back here; you're a valuable member of the team. Now, go back to work. I'll talk to you further this afternoon, and thank you, it can't have been an easy decision.'

*

'Molly, Molly, guess what.' The excitement showed on Annie's face. 'I'm going to the Front, to a Dressing Station.'

'You are what?' Molly's face paled as she plonked down on the side of her bed.

'I'm not sure when it will be, but it will be soon. Sister has just asked me and I've said yes.'

Molly hugged her friend. 'You're daft, you know, and I'll miss you so much, but I wish you good luck. I'd not be brave enough. How long for?'

'A few weeks, Sister said, but she was a bit vague about it; could be longer.'

158

Annie and Seamus worked their way down the ward. She wanted to talk about the plans but knew that this was the last thing her patients wanted to hear. Some of the less ill teased her about Daniel. They had seen her face light up when he came into the ward, they saw the hurried, whispered conversations.

Annie did her best to take the men's minds off what she and Seamus were doing to them, by talking about things she thought would interest them.

'Have you heard from your mother yet, how's the family? They'll be looking forward to seeing you when you're better.' She chatted to the men. 'Would you like me to write to your sweetheart for you? She would be glad to hear from you and I know how difficult it is for you to write.' Anything to attract their attention away from what she was doing to their broken bodies.

With further intake of casualties, Daniel pushed another stretcher into the ward. 'Hello Mr Braithwaite!' They tried to keep some formality in the ward. She looked down at the man on the trolley. 'What are the injuries?'

'We aren't sure. He has a broken leg, but he is so ill; there must be more to it than that. His torso is bruised and he is vomiting.'

'I'd better get Mr Rutter, the surgeon, to have a look at him as soon as possible.'

They lifted the injured soldier into bed and covered him with the blankets.

'Daniel,' she whispered, 'I must have a quick word with you.' She helped him push the trolley out of the ward

'I've not got long, got to get back. It's Bedlam out there.' Daniel was in a hurry.

'I'm going out to work at the Dressing Station; soon. Seamus will come, too. Will I see you before I go?'

'You're what? That is no place for a woman. What does Matron think she's doing, asking you? But I can't stop now to talk about it. What time are you off tomorrow?'

'Not till nine, that's if I'm lucky.'

'I'll try to see you then, but it won't be for long. We are just so busy all the time.'

159

*

Annie stood shivering under the dim light and pulled her blue wool cape tight round her. Daniel sprinted toward her.

'I thought you weren't coming.'

'Sorry, I had to borrow a truck and they were very difficult about it.'

'Daniel, am I making the right decision? Sister asked me yesterday, and I didn't feel I could say no, and it will be such good experience and I'll miss you so much ... and ... and ...' Tears were running down her face.

Daniel encircled her with his long arms, bent down and kissed her firmly on the lips. 'I'm getting very fond of you, Annie Scott.'

She stood back, the blush not visible in the darkness.

'There, now I've said it. Sorry if it has upset you.'

'No, no ... I think, I'm getting fond of you, too. But I am so confused; things here make everything seem unreal.'

'I do know what you mean, but I've not been able to get you out of my head. I think about you all the time.'

'Oh dear, I've just said I'll go to the Front.'

'I'll probably see you there. I have to go along trenches, collecting the injured. We may work together. But I still think you shouldn't be going; a Dressing Station is no place for lassies.'

'It'll not be for long and, now I have had time to think about it, I am quite looking forward to it, especially now you have said I might see you, Daniel Braithwaite.'

Chapter 27

Joseph

The men were herded, hand-cuffed together, the short distance from the railway station to where they had travelled from Scotland; a long, tiring journey during which guards had changed several times. Some had been kind and conversational, others hard and uncompromising. Maidstone prison was as welcoming as a damp Sunday afternoon; high, thick walls built of light-grey rag-stone, typical of the buildings of the area. It stretched from east to west, almost as far as the eye could see; the circular tower, reaching three or four stories high, overshadowed the wide gateway with its huge wooden door.

'At least, we will be under cover, not like in those terrible tents,' Joseph muttered under his breath, 'but I wonder how long they will keep us here; it doesn't look very friendly.'

They were roughly processed through reception and changed into prison uniform; their few possessions were examined and some taken away, but they could keep their Bibles.

'I'm glad we haven't got to wear army uniform,' observed Norman.

Soon Joseph, Norman and Bert were standing in front of the Governor. A tall, forbidding looking man, clearly ex-army, but Joseph felt he detected a potentially kind man under the stern look.

'I have to admit to you lot that I don't really want you here,' he began. 'You are not the usual run of prisoners that I get. Rules have been sent to me from the War Office, both you and I have to abide by them. You have been sentenced to ten years penal servitude and that is what you will get. You will do work of national importance which you will be expected to finish in the prescribed amount of time; you may get some remission but don't rely on it. You will wear prison uniform and be kept in solitary confinement, with one hour of exercise a day. During this period, you will not speak to each other or to anyone else, in fact you will not get into conversation at any time with anyone. You will be given three meals a day, of the same standard as the other prisoners, unless contravention of the rules means a punishment of bread and water. If you have any complaints about anything, forget it; you are here to be punished. Any comments or questions?'

Bert opened his mouth but was cut off. 'Good, dismiss,' snapped the Governor.

They were hustled off to cells.

Apart from a narrow bunk with a grubby blanket, there was a table and chair. Running under the tiny, high window was a pipe which Joseph assumed was for heating but was cold to the touch. There was a lidded, enamel bucket by the table. Trying to be positive, Joseph thought that the cell seemed like heaven, compared with the conditions they had endured at Henriville, in the crowded conditions of the one cell for all fifteen men, where they had to share one bucket, and the thin, wet tents of Dyce where they slept on the ground and were constantly cold; but it was hardly comfortable. In the corner of the cell was a pile of hessian, with needles and thread which he assumed was his work. Joseph sat on the bunk, his head in his hands and tried to pray, but nothing came into his mind. Instead, he saw pictures of his friends, the ones that had started together in Richmond but were now dispersed all over the country.

'We were all so determined to stick it out, stick together. How many of us are there left now, I wonder, and how many will there be at the end, when ever that will be?'

The last time he saw Norman and Bert was in the Governor's office. Goodness knows where they were now. He had got on well with the lads at Dyce and was sorry and sad to lose that contact with them. They appeared in his mind one after the other, a parade of faces, young and old, all tired and worn down. His prayer was now for their well-being. Then he thought about those who were in Maidstone Goal with him and wondered if he would ever be able to see them or make any contact.

'Time will tell, and I have that a'plenty,' he said out loud. 'I'll talk to missen each day, read my Bible a'loud and sing t'hymns to keep mi voice fettled.'

He stood on his bunk and rubbed a clean spot on the window. He saw the bare branches of a tall elm tree in the distance; remains of rooks' nests clung in the forks. He thought of the woods with their birds' nests at home.

Keys jangled in the door lock and a young warder came in,

peering through his thick-lens glasses, and set down a tray on the table: a bowl of transparent soup, a hunk of bread and cheese and a mug of weak tea.

Joseph realised how hungry he was. 'Thank you so much.'

The warder glowered at him. 'You are not to talk to me,' he said. 'You've been told.'

'Yes, I know, but it seems so rude not to say thank you for bringing me some food.'

The lad ventured a smile. 'That's how I was brought up, as well, but I'm supposed to make you stick to the rules.'

'We'll get on well, you and me,' whispered Joseph.

'Well, don't let me be caught, or I'll be disciplined. I could lose my job.'

'Sorry, I'll be very quiet.' Joseph felt he had made a friend and felt less abandoned and alone.

As the day drew to a close, the cell darkened; too dark to do any work or read his Bible. He pulled off his boots, tucked the thin, damp, smelly blanket round his shoulders and was soon asleep.

*

As the grey November morning light shuffled into the cell, he was woken by the door being opened. Joseph sighed; he would have to get used to the sound of keys again. He swung his legs to the floor. 'Good morning.' The smile died on his lips as the warder crashed open the door; he was not the young lad of yesterday. This man was huge. The uniform tight over his frame, a leather belt held his trousers up and his belly in. In his gorilla-like hands he held a tray with a meagre bowl of porridge and a mug of tea.

'Get up, and at the double!' he yelled. 'What do you think this is? A health resort? You are to have ten bags sewn before nightfall.' He thumped the tray onto the table, spilling half the tea. 'You will find you have everything you need in that pile.' After indicating at the heap on the floor, he slammed the door behind him.

Joseph laced on his boots and ate the porridge as quickly as he could; it was barely warm. Investigating the pile of hessian, he found that it was already cut to size into large rectangles; his job was to sew it into sacks. He had seen his mother teaching

163

Hannah to sew, but had never tried himself. 'Not a man's job,' he had been told. He was very clumsy, found threading the needle difficult. The edges of the hessian would not stay together while he tried to sew them.

When a tray of boiled potatoes and gravy with the inevitable mug of weak tea arrived at dinner time, he thought he had sewn one sack. He held it up for inspection.

'Is that all you have done? What do you think you are up to? This isn't good enough. What are you holding? What does it look like?' the man sneered.

If it hadn't been for the look of utter fury and contempt on the man's face, Joseph would have giggled. The sack was a sorry affair, lop-sided and clearly useless for carrying anything.

'You will have to undo it and start again!' the officer shouted.

'Sorry, I've never done sewing before,' admitted Joseph. 'I'm sure I'll get the hang of it soon and get better and quicker.'

'You'd better; and soon! Now get on with it.'

When a tea of bread and dripping was brought in, Joseph had completed one sack to his satisfaction, but his fingers were sore and stiff with the unaccustomed exercise.

'I have to keep track of t'days of t'week. Is't Tuesday or Wednesday today? Happen I mun' ask that young lad, I hope I see him soon, he'll put me right. I need to know when 'tis Sunday so I can hold Meeting for Worship.' He spoke out loud to himself. Joseph scratched a line on the wall above his bed. 'Six down and one across on Sunday – that will keep me right an' up to scratch.' Joseph laughed at himself. 'Is't that's where t'saying's from? Maybe.'

As he fell asleep, he heard a tapping noise on the heating pipe under the window. 'Typical to turn on the heating at night,' he said to himself as he drifted off.

Chapter 28

Annie

The bunkers were cut in to the hill; huge, curved caves of concrete covered with grass and turf. Annie stood in the operating theatre of the Dressing Station and took stock. Two long tables with the trays of instruments covered with a cotton sheet were ready; saws of different sizes, small ones for arms and heavy duty ones for legs; clamps for vessels and internal organs; thread to do the sewing; boxes of different sized pads and bandages. The anaesthetics had run out, sticks were provided for the men to bite down on when they were strapped down; they avoided operating here if they could, but some surgery had to be done, to stop bleeding, take off a mangled limb or to put a man back together as best they could before sending him on to hospital.

In the bunker next door, two rows of chairs ran down either side of the walls; down the middle, a double row of cots. Inadequate red blankets covered the stained canvas. The khaki coloured ambulance, with its painted red cross on its sides and top, had just left taking those with Blighties away from the Front and back to the hospital to be treated. These men regarded themselves as the lucky ones; injuries bad enough to be taken from the Front and sent back to England. They would see their families and get some home comforts; they didn't think about the possibility of what would happen to them when they were better and got sent back.

Annie could hardly even remember their names; they came and went so quickly. They cut off the shattered limbs, patched up the shrapnel wounds, after the pieces of metal were excavated, that tore out guts and obliterated faces; they comforted as best they could the ones burnt or blinded from the gas. This bunker was now ready for the next intake of broken men.

Other bunkers held further rows of cots, each with its occupants too ill to move, dying, who were taking their time to be transferred to the ever-growing graveyard outside. Looking after these, she found the most difficult aspect of her work. The overpowering stench of gas-gangrene hung over the men like a soft, wet blanket. The men themselves ceased to notice it; it

165

seeped into their lungs, clothing and hair. It was an everyday part of their journey to the end. Annie had got used to taking a gulp of fresh air in with her when entering and keeping a fixed smile on her face, hoping that the men wouldn't notice her distress. By the end of her shifts, she knew she smelt as the men did and she too ceased to notice it.

Two of these men took most of her time. Albert had three stripes on the now empty sleeve of his jacket that lay in tatters at the foot of his cot. Three times he had been injured, sent back to Blightie, repaired, recovered and sent back to the Front. He refused his share of the sparse amount of morphine. 'Give it to young Tommy.' Annie dressed his suppurating wounds three or four times a day. He had a stick thrust between his teeth to bite on; apart from his arm and leg, most of his internal organs seemed to have been ripped out by the shrapnel. To take her, and his, mind off what she was doing, she tried to chat to him about his family, his sister and brother. Annie didn't tell Albert about her brother who was missing, but she talked to him about the garden and the flowers and vegetables they grew. She grew very fond of Albert; his face, gaunt though it was with the constant pain, was beautiful, almost translucent. He had seen too much suffering in his life; he would be about the same age as Paul and Matthew.

In the next bed was young Tommy who shouldn't have been there at all. He had lied about his age. He was only fourteen but big for his age. His mother was so angry, so upset, but his father said, 'Let him go, if that is what he wants. He'll be back soon enough when they find out.' But they hadn't, and now he was in this hut full of noise and smells that he couldn't have dreamt about in his worst nightmares. It was said that he had been at the Front for only three days, in the mud and cold, before his legs were blown off. The men in the trenches could hear him screaming for hours before the stretcher bearers could get to him. Infection had got into his blood; it was consuming his body. Annie found it difficult to dress his stinking wounds; the waves of nausea came near to overwhelming her. He was delirious most of the time, crying for his mother. Annie would go back after her shift, to be with him, stroking his head, holding his hand; the skin dry and hot to her touch, she tried to quieten his cries which

166

frightened the other men by singing quietly to him the songs her mother had sung to her when she had been ill as a child. Tommy seemed to find them calming. The night sister would send her to bed when her head dropped to her chest. She had nightmares that muddled her brother and Albert, so that she would wake sweating and terrified.

Tommy and Albert died within hours of each other. Together for the last days of their lives, the two, man and boy, were buried side by side in the ever-waiting grave. The pastor said prayers over their wooden boxes as they joined their fellows; simple crosses were made to mark the place and the details entered into the register.

Annie made up the cots for the new intake, told herself to get on with it; that both of them were better off now, but she couldn't shake Albert, so like her brothers, out of her dreams. She asked Sister if she could write the customary, lying, short letter to Albert's parents, telling of his death: 'Fought for his country, brave to the last, not in pain.' The usual form which gave some comfort but told them nothing.

*

Annie sat down hard, head in her hands. 'Seamus, I didn't think it would be as bad as this; these poor men. It was bad enough in the hospital, but at least, they had had some care; clean water, morphine, anaesthetic. Now I know what and where it is all happening, it's too dreadful.'

'Dry your eyes, Annie. How long have we been on duty?'

'At least sixteen hours, Seamus, and I can't remember when I had a proper meal or sleep.'

'You are exhausted; I'm going to tell the Sister ...'

'No, please don't. I'll only get into trouble.'

'Alright, but I'll ask if you can go off duty. You're no good to anyone in this state.'

Sister could see the red eyes and exhausted state of Annie. 'Nurse Scott, Mr O'Connor tells me you haven't had a break for a while and you need to go off for a meal. I thought I told you to go at least two hours ago.'

'Yes Sister, you did, but then another intake arrived and several walked in and we were all rushed off our feet. Four men had to go straight for operations, two for amputations and two

167

more died, and the walking wounded had to be attended to, three of those were blinded …I just couldn't leave.' Annie was beside herself.

'Very commendable, Nurse! Now go, you are no use to me in this state. Go. Go. Mr O'Connor, will you please escort this young woman first to the Mess tent and then to her billet. And you can go off duty, too. I'll clear it with the Corporal. You've been here as long as she has. I'll see you both in the morning.'

As they left the bunker, Seamus took Annie's arm, supporting her. 'Have you heard from your young man recently?'

'Yes, he says there is a rumour of a big push at the Front coming soon. But you know what rumours are.'

'If it's true, we'll be even busier. Do you ever get the feeling that we are just a cog in a huge wheel; that we patch men up so they can just go back to the Front again?'

'There was a chap in here yesterday, with three wound stripes on his sleeve. This will be his fourth and last injury; he lost both of his legs this time, and his mind as well, if his behaviour is anything to go by; I'm not surprised, all this would send the sanest man mad, being sent back again and again.'

Seamus and Annie were sitting in front of their empty plates. They had been too tired to notice what they had been eating; they were trying to work up the energy to go to bed.

'Do you smoke?' Seamus was offering her the pack. 'No, I know you don't, not quite the modern woman, are you?'

'I don't like the taste and it made me cough when I tried it.' Annie stood up unsteadily and smoothed down her filthy apron. 'I'm off to bed, see you in the morning.'

*

The blackbird singing at the top of a dead tree roused her. In her half-awake state, it made her think of home, the Dales, the little cottage, her family. She kept her eyes tight shut, not wanting to lose the vision, not wanting to be reminded of the horrors of where she was. Reluctantly, she levered herself out of her narrow bunk and dressed in her dirty uniform; everything was dirty now, and lousy. As she wound up her infested hair and fastened on her cap, the face she saw in the mirror she barely recognised. When she put on her belt, it needed tightening again. She squeezed her swollen feet into her boots, wincing with the pain. 'Nursing, why did I ever think I could stand it?' she asked herself. As she crossed to the bunkers, night nurses were coming off duty; red-rimmed eyes, haunted expressions and crumpled uniforms told that they had had another busy night.

A constant stream of men arrived all day; some by ambulance, some carried by their mates on make-shift stretchers, others managed to walk, helping each other, one hand on the shoulder of the man in front. Annie and Seamus were kept busy sorting out the ones who needed immediate surgery from those who needed stitches and dressings that Annie could deal with herself; the blinded and gassed coughing up their lungs from the ones who were dying, for whom nothing but a kind word and a sip of water would help.

*

At the end of another long day, Sister came to both of them. 'Nurse Scott, you and Mr O'Connor have done very well today. I have another big favour to ask of you. You can say no if you feel you must.'

'What is it, Sister? Ask; we'll do it if we can, you know us.'

'Yes I do, and that is why I feel I can ask you. I wonder if you would be willing to go to the trenches for a short while, to the Advance Dressing Station. They have asked for reinforcements and I don't know who to send. I think you could do it. It is a very unusual request, to send a female nurse, but I feel you could cope.'

'Yes, Sister, I'll go if that is what you want; I'll be interested. It will be good experience.'

'I'll make sure you are properly kitted out. You'll go tomorrow. It will just be first-aid and maybe escorting the most badly injured back here. Just for a short time, while the others take a break for a few days. They haven't had any time off for several months. Now go and get some sleep.'

*

Annie was very embarrassed to find that part of the kit she was issued with was breeches; never having worn such a garment before, she found them bulky and uncomfortable, and the heavy, woollen fabric chaffed her thighs. She soon found out how necessary these garments were. She could never have maintained decency in her long skirts. The tin hat felt heavy and kept falling

169

into her eyes, until she was shown how to adjust the internal webbing. She was glad her parents couldn't see her; they would have been shocked.

'But they would be horrified at what I am doing out here if they knew; the only woman among all these men, with the smells, the taste of death, the terrible sounds,' she told herself.

In the pouring rain, she and Seamus plodged along the duck-boards which were laid at the bottom of the trench. It seemed to go on for miles, zig-zagging towards the Front. The pack she carried felt heavier and heavier. Mud squelched up through the boards, her feet were soon sodden. When they arrived, the Advanced Dressing Station appeared to be in a kind of cave dug into the side of the trench, down a short flight of steps. They drew back the gas curtain, held up a lantern and looked in dismay at the primitive facilities.

'We only sort them out, do first-aid, stop bleeding if we can, check on the bandages put on by the soldiers, tourniquets, wash eyes, put on fresh dressings, that is all we do here,' Seamus reminded Annie, 'we just do what we can and send them on, sort the living from the dead.'

'Seamus, what have we let ourselves in for?' She was horrified.

When the shelling started, Annie cowered in the corner, her hands over her ears. The shells screamed towards them, thumped down near, too near. The trench that they were crouching in was lit intermittently with a flash of brilliant light as Very Lights exploded. All the while the bombardment continued, they had little work to do. Soldiers were firing back, the dead and wounded left where they fell. Eventually, it stopped without apparent signal or reason. A last stray shell exploded near to where Seamus and Annie were waiting, bringing down a shower of wet mud and stones.

The wounded started to arrive; stretcher-bearers brought them in, a never-ending stream; comrades brought in their fellows, the walking and crawling walked and crawled. Moaning and groaning filled the small space. Annie learned that the quiet ones were either dead or beyond her help. The Chaplain was kept busy blessing all, Christian and Heathen alike. One after the other, they fastened on dressings, adjusted tourniquets, bandaged heads, arms, legs and broken bodies. They gave orders to the stretcher bearers who were taking the ones who might survive on to the Casualty Dressing Station for amputation and further treatment. The head injuries were terrible. There were so many of them, more than any other. Some seemed to have their faces smeared across their heads, almost unrecognisable as human. 'God help you,' Annie whispered to herself more than once. Giving water to some of these was impossible – no identifiable mouths.

Suddenly they were finished; the last one taken away, after hours and hours of non-stop hard work, there were no more left. 'Can we go outside? I need some fresh air.'

'Come on, I need a smoke.' Seamus helped her up the few steps and held aside the curtain.

Annie climbed up the steps, into the trench where a soldier handed her a mug of tea. 'Wot you doin' 'ere? Nice girl like you, but glad to see yer, Angel of Mercy, that's wot you are.'

'May I see over the top? I'd like to have a look.' She was curious and it had been quiet for a while.

'Got your tin hat on firmly? Let me go first.' The soldier climbed onto the fire-step and bent down to help her up. Annie couldn't believe her eyes; the desolation that lay before her was beyond description, it took her breath away. The landscape undulated as it had been torn by shelling. Not a growing living thing; the blackened remains of trees had fallen in all directions into the mud-filled shell holes, though one or two stood defiantly upright. Roll upon roll of barbed wire. A litter of rifles and tin hats showed where men had fallen. The bodies of horses lay where they had fallen, left to rot. The whole scene was barren, flooded, unimaginable, and indescribable. The sun setting behind it threw all into silhouette and bathed everything with a golden light. She stared at it all, speechless until the soldier handed her down again.

'In that last lot of shelling, did anyone gain anything, move up a bit, make it worthwhile?'

'No, not a foot; can't see the point, me, but then, no-one asked me, did they? Now, you can't stay there too long, you're a sitting target. Gerry is just over there.' He lit a cigarette, the flare of the match lit up his face.

A shot rang out. The man fell back into Annie's arms, with a bullet hole between his eyes. She held him as he died, her tears dripped onto his face, his blood seeped down through the duck-boards under her feet and into the yellow mud below.

In the dug-out, Annie broke down again, tears soaking her tunic. 'It was all my fault. If I hadn't asked to see over the top, that poor man would still be alive. I can't stay here, Seamus. Sister said it wouldn't be for long. I need to leave. I can't take it anymore.'

'Be strong, Annie. Here, eat this, the men have brought it for you specially, then lie down on one of the bunks and get some kip. You'll feel better after a rest. I'll wake you when we get busy.'

Each day was the same; shelling, a period of quiet while the wounded were tended, snatched meals, snatched sleep. Annie hardly stirred out of the little cave, feeling safer under ground.

Chapter 29

Daniel

The ambulance trundled its way into the dark, bearing its load. Daniel turned back to his dug-out. Most of the others were asleep; they slept where they dropped, but he was on watch, on duty, had to stay alert. He rolled and lit a thin cigarette and looked about him. He would have played his mouth-organ but didn't want to disturb the others. It had rained for days, weeks, everywhere was mud; nothing but grey, yellow, sticky, clay mud, sucking and squelching. As Daniel scraped the muck off his puttees and boots with his knife, he noticed a little movement out of the corner of his eye, a bright twinkling, a few brown whiskers, a furry body and a long, sinuous tail. A fat, sleek rat was staring at him, and he at it. Rats were so common here, but usually they just scuttled away.

'Hello,' he whispered, but then he remembered that this was not an English rat. *'Bonjour, ça va?'*

The rat held its silence as all good rats should, but it cocked its head on one side and appeared to listen.

'Are you hungry? *Tu fame? Je m'appelle Daniel, et tu?'* Still no reply but his French was being over-stretched; this conversation would have to continue in English.

'If we are going to be friends, I'm going to have to give you a name. As you won't tell me what it is, you are now called André.'

The rat didn't seem to mind and continued to regard Daniel with curiosity.

Daniel knew that the rat had plenty to eat in this field of death but slowly reached forward his hand, with a morsel of bread. André crept cautiously out of his hole, sniffing the air. Daniel crooned quietly to it, *"Sur la Pont D'Avignon, on e dansé, on e dansé ..."*, the only French song he knew. It seemed to reassure André who stretched out a paw, snatched the bread and sat on his hind legs to nibble at it.

'Attention André. Je pense, que j'aime la femme jollie. Bother, I can't keep this French up, you'll have to translate for yourself, sorry. What was I saying? Yes, what shall I do? There is this lovely nurse back at the hospital, all dark-haired and

mysterious, she's a cracker. Annie Scott they call her. I'm going to keep my eye on her; given half a chance, I'm going to ask her to marry me.

André seemed to be listening, and the two of them continued to talk for a few minutes, although André actually contributed little to the conversation, maybe because Daniel spoke only English; maybe he was just bored. A sudden movement made André scuttle away, down his hole again.

'Don't go, *ne pas partier, s'il vous plait, nous sommes jusque* getting to know each-other.'

But he was gone.

*

Daniel lay on his make-shift bunk in the dug-out. It was really only a wire frame with a blanket spread on it, but it kept him out of the mud. He thought of it as his, but it was only his as long as he made use of it; as soon as he got up, someone else would lay claim to it and he would have a different one next time, if he was lucky, wherever he might be. He was now proficient at sleeping whenever and wherever he could, regardless of circumstances. He felt he could sleep though a major bombardment; a bunk was a real and unexpected luxury. He was trying, unsuccessfully, to dry his spare socks over the heat of a candle. He gave up and stuffed the soggy article back into his pack.

He lived in his clothes, day and night, didn't take them off. They were encouraged to change their socks, to prevent trench-foot, but it helped little. There was usually nowhere to wash and dry anything. They all slept in their clothes, though they longed to take them off; lice had taken up residence in every seam, nook and cranny. Daniel was almost glad to have the sore on his shin where he had been injured; it took his mind off the itching and scratching. And the leg wasn't just sore; it was now painful making him limp. It ached all the time; sometimes, it even disturbed his sleep. He struggled up the steps to the trench outside, into the cold morning air, sat on the fire-step and took off his left boot, unwound the puttee, rolled up his trouser leg and removed the soggy dressing. It looked worse this morning, really angry. A red halo surrounding the mess, and it was bleeding again. It had seemed such a little cut when he had been caught in the shelling, though it had been very deep. He had tried to ignore it, but the mud had got into it. He dabbed at it with a field dressing and started fresh bleeding soaking down into his sock.

'Ow. Sod it,' he muttered to himself. 'Now, what can I do?' He hobbled over to the Officer. 'Serge, I'm sorry, but I'm afraid I have to show you this.'

'Bloody fool, Braithwaite, when did this happen?'

'A while ago, when I got caught in shelling. It didn't seem much at the time.'

'Why didn't you tell me sooner? You'll have to go to the field hospital and get it properly seen to.'

Daniel limped back to his bunk, to collect his pack and woke Hubert.

'Sorry, my old chum, I've got to go, leg playing up. Serge is furious with me. Look after yourself. I'll be back soon. You can have the bunk.'

'I told you, that leg needed seeing to, didn't I? You didn't take any notice,' grumbled Hubert.

'Yes. You were right, as usual; I should take more notice of you.'

'Stubborn bastard, aren't you? Anyway, take this, you may need it.' Hubert handed him his lucky rabbit's foot.

'You can't give me that. You've never been parted from it, you told me so yourself. Your sister gave it to you; you took it to your boarding school.'

'You can return it when you get back. And I don't need it, do I?'

'Well, thanks, old man, very good of you. I'll look after it; I'll give it back to you when I see you next.'

'Now, get going, you lucky beggar; a few days in a bed, lovely nurses, maybe see that Annie of yours, hot food, a bath and clean clothes and no lice.'

'You know, I don't want to leave. You'll be short-handed but orders is orders.'

The Sergeant called up an ambulance and helped Daniel up the step.

'Hang on, you have to take this poor sod as well, I suppose.'

A young German lad with half his guts blown away was posted into the ambulance on a stretcher. Daniel hadn't seen a live German really close up before. He looked at him; he was fair haired, same age, young and frightened. He didn't look evil or wicked, but just like someone maybe he had gone to school with or had on the cricket team, just wearing a different uniform. Had they been told lies? There was nothing monstrous looking about him. The boy seemed to be semi-conscious, moaning and crying out.

'*Vater, Mutter, Vater, Mutter. Wasser, Wasser. Komm, komm. Bitte, bitte. Hilf, Herr, Hilf.*'

Daniel got out his water bottle and lifted it to his lips. The German seemed grateful.

'*Danke,*' he whispered.

He lit a cigarette and held it for the lad; they shared it, down to the last drag.

'All aboard the Skylark; hang on,' called out the driver as he bumped them over the cratered road. They had only been going for a minute or two when a shell screamed towards them; it landed and exploded in the dug-out they had just left. The truck ground to a halt. Daniel looked back, earth flew up into the air in a plume and fell back slowly, oh so slowly; then bits of khaki, a helmet and a gas mask ripped past them,

'Oh my God, Hubert … and I have your lucky rabbit's foot. You stupid, stupid beggar.'

*

'Daniel, Mr Braithwaite, what on Earth? Why are you here? Why are you limping?'

'Oh Annie, Nurse Scott, it's my leg. It got injured when we were shelled and it's gone nasty. Serge is furious with me, sent me here to have it seen to.'

'Well, I'm sorry, but you'll have to wait your turn. That young German needs treating first, he's in a really bad way.'

'Please, do what you can for him. He looks so like one of the lads I was at school with. We've been told lies; he is not a fiend, just a young soldier, like our own, doing what he is told to do. He's just injured and frightened.' Daniel was nearly in tears.

'Do you speak German?'

'No, but I know a scared man when I see one, and the word for water is very nearly the same. I think he's been calling for his father and mother, as well, just like our boys. Can you help him, please?'

'Do you know his name?'

'No, I've just been calling him Fritz; he doesn't seem to mind. But I don't understand what he has been saying; the words sound the same. I gave him some water, all I could do for the poor beggar. I did understand "mother", though, almost the same as in English.'

'Well, get yourself bathed and changed and into bed, and I'll see to you as soon as I can.' She didn't notice the distress in Daniel, too focussed on the injured German lad. 'Here are some clean pyjamas.'

Daniel sat by the bed he had been allocated. He slowly took off his boots, peeled off his puttees and the filthy uniform, folded them and placed them carefully in a tidy heap on the floor. The habits he had learned in Richmond were now ingrained into him. He limped to the bathroom and had a very welcome bath, staying in as long as he dared, keeping his leg out of the water; he dressed in blessedly clean hospital pyjamas, hobbled back to his bed and promptly fell fast asleep.

When he woke, he sat in his bed and watched Annie at work. He had never had the luxury of just watching her; they had always been too busy. She bustled about, checking on her patients and seeing to their needs. He thought about Hubert. He asked and was told that he had been killed outright. He turned his face to the pillow and, at last, allowed himself to cry for his friend.

'Oh my dear friend, how am I going to go on without you? There but for the grace of God … but it can't be anything to do with God, can it? It proves that there is no God, doesn't it?' he argued with himself. 'A good God wouldn't allow all this to happen. Hubert was just in the wrong place at the wrong time. By my own stupidity, getting my leg hurt and infected; I am not dead and I am being looked after by the lovely Annie.'

'Now then Daniel, er... Mr Braithwaite.' Sister was watching. 'What have we here?' She carefully undid the field dressing. It wasn't a very big wound but it was very deep and full of pus. Annie cleaned it out with hydrogen peroxide, allowing the bubbles of oxygen to do its work. She swabbed it time and again. Daniel gritted his teeth and gripped the bedrail. He turned his face away as the tears started. He didn't want Annie to see how much pain he was in. Eventually, she packed it with sphagnum moss, put an iodine-soaked dressing over it and bandaged it carefully.

'Strict bed rest for you.'

'Yes, Nurse,' he said meekly.

'I'll ask Sister to get Mr Goodman, the surgeon, to look at it in the morning, but I think you have a Blightie. You'll be off to England. I'm off duty soon. Can I bring you anything before I go?'

'Annie, yes, could you please get me a pen and paper? I have a very important letter I need to write. Thank you.'

'I'll see you in the morning, sleep well.'

Dear Mr and Mrs Cartwright

Me and Hubert made good friends at Richmond Castle, he may have spoken of me, we trained together in the NCC. He was the best mate I could have asked for; he always looked out for me.

I know this is little comfort but this is all I can offer you. It may seem strange but he was one of the lucky ones, killed by an outright shell, he didn't even know it was coming, which is why all I can send you is this, his lucky rabbit's foot that he gave me before I came into hospital; I am sure he would have liked you to have it, he was never without it. I think one of his sisters had given it to him.

I will miss him terribly, as I know you will; I don't know how I am going to do without him while this show goes on.

Maybe I will be able to get in touch with you one day.

With a sad heart and my deepest condolences,

Daniel Braithwaite.

Please will you deliver the enclosed letter; thank you.

Dear Hubert's Aunt Hilda

I am so dreadfully sorry that my friend, your favourite nephew, is killed. He loved you, always spoke about you and the good times you had together, so much so that I feel I know you. I had hoped we would meet sometime, but I don't expect that will happen now.

He believed in your work with Mrs Pankhurst and I too hope you women get the vote very soon, you should; but I suppose that won't happen until this dreadful war is over.

We will all miss Hubert; I don't know how I'll get on without him.

With kind regards

Daniel Braithwaite

Daniel couldn't take his mind off Hubert, 'I'll miss you so much you, old mucker, may you find peace, wherever you are.'

He fell asleep again very quickly, exhausted by the long, unrelenting days at the Front, grief and, for the first time in months, no lice to disturb him.

Chapter 30

Joseph

Joseph counted up the blocks of scratches on the wall above his head. 'Twenty seven, six months, 'appen I've been here six months. I feel that t'sun may be shining, it'll be champion out.' His voice cracked with disuse. 'But what good's a beautiful day like this to me, every day is t'same, sacks, sacks and more sacks. At least, we'll not get mithered during what they call exercise.'

Standing on the chair at the slit window; he could just see the old elm tree in the park. Leaves of the purest, palest green, gleaming in the early sun were unfurling, the rooks busy mending last year's nests and chattering among themselves.

''appen there'll be folks walking in t'park today, maybe there'll be a band playing again, like it did at Christmas; that'd be champion.' He could hear the scream of gulls, hoof-beats as carts rolled by, footsteps and children in the street below, families out for their Sunday afternoon stroll.

He lay back on the bunk, watched shadows as they chased over the ceiling and tried to guess who they belonged to. Shutting his eyes, he wondered what his family was doing and pictured the scene at home. 'T'daffies and primroses will be over by now and t'bluebells in t'woods down our lane will be smelling graidly. I wonder if our Susie will have picked a bunch o' them and tak'n them into t'cottage and arranged them so that t'bells hang down over t'edge of the little yellow jug, like she did last year?'

He sighed, got up and counted the scratches again. May time. Did Susie dance with the other girls round and round the may-pole, making patterns with their ribbons on May Day or was she too old for that now, or did she wash her face with the May morning dew? He wasn't quite sure why they did that, but he had a feeling that is what all the young girls did, very early, just as the sun was rising. Supposed to make them beautiful, but Joseph knew she was already a lovely girl, didn't need washing in May dew. He fell to dreaming again.

He shook himself and counted the scratches again. 'Sunday, Sunday morning, Meeting for Worship, no sewing today.'

It had taken quite a battle, bread and water for days but they had won, no sewing on the Sabbath. He tapped on the pipe. Over the last six months, the men had worked out their own code which they used sparingly. The answering taps reassured him that it was indeed time for Meeting. They met in the Spirit, as they were not able to actually see each other. Joseph sat on his chair, to read from his Bible; he turned to Matthew's gospel chapter five.

"Blessed are the peacemakers: for they shall be called the children of God. Blessed are they that are persecuted for righteousness sake: for theirs is the Kingdom of Heaven. Blessed are ye, when men shall revile against you, and persecute you, and shall say all manner of evil against you falsely, for my sake. Rejoice, and be exceeding glad: for great is your reward in heaven: for so persecuted they the prophets which were before you." He found the idea that peacemakers had been persecuted down the many years comforting; he was not alone. The worse time here so far was when they had taken his Bible from him as a punishment. He had seen Norman in the exercise yard, run to him, spoken to him, taken his hand and was about to hug him when they were pulled apart.

He sat quietly, hands in his lap, and gave thanks for his family and prayed for their well-being, holding them in the Light. He thought about them one at a time, Hannah and Mother and Father; not for the first time, he wondered what they thought of this stubborn son. He prayed also for the leaders of all the warring nations and for the people involved, especially of Belgium and France on whose soil this terrible conflict was still raging. He rubbed tears from his face. He had had little real news for months but, by what he had gleaned and using his imagination, he found himself very distressed whenever he thought of it, which was often, it was after all why they were all here.

Another tap on the pipe indicated that Norman had judged the hour to be up. Joseph stretched himself and started on his exercise routine. There was little time, except after dark, for this as he still had great difficulty sewing his allocation in the time allotted every day, so he tried to make up for it on Sundays. He ran on the spot, lay on the floor to do sit-ups and press-ups, swung his arms around up and across his body; his stiff muscles and joints complained.

Then he smiled to himself in the memory of another triumph that had happened a while ago. One day, the young, myopic guard had arrived with the allocated sacking. 'Get on with it, the colliery is getting short.'

'Colliery? Are these coal bags?'

'Of course, what did you think they were for?'

'I'll not sew coal bags. That coal will be going to France.'

'Oh no, not again. You really are your own worst enemy, aren't you?' The young man shrugged his shoulders.

Joseph sat on the chair, put down his needle and folded his arms. 'No more coal bags.'

In front of the Governor, he explained. 'We cannot do this work.'

The Governor sighed. 'I was afraid this would happen if you found out.'

'You knew? You knew it was against our beliefs and you still let it happen?' Joseph was furious.

'You weren't supposed to find out. How did you?'

'I can't and won't say. I am not saying, just put it down to the bush telegraph.'

'Will you sew mail bags?'

'Maybe. Yes, I'll do that but you'll have to ask the others yourself. I can't speak for them.'

'Do they know? How did they find out?'

'Again, I can't and won't say.' His voice, unaccustomed to loud speech, cracked.

'Well, it's bread and water for you again, but I'll see what I can do. Dismiss.'

Joseph was marched back to his cell. When the guard had gone, he tapped out his message on the pipes.

The sacking was taken away and different quality of hessian given to him. The bags were much bigger, and they took longer to sew but he felt he had scored a very important victory. He laughed to himself again. 'Some sort of pacifist you are if you think you score victories.'

*

As the days lengthened and the amount of daylight increased, they were given more bags to stitch but, by now, Joseph had become adept; his fingers had got used to the sewing, he had grown calluses and didn't get so sore or stiff anymore and the new fabric was easier to work, so he worked more quickly

He had a little time of light to himself first thing in the morning. After his prayers, he used this time, occasionally, to read and contribute to the newsletter that Bert had started. Written on toilet paper, with smuggled pencils, it was hidden behind the lavatory cistern. When the men went to slop out, they took it in turns to feel for it, take it away, write some more and return it for the next man. It had pictures, cartoons, stories and jokes, all in miniscule writing. It was a great diversion and entertainment; it kept them amused and informed.

*

As spring moved into summer, Joseph's cell stayed cold and damp; north facing, it never had the benefit of any of the warmth of the sun. He felt that he was living under a stone. He became sad and withdrawn, barely speaking to the young, friendly warder. He occasionally saw Norman or Bert in the exercise yard and greeted them with a narrow smile. The promise made to himself to speak, sing and exercise lapsed and he sewed the bags automatically without thinking. His mother couldn't visit; she couldn't spare the time or money for the seven hundred mile round trip. He felt abandoned, almost forgot why he was there. He was allowed to write and receive one short letter a month, but what could he write about? His only diversion, his only pleasure was the only thing that changed; the one thing that stopped him going mad was the old elm tree in the park opposite his cell window. He took to standing on his bunk several times every day, to see the rooks building their nests, bringing up their chicks and watching them fly off. His back hurt from bending over the work and the toothache that had started soon after they arrived had turned into constant pain. He asked to see a dentist, but the request was denied. On Sundays, if the band was playing in the park, it seemed to intensify his feeling of being cut off and abandoned.

Chapter 31

Daniel

Daniel was back in hospital, in North Yorkshire.

'Yes, Sister, no, Sister, I quite understand, Sister.'

Sister wasn't quite sure if he was laughing at her. She was never quite sure with these men, the ones who were getting better and would be out soon. There was a sort of gallows humour among them. She sighed.

'You can go outside for a little while, not long, I don't want you getting chilled.'

Daniel tucked his mouth-organ into his pocket and made it down the steps on his crutches with great care, one step at a time. His leg was getting better quickly, too quickly.

'Why couldn't it do it slowly, so the war will be over before I have to go back?' he muttered under his breath.

He found a seat at the end of a patch of over-grown grass, took out his tobacco tin and rolled himself a cigarette. Cowslips were showing through the grass, a creamy yellowness, the colour of butter. He looked at them and thought of his home where they grew in profusion all over the hills and then thought about the flowers he had seen in France.

'Red poppies; the colour of blood. Do they only grow where blood has been spilled? Will France be covered in red poppies for ever?' he mused as he dragged in the smoke. He shook his head, to clear the memories from his brain.

Thinking about France, he played some of the tunes that he had learnt there: *"Pack up your troubles in your old kit-bag ..."*, *"It's a long way to Tipperary to the sweetest girl I know..."*

'Only, she isn't in Tipperary; she's in France. I wonder if I'll see Annie here before I go back.' He shuddered at the thought of going back. 'But she is the only reason I want to go back to France. I wonder how she is doing; I do miss her. And Hubert, I do wish I could have you here with me, I miss you so much, as well. But at least, you are out of it now, not like some of these poor souls in here.'

Daniel made good progress. He spent a long time in Catterick Garrison Hospital. His wound was healing up well, after a very difficult start; he had been very ill with septicaemia.

It had been deeply infected, but now seemed to be clear. He had been in hospital weeks and weeks, had had an operation to clean out the wound. There had been some talk of him losing the leg, but the skill of the surgeons and nurses had saved it.

He was now in a rehabilitation hospital in Northallerton; the County Hall had been requisitioned for the duration of the war. The Board Room was now a ward; it was panelled in oak, and had very fancy chandeliers and fluted columns either side of the big fireplace. The thirty-two beds were packed close together, almost touching, with just enough space for the nurses to squeeze in, to tend to them. He had, by now, got used to being free from lice and mud. He had even forgotten about his little rat-friend, André. Weeks ago, when they made the crossing, the sea had been rough. He was very sick, so was nearly everyone on board; it stopped the boastful ones. On reception in Portsmouth, they had been put in temporary accommodation; so crowded, it made this ward seem spacious. They had been sorted out; the ones with head and facial injuries, who would need skin grafting and other plastic surgery, were sent to specialist hospitals Some of the men who had lost their minds, who were no use to anyone, least of all themselves, were sent on the long journey to an asylum near Newcastle-on-Tyne, to see out the rest of their days, to be cared for, maybe to get better, maybe not.

Daniel didn't like the Vale of York. He thought it flat and uninteresting, but he was glad to be here; it was at least nearer to his home. Ma was able to get to see him occasionally and even Susie had got leave to visit once. Visiting was restricted to weekend afternoons; the nurses said that visitors got in the way and upset other patients who had no-one to visit them; he wasn't sure.

'At least, I don't have far to walk from the station, it being just across the road, Danny, but the train is very crowded with so many folks coming to visit,' grumbled his Ma.

'Where is Susie? Why couldn't she come this time?'

'Couldn't get the day off. Maybe she'll be able to come next week. See here, I've brought you some eggs and I've baked you a bit of a cake.'

'That's grand, Ma, thank you so much. The lads will be pleased. I have to share it round, you know.'

'And I've brought you more tobacco; I don't like you smoking, Danny, but I suppose it gives you something to do while you are in here.'

'I got really into it when I was in France. As you know, I didn't smoke much before I went. Mr Fosdyke wouldn't have his staff smoking, said it wasted too much time.'

'Good for him. Always thought him a sensible man; he always asks after you when I see him.'

'Ma, I've summat to tell you. I've met this grand nurse, Annie Scott they call her, raven hair, blue eyes, with that colouring I wonder if she has Irish blood in her. She's a right beauty, you'll really like her.'

'Will I? Just because she is a beauty as you call her, doesn't necessarily mean she is someone I'll like. And when will I get a chance to meet her if she is in France?'

'I know she has some leave due. I'm hoping that I'll still be here, at least in England, when she gets some home leave.'

'Oh Danny, you're not going back, are you?' Elsie's voice became a cracked whisper. 'Haven't you done enough already?'

'Unfortunately, as soon as I am fit enough, I'll have to go. I'm still in the army, under army orders. I have to go when I am sent, and they do need me. I do a good job and I can look after myself.'

'If you took care of yourself properly, you wouldn't be in here now, would you?'

'That was just bad luck. I'm alright. I really am.'

'So this Miss Scott, where does she hail from? Where does her family live? You said she is a nurse; is she a proper trained nurse or one of those lovely VADs?'

'Oh yes, she's a proper nurse; did her training in York. Her family comes from near there, so she is a true-born Yorkshire lass and her father is a school teacher. I hope she'll be able to come up to visit me, and then you can meet her, unless I go to see her.'

'Well, it's a good thing she's one of us; nothing like your own folks, though York is a bit far away.'

'Ma, you're priceless. Just you wait till you meet her. She'll charm you as she has me. I'm hoping we'll be wed, but that will have to wait until all this is over. I've not asked her, in case you wonder. I have yet to meet her father.'

The surgeon, Mr Fuller, did ward rounds every week on a Wednesday, and his junior Dr Allen, came every day to see all the patients. They were both pleased with Daniel's progress.

'Soon have you back out there, my boy, if you carry on as well as this. Well done, Sister, you've done an excellent job on this one.'

Apart from missing Annie more than he would have guessed, he dreaded the idea of being discharged, in spite of his bravado in front of Ma. The bitter cold and the oozing mud held him in fear; the scream of the shelling, the cries of the men he tried to help, the terrible smells, the bleakness of everything, the exhaustion, the rats, the constant lice, the food that always tasted of petrol; the whole idea made him feel desperate.

He sat on his seat, in the twilight. It was getting chilly.

'Now then, Mr. Braithwaite,' sounded the cheery voice of Nurse Ashton. She found Daniel sitting by himself. 'Sister said you could come out for just half an hour. That must have been an hour ago. We missed you, aren't you getting cold?' She pulled her cape closely round her shoulders.

'I can't go in.'

'Why ever not? Now, take my arm, I'll help you in.'

'I can't face it, I can't go on.'

'What ever do you mean; you are doing so well?'

'That's the problem, I'm doing too well. They'll send me back soon, all that …'

'It won't be for long, it must end soon, surely.'

'It had better. They'll run out of men to kill and maim, soon. They said it was supposed to end by Christmas. But which one? We've had two, or is it three? I've lost count of the days and years. They didn't tell us that.'

'Now then, Mr. Braithwaite, Daniel, you know you'll get leave at home before you go, at least a week. You'll see all your family, get yourself ready. I hear you're one of the best stretcher bearers they have; they need people like you.'

'Can I stay out here in the garden for a bit longer? I'll not stray. I'd like to see the starlings as they fly in their amazing formations; the sound of their wings, thousands of them, the patterns are wonderful, and the rooks as they head off for their nests for the night are comforting, timeless; great flocks of them swooping and curling round in huge swirls, making an extraordinary display.'

'Alright, but don't be long, you'll have Sister after me if you're not careful.'

As the sun set behind the distant hills of the Yorkshire Dales, Daniel took his mouth-organ out of his pocket and played his 'own' tune, Annie's favourite: *"Oh Danny Boy, the pipes the pipes are calling ..."* He found comfort in the music; it reminded him of his father who had taught him the tune and of Annie who had sung to him as he played.

Chapter 32
Annie

Annie had been home on leave. She felt rested and relaxed from sleeping in her own bed and Mother's good food, but when she returned to the hospital she was feeling lost and lonely; she found that both Seamus and Molly were also on leave and she didn't get on well with Seamus' replacement. She struggled on and, to make it worse, Daniel was still in England, in spite of his good progress. At last, she saw Molly's hat hanging on the peg behind the door.

'Molly, Molly, guess what, he said he loves me.' Annie's eyes where shining as she saw her friend.

'Yes, and it's good to see you again, too. So you did see Daniel while you were on leave? I knew you would, what did you say?'

'Oh, sorry, Molly, did you have a good leave? Give me a hug; I've missed you so much. We had a wonderful day together, had a picnic in the woods, we didn't stop talking. I didn't like it when an aeroplane went over; reminded me of the war. Daniel said that they were going to take paying passengers one day; you'll not get me up in one. He came on his bicycle, said because of his leg it is easier than walking. We had a lovely day.'

'Stop, stop. What did you say when he said he loved you?'

'Well, I told him I love him, too.'

'So? Did he ask you to marry him?'

'Yes and no, not really, but he will. He said he wanted to, but I wouldn't let him. I don't want him to, until all this is over. We've only known each other here, really. It is all so artificial.'

'Oh, Annie, I am so happy for you. So you had a good break?'

'Yes, it was so good to see Ma and Pa again, to have some of Ma's home cooking, to sleep in my own bed. Did it really take me being out here, to appreciate all that?'

'Have you heard about Matthew yet?'

'No, nothing, and the worry is wearing Ma out. I am really anxious about her. Now, did you have a good leave? Tell me all about it.'

The next morning dawned bright but very windy. The nurses had trouble keeping their caps on and their cloaks pulled round them as they crossed to the main building of the hospital. Leaves were chasing round in little circles on the wide stone steps, big beech trees were being stripped of their leaves. Small birds were blown off course or stayed close to the ground, pecking at insects and fallen seeds. It could have been an idyllic scene; the elegant chateau looked unkempt but showed little of the pain and suffering within its walls; doctors and men and women in uniform scuttled across the barren grass, from hut to hut.

Annie stopped as they entered the ward. 'Molly, with all the lovely Yorkshire air that I've been having, I had forgotten the dreadful smell of this place.'

'Well, I'm afraid we'll have to get used to it again.'

Annie was delighted to see Seamus again. 'Did you be having yourself a good break, young lady? You've put on weight, I'm glad to see, and there's a sparkle in your eyes.'

'Oh, Seamus, it's good to see you. Yes, it was so lovely to be home, so difficult to come back, but this is where I belong for the time being, so long as I'm not sent to the Front again. Did you have a good time with your family?'

'Yes, I did, but were you seeing your young man again? He was home with that injury, wasn't he?'

'Yes, we managed to spend a lovely day together. He came on the train with his bicycle; you'll not get me on one of those things, it looks so unstable, but Daniel manages alright, though he did say he fell off several time while learning.'

'There's something you're not telling me, isn't there?'

'Maybe, but it will have to keep. It looks like Sister's on the war-path.'

'Good morning, Staff Nurse Scott; Mr O'Connell, I trust you are suitably refreshed?'

'Yes, Sister, thank you, Sister.'

'You and Mr O'Connell make a good team. I think she has probably missed you. So you'll work together again; now hurry, the night-nurses want to go off to bed.'

They stood round the big mahogany desk in the middle of the ward, the wind rattling the window panes; the men in their beds

190

pulled their blankets round their shoulders, some were sleeping, some moaning, tossing and turning.

'Nurse Scott, I want you and Mr O'Connell to see to those ten men on the right-hand side of the ward, there are not so many of them, but all of them have deeply infected wounds. It will take all your skills to clean them up. I trust you to do your best.'

'Yes, Sister, of course, Sister.'

'And no chattering over the beds! You know it upsets the men, whatever news you have will have to wait.'

'No, Sister, of course not.'

Annie took off her cuffs, rolled up her sleeves and smoothed down her apron. She and Seamus worked their way down the row of men. There were Privates, Corporals and Lance-Corporals; the ward couldn't accommodate difference in rank. Every one of them was ill with gangrene or septicaemia. Annie and Seamus worked skilfully, removing foul dressings, cleaning with hydrogen peroxide and packing wounds with iodine-soaked sphagnum moss. The men were so brave and tried not to cry out, but sometimes a yell would break out, nearly always followed by an apology. Some of the men were too ill to know what was going on. At the end of the ward, tucked behind a screen, was a young German lad; he had head and abdominal injuries. He, too, was unaware of his surroundings, was delirious and crying out; his wounds were particularly difficult to dress.

'*Wasser, Wasser.*' He cried out constantly, but suddenly he seemed to be lucid and asked, '*Sprechen Sie Deutsch? Ich verstehe nicht.*'

Annie had learned a few German words so could tell him that '*Ich Eine Krankenschwester,*' but was afraid that her accent was so bad he wouldn't understand her.

'Why is the word for nurse such an ugly word?' she wondered.

All she could tell the lad was '*Ich spreche kein Deutsch*'. It didn't really help anyone to say she didn't speak German. She did what she could for him.

At the end of the morning, Annie felt exhausted and filthy, her apron was stained and crumpled, however much she tried to smooth it down, and her cap was awry.

'Nurse Scott, you and Mr O'Connell go off for your dinner

break now. And when you get back, I want you to tidy up the store room. I can trust you to do an efficient stock take. I am sure we are getting low on some things.'

'Yes, Sister, thank you.'

'I've missed these stodgy meals.' Annie laughed as they sat down together in the Mess Hut. No-one minded or even commented on nurses and orderlies eating together, the usual conventions of army and hospital life were blurred and forgotten in the stresses of war. Annie and Seamus were seen as friends and a team.

'Now then, will you be telling me about your break? You were going to be telling me about your young man, Daniel. Is he back in France yet?'

'Yes, I think so. I expect he is here again. I came back well ahead of him. He was glad we weren't on the same boat as he didn't want me to see him with sea-sickness. And, yes, I told you; we went for a lovely walk. He brought his bicycle on the train to Masham and cycled to my village. We walked through the farm and had a picnic in the woods. It was a beautiful day; the beech trees in full leaf, birds singing, swallows swooping and diving among the farm buildings; perfect. I even took little Rover who is completely healed now.' Annie's eyes shone as she told him all about it. 'The only thing that spoiled the day was an aeroplane flying low overhead; it reminded us of being here.'

'Yes, yes, but what happened?'

'I told you, we had a picnic,' Annie teased.

'Nurse Scott, I'll swing for you; what happened?'

'Oh, you mean did he ask me to marry him? Well, no; if that's what you mean.'

'But are you disappointed?'

'No, not really, we did talk about it, but I wouldn't let him. I can't make promises out here. We can't commit to each other when none of us knows what is going to happen.'

'What do your parents think of him?'

'Well, they didn't meet him, of course. I'm not happy about him coming back. I don't think his leg is really better, but I couldn't dissuade him. He is committed to seeing this out, whatever the consequences; though I know he doesn't really want to.'

They finished their stew and dumplings and bread and cheese and washed it all down with a mug of tea, and then it was back to the ward. They were set to counting bandages, dressings, rolls of cotton wool and gauze, syringes, thermometers, tubing and bottles of peroxide and iodine. They made a list of all of the items in the stock-room and left it on Sister's desk.

Then it was back to the patients, to re-do dressings and make beds.

Annie spent some time behind the screen, holding the hand of the young German soldier. She bore him no malice; he was just like the other men on the ward, young and doing what he was told. She had listened to Daniel's story of the other Germans that he had rescued; all frightened and hurt, no different from the English boys. Somehow, this one reminded her of Paul and Matthew; it must have been his heavy, floppy fair hair and blue eyes. She didn't speak any German, but understood.

'*Mutter, Mutter, Vater, Vater,*' All Annie could do was sing quietly to him.

'I'm so sorry I can't understand you. I wish I could.'

'*Verstehst du mich, Fräulein? Es stimmt nicht.*'

When Annie gave him water, he was able to thank her; she understood that.

'*Danke schön.*'

He was a son to a mother, like all her other charges. She doubted that he knew where he was.

193

Chapter 33

Joseph

It was bitterly cold in his cell. Joseph's feet were swollen with chilblains. He had great difficulty pulling on his boots; the socks he had been issued with were too small and too thin. His knuckles were stiffening up again; he was now finding his sewing tasks nearly impossible. Constantly being reprimanded and punished for not meeting requirements, bread and water was his most common dinner. Working in the poor light that winter, his eyes were strained; his teeth hurt all the time and were loose. He had still not been given a chance to see a dentist, in spite of asking several times.

He often had dreams of open spaces, clear horizons, clean air, sparkling rivers, and his family; but waiting for him when he awoke was the dank, dark reality of his cell. Occasionally, through the bars of the high narrow window came the sounds from the street below, but since the snow fell, even that was muffled and he heard hardly a thing, except the grating of keys in the lock, the slam of cell doors and the shouts and cries of his fellow prisoners at the abuse of the warders.

Yesterday, being Sunday, he had no sewing to do, he had sat on his bed, unable to motivate himself to move. He had seen Norman in the exercise yard and tried to smile, but this unaccustomed expression made him feel that his face would split. The cold got into his bones; he tried to exercise to warm up but found it nearly impossible. This morning, he asked again to see a dentist, but was told that that was a privilege he would have to earn.

He stood on the bunk and looked out. There had been a further sprinkling of snow in the night; the world looked changed, beautiful, the sun sparkled on the roofs and trees. His elm tree looked magical; as it shook gently in the breeze, little droplets of ice rained down from the branches, sending a scattering of shards of light. Joseph found it difficult even to appreciate this beauty; all life seemed to have left him.

The young warder arrived with the week's allocation of hessian and some more thread.

'Less for you this week,' he whispered.

194

'Why, what have I done to deserve this unexpected treat?'

'Nothing, but you have tomorrow off.'

'Again? Don't tell me, we are having Sunday twice this week.' He tried to smile.

'Well, in a way, yes. Tomorrow is Christmas Day.'

'How did I manage not to work that out? So we're having a party? A chicken? Singing? Gay hats?'

'Well, no, I don't think so, but I think the Governor does have some sort of treat for us all.'

'What? Tell me, please.'

Footsteps were heard outside, the warder's tone changed and in a loud voice, he said, 'So you can get this lot done quickly, no slacking.' He winked at Joseph.

Joseph sighed. 'Christmas or no Christmas, I still have this to do.' He pulled the chair close to the window, took up the first piece of the fabric and started sewing. He had been doing this for so long that he felt he could do it in his sleep.

The day came and went, with no sign of the promised treat. He had tapped a short message to Norman and Bert on the pipes, using the code they had managed to devise.

'That warder was raising my hopes unnecessarily,' he muttered to himself.

As he was preparing to say his evening prayers, the cell door was suddenly opened, no-one came in and the door was left open. Carefully, Joseph struggled to his feet, tentatively made his way out onto the landing and looked down. All around, men were coming out of their cells, leaning over the rails, looking at the floor below them. Ranged below in a circle was a group of their warders and the Governor. They were singing. Carols, Christmas carols. *"Hark the herald angels sing, glory to the new-born King ..."* Joseph took a deep breath and quietly joined in; soon, the whole wing reverberated with the joyful sound of men singing. At the end of *"Away in a manger, no crib for a bed..."* there wasn't a man who didn't have tears in his eyes. *"Yea Lord we greet Thee born this happy morning..."* The circle of men dispersed, the prisoners went back to their cells. Joseph fell to his knees and cried. 'What a gift, I must somehow find a way to thank the Governor.' Joseph said his prayers and thanked God for the Christmas present from the Governor.

On Christmas Morning, breakfast was just the same as any other day, but maybe there was just a little more porridge, and maybe it was just a little bit hotter than usual.

Being a holy day, they tapped to each other that Meeting for Worship would be at the usual Sunday time. Somehow, it was deeper, more meaningful; there was a feeling of some hope in the air.

Christmas Day dinner included an extra ration of meat. Joseph really enjoyed every mouthful. As the light faded, he stood on his bunk, gazing at his elm tree. Through the window, he could hear a distant brass band playing carols. He sang along with the tunes, and no-one came to tell him to stop. But the day ended as all other days had, a scratch on the wall above his bed, prayers and dirty, thin blankets. The next day, it seemed like it all had been a dream.

*

The door opened. 'I don't know what you lot have done to deserve this,' complained the Officer, 'but the Deputy Governor said you were to have an extra letter to receive and write. So, here is yours, it's been read as usual, it's from your mother. And here is a sheet of paper and pen for you to reply; don't seal the envelope – we still have to look at it, as you know.'

Joseph sat speechless, his mouth opening and shutting, 'Th ... th ... th ... thank you, I don't know what to say, tell the Deputy Governor thank you.'

"Christmas 1917

My dear Laddie Joseph

We miss thee so much at this Christmas-tide and hope that thou can have a little bit of a celebration to mark the birth of our Lord. As usual, we will go to Meeting for Worship, even though it will be a Tuesday and will again pray again for thee to be well. All the Friends send their prayers and love to thee and are holding thee in the Light.

Hannah is doing well in school; we are hoping that she will be able to stay till she is fourteen. Jacob

196

*has started his apprenticeship and is doing well;
working hard, Mr Ventress is pleased with his
progress.*

*Pa is starting to feel badly; he is nearly forty-five
you know, and is feeling stiff and arthritic in the
mornings; he's fair mithered about it all.*

*I have been busy with preparations for Christmas.
Uncle George will be with us in our celebrations and
we will join the other churches for carols in the market
square as usual.*

*Look after thyself as well as thou art able, our
thoughts and prayers are with thee as always.*

*With all love and our prayers from thy loving
family, we miss thee so very much.*

Ma."

Joseph pictured all the family at home. He knew that he was in
their thoughts and prayers, and that knowledge helped to sustain
him.

As Ma and Pa weren't expecting an extra letter from him, he
decided to write to Uncle George instead. He had to think hard
about what to write, as he had only the one sheet of paper and no
more would be given to him for a month.

"Christmas 1917

Dear Uncle George,

*You will be surprised to receive this, but an extra letter
is a Christmas gift from the Deputy Governor. He is, I
believe, a kind man but is controlled by those above
him. I hope he is not reprimanded. He also allowed us
to join in with the Christmas carols and gave us an
extra but small ration of meat with our tea.*

*I can't say this to Ma and Pa as they would only
worry. I don't know how I keep going. I am constantly
cold and hungry, I have chilblains, arthritis, terrible
tooth-ache and a constant cough, my voice is weak as I*

197

hardly ever talk; we are supposed to remain silent; it's driving me near to madness. I do talk whenever I can, though it usually incurs a punishment, bread and water. Because of the work we have to do, my eyesight is going. I have an allocation of mail bags to sew every day and only poor daylight to do it by; these long nights and short days really do limit the amount of time I have to work in.

My only comfort is my Bible which I try to read every day, but that is also limited because of lack of light in the short winter days and pains in my eyes.
But I still know that I am doing the right thing. I could give up at any time and be sent to the Front but that would be so wrong and against everything we have suffered for so far. I have stuck it out this long and the war cannot go on for ever.

Please keep a watch on my family, hold them and all of us in the Light.

Your loving nephew,

Joseph."

Next evening, at slop-out, Joseph slid his hand behind the cistern and found the tiny 'newsletter'. He secreted it into his belt, hiding it carefully. In his cell, he removed the pages that he had written previously and put them to one side, ready to flush away; taking two sheets of saved toilet paper, he wrote a letter to his fellow inmates about his feelings.

"Carols, wonderful, I was moved to tears. It made me remember the time at home; we would join our Anglican brothers and sisters for carols in the market place on Christmas Eve, singing as loudly as we could with such joy. The next day, we would go to early Meeting for Worship before giving each other the little gifts that we had made and tucked away. At dinner time, we would have the roast chicken that Ma had cooked for us and the pudding which had been made in the autumn where,

198

hidden, we might find a silver thrupenny piece if we were
very lucky. Of course the animals had to be tended
morning and evening, but even they seemed to sense the
specialness of the day.

My blessings on you all."

He tucked the thin papers under the mattress, ready to take them back next time he had a slop-out. Remembering all this and writing it down made him feel calmer and less depressed. He took up his Bible and read the words "In the beginning was the word and the word was God ..."

*

Joseph looked forward to the next episode of their newsletter. They knew it couldn't last, would be found eventually; it was. The little newspaper was found, the most important way of keeping in touch, keeping their spirits up. No-one confessed to being the instigator and no-one told any tales, so the culprits were never identified; it had kept them going for months. However, it was bread and water all round again for many days.

Chapter 34
Annie

Annie took off her coat and hung it on the peg by her bed. She removed her hat. As she threaded Grandmother's hat-pin through the band, she caught her hand on it.

'Ow. I can't have been concentrating; I've never done that before.' There was a sizeable deep wound. 'Bother, and now it is bleeding.' Annie wound a handkerchief round it.

'Let me have a look at it,' said Molly.

'Don't make a fuss. It is nothing. It'll be fine by morning. Now then, Molly, do you know how the French celebrate Christmas?'

'No, but does it matter? Everyone here is English.'

'No, they aren't; we have Irish and Scottish staff from Britain and some French orderlies.'

'Well, I think we will have to have an English Christmas, if possible, for the sake of our men. Most of them are British; though, of course, we do have a few others, not only French but those two German patients, Heinrich and Claus.'

'Well, Sister has asked me to organise the Christmas Eve carols, you know, like the ones we do in hospital at home. We will need to have a few rehearsals.'

'Have we got any carol sheets, so we all sing the same words?'

'We could write some down and hand them out.'

'I'll ask Sister, see what she suggests.'

Rehearsals were arranged and the nurses and orderlies who could get to the Recreation Hut after their shifts joined in. They found that they had a repertoire of a dozen or so carols which they felt would be sufficient. Most of them knew the old carols from their childhoods, but it was interesting comparing the variations from different churches; they had to agree on the words they would use.

*

At about nine o'clock on Christmas Eve, all the patients were settled for the night. The wards were in darkness, except for dim lights over the beds of the really sick men and over the desk in the middle of the ward, where the night-nurses sat. Annie and the other day nurses took up their positions; they were all wearing clean aprons and caps and had turned their capes inside out so that the red lining showed. Behind the nurses, a few of the stretcher bearers, including Daniel, and some of the doctors and orderlies were tagging along to help give voice. They were all welcomed and handed a sheet with the words to sing. Each nurse carried a jam jar on a string tied up the same way as little boys do when going out to catch tiddlers; the candles in the jars threw a warm glow onto the bright faces of the young girls. They crossed the wide lawns, the moon shining clear and bright above them.

'Ready?' said Annie, as she smoothed down her apron. 'You know what we are going to sing?'

The doors of each ward were opened and the nurses trooped in, singing softly *"Away in a manger, no crib for a bed..."*

They walked slowly, so slowly down one side of the ward and up the other. *"Yea Lord we greet you born this happy morning..."* Some of the men joined in, others openly cried, there were a lot of handkerchiefs used. All of them thought that they had been visited by angels. Annie was particular when they got to ward three at the screened off area where the two German lads were being nursed; they sang especially for them *"Stille Nacht! Heilige Nacht! Alles schläft, einsam wacht ..."*

'Danke, danke.'

'God bless you all,' the men whispered to the nurses, deep in thoughts of home.

As they passed by, a young patient cried out. A night nurse hurried over to him, stood by his bed, held his hand, listening for a few moments, then she closed his eyes and covered his face with the sheet.

The choir visited all the wards in the hospital, and in each the reception was the same; the men were reminded of better times in the past and wished for a bright future.

The nurses and some of the stretcher bearers, doctors and orderlies assembled in the Mess Hut. The cooks had managed to make some mince pies and there were steaming mugs of cocoa. One or two of the men poured in a surreptitious top-up from hipflasks that they had hidden in their pockets; Matron chose not to notice.

They stood in a circle and gave a rendition of *"We wish you a*

Merry Christmas and a Happy New Year ..."

Daniel put his arm round Annie; Sister Jackson looked the other way. 'Happy Christmas and a peaceful New Year, my dear, and let's hope that next year brings an end to all this.'

'Amen to that. Peace in the New Year to you too, Danny. May we all live to see the end of it.'

He kissed her on the top of her head 'I've got to go.'

They went out into the cold midnight, their breath making little clouds before them; they looked up at the stars. 'Strange to think of all these stars shining the same on everyone, young and old, ill and well, British, French and German; the heavens are there for us all.'

'Another year of war, when will it end?' Annie asked.

'It has to end soon, it cannot carry on like this; there will be no-one left to fight, soon.'

'I'm not sure I can take much more of it.'

'If you can't take any more, you are at liberty to go. I have to stay and carry on.'

'I couldn't leave you, Danny, even if I wanted to. It is seeing you regularly that's keeping me going.'

As Annie reached out her hand to Danny, he said, 'What have you done to your hand?'

It's nothing, just caught it on my Grandmother's hat-pin, it's fine.'

'Well, look after it, won't you. I love you. You know that, don't you?'

'Yes, I will and I do, and I love you. You look after yourself; don't let anything happen to you, will you.'

'Goodnight, God bless.'

Chapter 35
Annie

Annie woke feeling feverish and in pain. Her hand throbbed; she could feel the rhythm of her heart beating in it. Yesterday, it had looked a little swollen, but today it was really nasty looking, inflamed, angry. She panicked. She thought she had been so careful. She always washed her hands as thoroughly as she could, but they had run short of carbolic soap and were having to make do without. That young German lad, Heinrich, the one who, in spite of their efforts, had cried out for three days and long nights before eventually dying. His abdominal wounds had been particularly difficult to dress without getting the gangrenous muck onto her hands; they had been deep and almost impossible to treat. Ironic, she thought wryly to herself, to get an infection from a German! Her hand throbbed, her arm ached, her head hurt and she was sure she had a high temperature. She felt cold and sweaty.

'Molly, Molly, wake up. Help me, please.' Molly was such a sound sleeper that Annie had to stagger over to her bed, to shake her friend.

'What? What's up?' Molly rubbed her eyes.

'Please. Help me, Molly.'

'Now, what is it?'

'It's my hand, my arm.'

Molly sat up, scratched her head and ran her fingers through her hair. 'Now then, show me. Oh, I don't like the look of that. Where did that come from? Is that where you caught yourself on that your Grandmother's hat-pin? How's it got like that?'

'Yes it is. I must have got infected matter into it when I dressed poor Heinrich's wounds. You know we've had no rubber gloves for weeks and we have been running short of soap. What am I going to do?'

'Poor Heinrich, indeed! Poor Annie, let's have a proper look.' Molly snapped on her torch. She looked at her friend's arm and felt her forehead. 'No, I don't like the look of that at all and you feel pyrexial.'

An angry-looking, red line ran up Annie's arm, from the site of the scratch to beyond her elbow. 'Come on, I'll help you get dressed and take you to see Sister, see what she has to say.'

Molly helped Annie into her clothes and tied her long hair up with a ribbon, fashioned a make shift sling from a scarf and wrapped her cloak round her.

Shivering, Annie leant against her friend as the two of them made their way out of their quarters, through the cold morning air and across the muddy grass to the hospital. As soon as they got to Ward Three Molly sat Annie down on a nearby chair and ran into the ward.

'Sister, Sister, please come.' Molly was flushed with the exertion and worry.

'Now then, Nurse Williams, what on Earth is all the fuss and hurry? And how many times have you to be told not to run? And why are you half-dressed?' the night Sister asked.

Molly put her hand to her head. She had forgotten her cap and her hair was dishevelled. 'Sorry, Sister, but it's Annie, Nurse Scott, she's just woken me. She's in a bad way, she's by the door, please come and see.'

Sister Walker bustled along and took one look at Annie. 'Nurse Williams, find a wheelchair quickly. Come with me, my girl.'

There were no separate facilities for ill staff and no ward for females, so screens were pulled round the end bed; Molly helped Annie onto it.

'Let me have a look.' Sister thrust a thermometer under Annie's tongue while she rolled up the sleeve of her dress. 'I don't like the look of that, not one little bit; we'll have to get Mr Goodman to have a look at it, as soon as he gets here. Nurse Williams, go and get Nurse Scott's night clothes and washing things, and while you are there, get yourself properly dressed.'

'Yes, Sister, as soon as I can, Sister.'

Sister looked at the thermometer. 'How high is it, Sister?' Annie wanted to know.

'102 degrees, much too high. We must get it down. Have you had anything to eat or drink today?'

'No and I'm not hungry.'

'Well, I want you to drink. I'll bring you something.'

Annie's hand shook as she tried to drink the cold water from the cup that was held to her lips. 'Now then, my girl, how did this happen?'

Annie tried to explain about Heinrich's infected wound and Grandmother's hat-pin, but she lost the thread and got confused.

'Never mind, it doesn't really matter how it happened. The important thing is to get you better. Nurse Williams, have you any idea when this started?'

'A few days ago, I think. She scratched her hand and would not get it seen to, she thinks it got infected from Heinrich Schultz' wound.'

'Oh dear, as long ago as that, and Mr Schultz had gas-gangrene.'

When the day and medical staff came on duty, Sister Jackson showed Mr Goodman the swollen, hot arm and hand.

'I'll have to operate, let some of that infection out; let's hope we are in time. Get some hot compresses onto it in the meantime; see if we can draw out some of that infection.'

Molly and Seamus took it in turns to tend to Annie, putting cool cloths on her forehead and hot fomentations on her arm and hand. At midday, she was wheeled down to the operating theatre where, under meagre anaesthetic, Mr Clarkson opened up the infected area so the pus could run out; the smell confirmed the diagnosis of gangrene.

Back on the ward, Annie's arm was supported by a sling on a pole, to keep it high above her heart, and the wound was constantly irrigated to wash away the infection. Molly and Seamus were kept busy all day, tending to her; they barely took any time for meals. Annie became delirious, calling out for her mother and for Daniel; she had no idea where she was. Her temperature continued to creep up. Damp sheets were laid over her and the window near to her bed kept open. Her cries and mutterings mingled with the groans and cries of the men on the ward.

'We really should send her back to England for treatment, but she is too ill for that. We shouldn't really be nursing female staff here. Luckily, she doesn't know what is going on.'

'But where else can we nurse her?' asked Mr Goodman. 'You are the best person to look after her, you and her friends, Mr O'Connor and Nurse Williams. It's the best we can do for her.'

'Matthew, Matthew, is that you?' In her delirium, Annie

thought she saw her brother.

Mr Goodman and Sister continued to be very worried about one of their favourite nurses. 'Her temperature is still going up, it's 104 degrees now, we can't keep her cool enough; I think we must cut her hair, that might help.'

'Nurse Williams, you are Nurse Scott's closest friend; would you like to be the one to cut her hair, as short as you can manage? It will help to cool her down; her pyrexia is getting out of hand.'

Molly was shocked. 'She has never cut her hair in all her life.'

'It's her life we are trying to save, Nurse. If you can't do it, I'll have to.'

*

Daniel felt very tired and depressed. He had been on the go, non-stop for hours, or was it days? He was so exhausted, he hardly could tell day from night. The bombardment seemed to be unceasing. Shuttling the wounded back to the Dressing Station, collecting them from No-Man's Land, and the constant terror; it was no longer fear, he was constantly convinced that every day would be his last.

He had a letter in his tunic pocket. He didn't recognise the hand writing and was barely interested in it, and hadn't yet had the time to read it. He was worried that he hadn't heard from Annie. 'However,' he told himself, 'if I am busy, so is she.' He told himself not to be silly. 'She'll write when she has time. When did you last write to her?' he asked himself, 'it must be several days.'

'That's the lot,' a voice called.

'What, no more?'

'Can't find any more, not till next time, unless Fritz takes a pot shot at some idiot who sticks his head above the parapet.'

'Tea all round then?'

Daniel took the mug of murky-looking, brown fluid that smelt of petrol and tasted worse, but it passed as tea and now he scarcely noticed. He sat down, away from the others, rolled a cigarette, pulled out the letter and opened it carefully with his pen-knife.

"Dear Daniel,
I am sorry to have to tell you this but Annie is
in hospital"

'Of course she, is she's a nurse,' he muttered.

"She is very ill. She has an infection in her
hand which the surgeon says she might lose.
If you can get here to see her, I am sure she
would like that.

Don't leave it too long.

Yours truly.

Molly."

'Sir, Sir. I have to go, go to the hospital, I'm taking an ambulance.'

'Don't be a fool, boy ...'

But his words fell into empty air as Daniel drove away.

*

Daniel arrived in the ward, out of breath and looking exhausted and filthy.

'Sister, Sister Jackson, I've heard from Molly about Annie. Where is she? I must see her!'

'Mr Braithwaite, I'm glad that Nurse Williams has informed you about Nurse Scott. You two are very close, I understand, but you can't just come barging in here like that. She is resting and I don't want her disturbed.'

'I won't disturb her. I just want to see her.'

'Right, I understand but I need to talk to you about her and ask you some questions. You go into the bathroom, look at yourself in the mirror and try to clean yourself up a bit. I'll put the kettle on and I'll meet you back in my office in a few minutes.

Daniel hadn't seen his own reflection for some time and was surprised and horrified by what he saw; his face was streaked, his hair muddy, his uniform filthy. He ran a bowl of water and

207

dunked his head into it. He washed his face and hands and did the best he could with his hair by combing the muck out of it with his fingers. He straightened his uniform and rubbed his boots on the back of his trouser legs, to clean them a little.

'Now then, lad.' Sister indicated a chair, 'what do you know of what has happened?'

'Only what Molly, Nurse Williams, told me in her note, that Annie, Nurse Scott, has an infection in her hand and that she might lose it.'

'Well, that is true enough. She has been tending some very sick people, as you know, with very nasty infections. It seems that she hurt her hand while off duty, and that has become infected. As you know, these infections can get very much worse in just a few hours. I'm afraid your friend is very poorly. Mr Goodman, who I believe treated your leg, has opened up the area and we are irrigating it, but it is not much better. We believe that she has gas-gangrene: she ought to go to England, but she's too ill to move yet. How is your leg, by the way?'

'She's more than a friend; I hope we will be married after the war is over. My leg still gives me trouble on and off and sometimes it gets very red and hot, but I haven't got time to worry about that now. What is the prognosis for Annie?'

Sister Jackson ignored Daniel's use of Annie's Christian name. 'We are having great difficulty controlling her pyrexia. We've had to cut off all her hair, hoping that ...'

'You've done what?'

'I know; Nurse Williams said that she had never had her hair cut before, but we felt it might help to bring down her temperature. You can come and see her now, but I am afraid your young lady is a very changed woman. You are going to be shocked.'

Molly's attempts at hairdressing had left Annie's hair sticking out in all directions.

Daniel stood by her bed; he had hardly recognised her, shorn hair, yellowing skin and sunken eyes made her look so old.

'Hello, my beautiful hedgehog.' Daniel found it hard to look at her; she looked so different.

Annie opened her eyes and smiled a weak smile. 'Oh, it's you. Thank you for coming.' She fell into a semi-conscious state again, her good hand clasped round her gold locket.

'So is she going to lose her hand?' Daniel asked Sister Jackson. 'Does she even know who I am?'

'To be honest, yes, in all likelihood. We are doing all we can do at the moment. I am just waiting for Mr Goodman. As to knowing who you are – at times, yes, I expect so.'

He sat with her, stroked her good hand and talked softly to her about their plans and hopes for their future together. When he got only inconsequential replies, he realised that she didn't understand a thing and may even not know who he was. He changed the cold compresses on her forehead and held the cup to her lips, to get her to drink a little.

'Braithwaite? It is Braithwaite, isn't it? Didn't I operate on your leg a while ago? How's it doing?' Mr Goodman was doing a ward round.

'Well, up and down, good days, bad days, but it's well enough to work with. It's worse when I'm tired, but what about Annie?'

'Good show; well, get the leg looked at when this lot's over, won't you, back in Blighty. Now, this is your young lady, isn't she? You'll have to do; no time to contact the parents and she's not well enough to understand. Got to get that hand off. Infection in her blood stream. Maybe too late already, but got to try. Will you give us the go-ahead?'

'If I must, if that is the only thing that will save her life.'

Annie was lifted onto a stretcher and wheeled to the operation theatre.

Seamus took Daniel to the Mess Hut and made him eat. 'You must eat; you'll be no good to her if you pass out.'

Daniel had no appetite. 'What if she dies? She and I, we …' Tears crept out and ran silently, dripping off his chin. Seamus looked the other way until he heard him blow his nose.

'Yes, I know, she told me. I can't comfort you. You know as well as I do that her chances are very slim, but Mr Goodman's the best that we have. He'll do all he can for her. Now, shouldn't you go back on duty?'

Daniel had forgotten the ambulance that he had taken without permission. 'Serge will be furious with me, I suppose. I could get court marshalled; Absent Without Leave, removing an army

209

vehicle. What am I going to do?' He buried his head in his hands.

'Have you any leave owing? Well, go back, explain the situation and ask for leave; they can only say yes or no. Annie will be out for the count for some hours yet.'

Next day, Daniel was back on the ward, sitting by Annie's bed. She was still delirious, but her pulse and respiration were not so rapid. Sister Jackson said that they hoped that the amputation had been in time. But Annie was restless, plucking at the bed clothes, muttering to anyone and no-one, to Matthew, to Daniel, to her parents and to Paul. Daniel felt so helpless. He tried to talk to her, but he was sure that she wasn't really aware that he was beside her.

Daniel stayed by her bed all day and all night. Sister Jackson didn't really approve, but she was now short staffed and the presence of this very sick young woman made even more demands on the nurses. He helped them with her care. He dozed on and off, sitting by her bed, holding her hand, with his head resting on the bed, near to hers.

As daylight crept into the ward, it was clear that Annie was worse. Her temperature was too high to record, her pulse was weak and rapid, her skin yellow. Her arm, what was left of it, was discoloured and still giving off the typical smell.

In the morning, Sister Jackson asked the chaplain to visit her and give her communion and a blessing. Molly found a candle, lit it and set it beside the bed. Annie seemed to be watching the flame. Daniel felt sure she was better; she looked more peaceful, she even opened her eyes and looked at him.

'Danny? Danny?' Annie looked at Daniel as if seeing him fresh.

'Annie, Annie my dear. Yes it's me, please tell me, when you are better, please, you will marry me? You will, won't you, when you are better? Please, say yes.'

Annie smiled and nodded her head. 'Yes please, yes, of course. I love you, my Danny boy,' she whispered and closed her eyes. At midnight, Annie took one last, deep breath and sighed it out; she took no other.

Daniel sat with her, sobbing into her pillow, until she was wheeled away. He took her locket and put it round his own neck.

'I'll keep it for ever, dearest Annie.'

210

Chapter 36

Daniel

The war continued to rage, neither side making much headway. The snow and frost had frozen the mud into deep, hard craters, the men slipped and slid about. They were always being warned of the danger of frost-bite. Daniel was bitterly cold, could never get warm but didn't seem to care. He sat in the dug-out, picking at the single 'wound stripe' on his sleeve. He had seen men with three or four and wondered how they managed to keep coming back. He held his head in his hands, looking at his mouth-organ, wondering if he could ever play it again and turning Susie's stone over and over in his hand.

'What sort of luck has this brought me?' he muttered to himself. 'But, I suppose Susie didn't promise me good luck; just that, when I wanted to think of home, to hold it. Well, I want my home now.' He shouted out, 'I want to go home, now; I can't take this much longer. Serge, send me home.'

'Come on, chum, pull yourself together. Stop being like this. We all want home and you must eat.' Jack had appointed himself to look out for Daniel; he wasn't doing very well at it. He knew that Dan had only been back from being wounded a little while, when his girlfriend had died; he seemed to have lost the will to live. He just wouldn't do anything; not eat, not talk – he just worked like a zombie.

'I can't, I just can't face food. Why should I? It all looks and tastes the same.'

'But you will make yourself ill if you don't look after yourself.'

'Why should I care? I have nothing to live for now.' He reached beneath his tunic to touch Annie's locket.

Daniel had only just managed to avoid being court marshalled after taking the ambulance. But they couldn't afford to lose him, and the Sergeant had some sympathy for him and had given him a good dressing down and many threats.

Daniel sat for hours, just smoking or else ceaselessly limping up and down. When shelling stopped and the time came for them to collect the injured from the battlefield, he took unnecessary risks; he wanted to be killed, but he seemed to be charmed –

none of the bullets fired at him found their mark.

During quiet times, he would disappear for hours on end, taking his mouth-organ with him, playing the same tune, the *"Londonderry Air"* over and over again; *"If I am dead as dead I well may be, you'll come and find the place that I am lying and kneel and say an Avé there for me ..."* 'But you'll not come and find my place, I'll find yours, I promise.'

Jack tried to coax him out of it but was quite unsuccessful. 'Come on, Dan, mate, can't have you fading away. Annie wouldn't like that, and what will your family do if you get hurt.'

'Leave me alone. Please. I don't want to talk about it. Can't.'

He went to see Molly at the hospital, but she was out celebrating the decision in the House of Lords that would give women over thirty the vote; most of the nurses were. But as she was the one person he felt he could talk to, he got angry with her for not being there. 'Where the hell are you when I really need you?' he yelled at the sky, as snow fell in great drifts around him.

He continued to drive the ambulance, taking the injured into Ward Three. He always found himself automatically looking out for Annie, before he would remember; he found tears came suddenly, it embarrassed him. His leg hurt, he rubbed it constantly. It was red and inflamed.

One day, Sister Jackson caught him sitting in the corridor; he had unwound his puttee and was looking at his leg.

'Let me have a look at that,' she demanded. She examined the wound. It was hot to touch, swollen, with red edges, white in the middle. She took his temperature. 'One hundred and one! How can you be working? You must be feeling so ill.'

'Have I a Blighty?' He echoed the question he had been asked so many times in the past.

'Hmm. Definitely, I would say, but we will have to ask Mr Goodman to see you again. Bed, you! I'll tell your CO.'

Once again he bathed, put on hospital pyjamas and lay in the blessedly clean, louse free bed. He immediately fell into a deep and dreamless sleep. Sister Jackson got a message to the Sergeant, to say what had happened and she asked that Jack would bring all Daniel's belongings when he next came to the hospital. Mr Goodman came to have a look at the leg.

'I'm not surprised. He has an abscess, probably osteomyelitis.

It looks like the infection has been grumbling away for some months. Now he is so run down, it's flared up; he hasn't been looking after himself, I suppose, not since his young nurse died. I need to take him to theatre and drain that; get the pus out. See what we have.'

Sister Jackson tried to explain what was to happen. 'Do you understand? Really?' But she doubted that he did; he had become very ill, semi-conscious. That afternoon, he was lifted onto a theatre trolley.

He spent many days ill, too ill to be moved. He called out for Annie, for his mother, for little Susie. He tossed and turned in the bed, his temperature raged up and down.

Molly stayed by his bed, cooling him with damp cloths, holding a cup so that he could drink. He grabbed her hand. 'Annie, my dear Annie, you've come back.' When he occasionally opened his eyes, he realised it was Molly and would cry again.

He was too ill to have it explained to him what had really happened. Sister Jackson allowed Molly to tell him.

'Listen to me Daniel; Mr Goodman drained the abscess, but then the infection got into your bloodstream. A few days later, you had to have another operation. I don't really know how to tell you this – Mr Goodman had to take off your leg to save your life; you've got no leg below the knee.'

'Show me,' he demanded. 'Why does it still hurt, just as much as it did before? I don't believe you. You are making fun of me.'

'I'm not, Danny. I'm really sorry. It's the nerves, they don't know yet that the leg is gone,' she explained, 'it can take a while for them to get used to it.'

'Don't call me Danny, only Annie calls me that,' he snapped. He turned his face to the wall and cried. 'Annie, where are you?'

*

Spring was creeping over England when the boat carrying Daniel and other wounded soldiers landed in Southampton. The first stop, after a short time in the Assessment and Transfer Hospital in Southampton, was Catterick Garrison. He had little memory of the journey, only that he had been very sick on the crossing and the rail journey had been a very long and exhausting time. Set in

213

the North Yorkshire Riding, Catterick had a well-equipped hospital and they treated the wound on what was left of his leg. He could smell the fresh air and hear the welcome sounds of newborn lambs and sky larks when he sat outside in the grounds in the pale sun. It was not too far from home, so his mother and Susie came to visit him when they could.

'Hello my son. You are looking better today.'

'Have you still got my little stone?'

But after the initial pleasantries, he had little to say to them; how would they ever understand? It wasn't just the loss of his leg, it was the loss of Annie who he couldn't stop thinking about. And it was the recurring nightmares. Every night, he woke screaming, thinking he was hearing the shells, the cries, seeing the Very Lights, the desolation, the mud. He pulled the blankets over his head, hoping to shut it out, but it didn't help. But other nights he dreamt of Annie and the walk they had when they went to the woods, or the dances they had been to, the concerts. He even dreamt of the wedding they didn't have. When he woke and found that she wasn't there, he cried again. He wasn't the only one troubled by dreams, there were others much worse off than he; they were transferred to the asylum in Newcastle, to be cared for. A psychiatrist came to visit people like Daniel, got them talking about their experiences; gradually, the nightmares became less frequent. But still, any sudden loud noise or flashes of light had him cowering under the bed clothes.

When he was well enough, the nurses took him out in a wheelchair in the grounds; he could smell the clean air as he sat in the chilly sun, wondering what had happened to him and what would now become of him. Would anyone want a cripple like him? How would he support himself? He could hardly expect his mother and Susie to. He made good progress and was eventually transferred to the County Hall Hospital in Northallerton. Some of the nurses recognised him from his previous time there and greeted him as an old friend. They put him through intensive physiotherapy to strengthen his muscles, fitted him with a wooden artificial leg and taught him to walk on crutches. It was a long, slow, painful process.

'I'll never learn to walk on these,' he complained as he fell again.

'Yes, you will. You are a very determined young man and we know you can.'

'I don't feel like it today,' he sulked.

'Sorry, but the only day off you can have is Sunday and that is only because I have to have a day off.'

The relationship between the men and their physiotherapist was one of love and hate. She goaded them on, and under her care they achieved far more than they believed they could and she shared in all their little triumphs; as they gained strength, they learned to manage on their own.

*

One day in November, they were going through their usual exercise routines. Daniel had fallen again and was feeling angry and depressed. They heard a shout, running feet, more shouting. The door of the ward was flung open; a dishevelled looking man appeared in the doorway.

'It's over, it's over. The Germans have signed. The war is over.'

Some men joined in the cheering and shouting; waved their sticks and crutches. The nurses looked stunned and hugged each other and the men; they danced round, waving and singing. Daniel burst into tears.

There was to be a street party. Those who were well enough were bundled into wheelchairs, tucked round with blankets and pushed by nurses and orderlies into Northallerton High Street. The banners, the noise, the cheering, the singing; people hugging and kissing complete strangers. Daniel was quite overwhelmed by it all; it was too noisy.

'Please, will you take me back to the hospital, Nurse? I am so glad it is all over, but nothing will bring back my Annie. We were to be wed as soon as we had peace. I'll never be married now, I know that.'

*

Daniel was due to go home. The doctors and other staff felt that they had done all they could for him. He could manage well enough on his crutches and could get about. He was glad to be home, as he needed the peace and quiet that only their little cottage could provide. He spent hours in his bedroom. He hardly spoke to anyone; nightmares troubled him. Slowly, he adjusted to

215

his new way of life. He wanted to carry on with the garden and, although he couldn't get down to it, he did what he could and helped his mother and Susie. He wanted to support the cricket team but found that they were so very short of men. The war had taken too many of them; there was no team to support. What team wanted a one legged player?

He realised he had to think about his future, so he went to see Mr Fosdyke at the bank, who was very pleased to see him.

'Now then, lad, I expect you'll be wanting your old job back,' he said, eyeing up the medals on his chest, the pinned up trouser leg. It would do the bank no harm to be seen to be employing a wounded soldier. The young women he had had to take on were never there long enough; found that the demands made on them were too onerous. The last one left when her young man came home, badly injured.

Chapter 37

Joseph

The change from summer to autumn had brought a dazzling display of gold and yellow to his elm tree; all the rook chicks had fledged and long gone. Standing on the chair, looking through the dirty little window, Joseph watched starlings wheel and cry in their thousands as they too took off for warmer places; they left the gulls to scream their lonely call. One cold and icy morning, all the leaves from the elm tree fell and scattered in the wind like so many hopes and promises, exposing its bare branches and the rooks' nests. Alone again and miserable, he fell to having long conversations with himself, couldn't think of a future; it had disappeared, along with his convictions. He hardly noticed the pains in his teeth and hands anymore. He felt abandoned.

*

On a day like any other, Joseph thought that it was probably November – he had forgotten several times to keep count of the days, to make the scratches on the wall, so was not able to tell exactly. He was dreading the onset of winter; the cold of the last two had been terrible. He wasn't sure he would survive another.

There was a great shouting all over the gaol. He could hear footsteps running up and down the corridors and landings, with shouted words: 'Victory! Peace at last!' It took a while for it to get into his head. He banged on the cell door, on and on, until eventually he was heard and the door was opened.

'What is going on?' he demanded.

'The war is over, armistice, the Germans have given in, we've won.' The young warder was flushed with excitement.

'What about us?' asked Joseph.

'I have no idea, mate, no orders.' And he slammed the door shut once more.

Joseph dropped to his knees, tears soaking down into his shirt. 'It's over, thank God.' He tapped on the pipe, made contact with Norman for the first time in over a week; maybe there was some hope of release.

'I'll die if I stay here much longer.'

But the Governor had no orders. The men had been given ten years. Maybe that is what they would serve; elation gave way to depression, another eight years to go. Mail bags continued to be the order of the day; day after day, week after week.

The Hessian was delivered every Monday, the allotment had to be filled, punishment for insubordination of bread and water continued. Christmas came and went. A different Governor gave them no treat this time around. Joseph felt suicidal, his joints hurt, his teeth were loose, his hair was falling out. Only his unfaltering belief in God and the overall goodness of all mankind kept him going. His faith was stretched further than he thought was possible. With no war going on, the incarceration seemed futile. The atmosphere in the prison changed, the attitude to the objectors became one of irritation and intolerance. New staff, some of whom had served at the Front, had no understanding of what these men were inside for.

Winter came, ice formed on his cell walls, snow blew in through the ventilation gap above his window, and the water he was given to wash in had a rime of frost on it. Fog enclosed the gaol; the view from his window was so restricted that he sometimes couldn't see his elm tree. Mail bags were sewn day after day, the monthly letters gave a little relief, but it was only temporary.

Then, one day, he felt a strange warmth in the air, birds were singing in the trees, people's voices and children shouting at play could be heard in the street below. Looking from his window, he could see the elm tree was turning green, the pinky green that covers a tree just before the leaves break out. Joseph sighed a deep sigh.

'I've survived another winter, thank the Lord. Will I survive another?'

He tapped on the pipe to talk to Norman; spring gave them some hope of release.

*

Joseph was back home and life had returned to normal. He was playing cricket with George and the lads again; they were beating the team from Middleham by an innings and four runs. He was being carried on the shoulders of his team mates for having made a half century.

The door crashed open; his dream was shattered.

'Get up you. You have to see the Governor today. Now. Get

up, you lazy scum.'

He rubbed his eyes and fought his mind back to the present; the cricket and the sunshine, the smell of cut grass evaporated in a cloud of lost hopes and disbelief. All he could see was the damp ceiling, the pile of Hessian in the corner waiting to be stitched, felt the cold. He struggled to sit up.

It all seemed so unfair. The war had been over since November, but they were still here and it was spring. Not that you would know it, no sunshine ever came into this cramped cell. Another of his recurring dreams, nightmares, was that he never got out, like the girl in the fairy story he never finished his task and wouldn't be released until he had; he had no magic goblin to help him.

'And a very good morning to you.' The vow he had made to himself to be polite now was a habit.

'No talking. Silence!'

'Sorry, I was still asleep, still dreaming.'

'Well, stop dreaming now, the Governor wants to see you.'

'Before breakfast?'

'Yes. Now. Get up. Get a move on. And no talking.'

'Good day to you, Mister Metcalf,' said the Governor.

'Eh up. Mister?' thought Joseph. 'He's never called me Mister before. I wonder what's up?'

'You and your comrades are free to go. The Powers That Be feel that there is no point in keeping you at his Majesty's pleasure, and the expense of the tax payer, any longer; we don't see why we should go on housing you. I don't know if I am glad or sorry to see you go. You have been the most difficult, awkward, well-mannered convicts I have ever had to deal with. You can go today, if you like, and we'll do our best to find you some civvies. Or you can wait a day or two, when your family can send you some of your own clothes.'

Joseph was stunned, rooted to the spot. He shook his head and wondered if he was still dreaming. He held on to a chair, to stop from falling over.

'I... I... I don't know what to say. I'll go today and take my chances; no-one is expecting me, I suppose?' He was having difficulty with his unaccustomed voice.

'No, it's up to you to contact them. I'll give you a travel

warrant so you can get home and money for food for the journey. I expect it will take you a while to get from Maidstone to your home, won't it?'

'That will depend on the trains. I suppose they are still running.'

'Guard!' the governor called out.

The officer entered the room, clicked his heels together. 'Yes, Sir.'

'Take this gentleman.' The man's jaw dropped at the *gentleman*. 'Take this gentleman to the clothing store, get him kitted out, let him collect his personal belongings such as they are, give him a bottle of water and some bread and cheese and bring him back here before he goes.'

It wasn't until he was trying on civilian clothes that Joseph realised how wasted and thin his body was; no exercise and poor food with intermittent bread and water as punishment for years had taken their toll.

He tapped on the pipe before realising that Norman would also have been given the opportunity to leave. 'I'd like to see my friends before I go, please.' He was let into their cells. The three men embraced.

'May God go with you, my friends; come and see me sometime, and go to a Quaker meeting in your area, you'll like it,' said Bert.

'I've been thinking about that,' said Norman. 'I'm going to join my local Meeting as soon as I can.'

'Don't be too hasty. Think about it. We have been through a lot, it will take a while to adjust to being home, I expect.'

The Governor shook hands with Joseph, Norman and Bert. 'I don't, and never have or will, agree with your stand but I do admire the way you have all have stuck to your convictions and taken the consequences. I wish you the best of luck.'

At the gate, Joseph turned to the guard. In a cracked voice, he said, 'Thank you, you have looked after us as well as you could. I bear you no malice. You did what you had to do.'

It was the guard's turn to be lost for words.

A thin April sun was shining through the intermittent clouds as the gate slammed shut behind him. He embraced his friends.

'May God go with you both. Write when you have time.'

For the first time since he had been taken by Fred Harker three years ago, Joseph was free. He breathed in the fresh air, turned his face to the sun and wept. The tears coursed down his face so that passers-by wondered what was up. He was free to move where he wanted to and free to speak; though not having been allowed to speak out loud for more than two years he found this difficult, but he managed to ask directions to the station. The noise of the people and traffic and the train, all confused and worried him, gave him a headache. Everything seemed so different from the world he had left only three years ago.

'Maybe I'm remembering it wrongly,' he wondered as he stood outside the station.

*

The third-class compartment was crowded and uncomfortable, with hard benches; people coughing, sneezing and spitting, some looked really ill. He pulled on the leather strap, to let some fresh air into the carriage,

'Shut the bloody window!' a voice shouted out. 'Do you want us all to die of new mown 'ay?' Joseph smiled to himself and guessed he looked terrible, as well. He had bronchitis; he had got so used to the cough that he had had since they were in Dyce that he hardly noticed it.

'What you got to grin about, chum?'

'I'm going to see my family. I haven't seen them for years.'

'Why, were you been? At the Front? You don't look like a bleeding soldier.'

'No, I'm not, never have been. I've been in Maidstone Gaol.'

'Hm, what you done?'

'Nothing, that was my crime, I did nothing.' Joseph laughed.

'You're mad, you are, mate; mad, bloody bonkers.'

'Yes, I probably am, but I stuck it out, stuck to my guns.' He laughed again at the irony and contradiction of what he had just said. 'Would you like a cigarette?' offering to roll him one.

The man shook his head. 'Got my own, thanks, chum.' He shrugged his shoulders and turned back to his newspaper, dragging on his cigarette, coughing and spitting.

Joseph watched the world go by outside the grimy window. The daffodil blooms were fading in people's gardens, the blackthorn blossom was over and the may trees just starting to

221

show pink; new leaves were appearing on the willow, elm and oak trees. By the time the scenery changed to the built-up area of London, the rhythm of the wheels over the rails had lulled him to sleep. He slept until the train pulled into Victoria Station. By asking directions, he made his way across London by bus to King's Cross. He found the unaccustomed exercise difficult. He was glad that everyone seemed to be in a hurry; no more awkward questions to answer, but people were helpful enough and smiled benevolently at his Yorkshire accent. While he waited for the overnight sleeper to York he went into Lyons Corner House and ordered fish and chips, but found he was unable to eat it, the food was too rich for his starved stomach, he drank the tea but reluctantly left most of the food, it made him feel sick.

On the train, he found a corner seat, pulled his cap over his eyes and, in spite of the hard seats, slept until York, when it was time to change for Northallerton. It was just getting light when he changed again for Masham.

The church clock was striking twelve, when the branch line train chugged into the station.

'Well, this is where it all began,' Joseph said to himself. 'Darlington, Richmond, France, Scotland, Maidstone and London; I never expected to travel so far in all my life. I never even expected to get as far as London. Not that I have seen much of any of those places, and I have no real desire to go back to them.' He had to make several stops, to catch his breath, as he walked up the hill.

He was delighted to see George Calvert, his cricketing friend, outside the station. George stared at him in disbelief, turned on his heel, his empty sleeve flapping against his side, and was gone. Joseph's greeting died on his lips, the hand that he had raised to shake his friend's dropped. As he staggered down the road toward his home, he fancied that people glared after him and pointed, backs were turned and doors closed.

*

'Joseph, Joseph, my dear son, is't really thee? Come in, come in; we've been hoping but not expecting thee; there have been rumours.' His mother broke down in tears of joy as she hugged him to her.

The family sat down together. Joseph realised how long he

222

had been gone when he saw his now grown up brother, Jacob, eighteen, with the calloused hands of a working man and Hannah wearing long skirts and her hair up in a new fashion.

'How was it in prison?' Hannah asked as she put her arm round his shoulder.

He put his head in his hands and was silent for a few minutes. 'I'll not say, 'tis behind me now, let's talk of other things.'

Over the evening meal, he found that all was not well in either the village or his family. Many of the men of the village were dead or injured in the war; families had been wiped out by the Spanish Influenza. The Metcalf family had been spared the flu because no-one would associate with them; many thought that Joseph had taken the coward's way out by refusing to fight.

Joseph went to bed, with a heavy heart, in the room he shared with his brother. His family had also had to take the consequences for his convictions. Again, he wondered if he had made the right decision. He missed his old friend Norman; he needed to hear his wise counsel.

He was tired, so tired, sleeping until midday. Walking into the village, he found that of the cricket team there were only two that were sound in wind and limb. Of the others, a couple were in wheelchairs, paralysed from shrapnel wounds in the back. Some had terrible facial injuries and were still being treated in hospital, hoping to have the new surgery that was being developed. One had been gassed and could scarcely breathe, and one was in the asylum, having lost his mind. Others were dead, either in the trenches or of the flu. Anyone alive didn't want to see him, made excuses, found they had urgent things to do. At the cricket pavilion, he found it shabby, paint peeling, pitch overgrown and, rubbing the dirty windows, he could see inside the whites of all the team hanging as they had been left as men had been called away.

Joseph found that no-one wanted to know him; he didn't even hear from Daniel. He tried going to his house, but the effort made him breathless. He had to turn back.

*

A few days after returning home, his cough worsened, his limbs hurt, his head ached, he was running a high fever; he shivered and it hurt to breathe. The doctor was sent for. He took his pulse, checked his breathing rates and shook his head.

'Come through London, did he? He's picked up the Spanish flu. Nothing I can do for him. He needs good nursing. Sponge him down to lower his temperature, give him lots of fluids to drink. Inhalations might help, but you must pray. He may pull through, but in his weakened condition... I'll come back in a few days to check up on him. It's up to you now. Keep the windows open; fresh air can help, but keep him warm, maybe a nip of brandy, keep his heart going.'

Jacob was sent to buy the brandy; no-one in that house had ever drunk any alcohol before. Mother and Hannah took turns looking after Joseph, sleeping in his room, keeping him warm, sitting him up to help his breathing, getting him to take sips of water and brandy. He developed pneumonia; the doctor came every day but couldn't help.

He fell into semi-consciousness and delirium, shocking Mother and Hannah by talking about the prison cells he had been in, crying out, suddenly sitting up and falling back, the nightmares of his recent reality coming back to haunt him. They couldn't really believe what they heard. His breathing became shallower and faster, his pulse thinner and weaker, his temperature soared. He lost consciousness.

In the early hours of a soft spring morning, the blackbird singing at the top of a nearby tree, his mother and sister holding his hands, Joseph took his last, difficult breath.

*

A letter arrived from a Corporal Jones for Joseph, with a pencil drawing of the tower of Richmond Castle. Joseph's mother sent it back, marking the envelope 'deceased'.

Chapter 38

Post-script 1

The new War Memorial was inscribed with carvings of strange animals, an eagle, a lamb, a pelican and a few human figures. The rain dripped off the hats of John Scott and his son Matthew as they stood outside the village church; Matthew rested on his crutches.

'I suppose all those figures mean something, but I'm blessed if I know what it is.'

'There is Paul's name, Pa, but why do we never see women's names on memorials like this?'

'They decided only to list those who died in combat. If you weren't a combatant you didn't get listed, regardless of the manner of your death.'

'Not only did the war take Paul, but also the two women of my life: dear Annie who died of the infection she got from one of her patients, and Ma died of a broken heart; losing Paul, not knowing where I was and then Annie dying, it finished her.'

'Thousands of men were wounded or gassed. Others, like you, have been broken by being locked up by the Germans for most of the war. The treatment you got in the German Prisoner of War Hospital was terrible. Look at you; you were only at the Front for such a short time before you were captured. You all gave your lives, but because you weren't killed you didn't get your names on memorials, either. You got a medal; a lot of good that will do you.'

'Well, at least it is some sort of recognition, and some say I was lucky to have avoided having months or even years at the Front; but the conditions we had to endure were hardly the height of luxury.'

'Huh, some say that the lucky ones were the ones that died; they don't have to live the rest of their lives as cripples like you.'

'It's not just us with broken limbs; what about the gassed men who will never be able to work again? They can hardly breathe, and the ones with shell-shock? They'll never leave the asylums; no longer able to look after themselves. They say that some are gibbering idiots with their minds gone; no memorials for them either.'

'War is a despicable thing; how can we make the politicians realise that there must be other ways of resolving these problems? I hope and pray that we never see the like again.' John looked worried.

'Don't hold your breath; have you seen the papers? The way the present lot are going on, it wouldn't surprise me if we didn't have another one before too long.'

'May God help us. But I fear you may be right. The newspapers are full of war gossip.'

As they turned to go into the church, the hymn that was being sung was *"Fight the Good Fight"*. Matthew knelt on the hassock, next to his father and wept.

Chapter 39

Post-script 2

They drove for many miles though the French countryside, in the little black Austin Seven, Seamus' pride. It had taken a while to find the place as it all looked so different; the mud had gone but huge craters remained, now covered with wild flowers; grass grew and poppies bloomed; few reminders of what had been. The roads had been rebuilt, many houses were mended, gardens and fields cultivated. Piles of rusted, twisted metal, live shells that had been dug up by farmers, were heaped by the roadside for collection. It seemed that life was returning to this country that had been so badly damaged. But the landscape was dotted with huge cemeteries; row upon row of white headstones, thousands and thousands, apparently all the same; acres and acres of them, as far as the eye could see. When they got up close, they could see the names and ranks of those who were buried there; so many of them, it was quite over-whelming. Among the headstones, small groups of people wandered; individuals stopped, read the inscriptions, laid flowers or little crosses, cried, knelt or stood quietly, thinking, remembering.

*

They had had to stop to study the map, ask directions, but Seamus eventually found the Chateau that had been the hospital where they had worked. He and Molly took turns pushing Daniel's wheelchair along the narrow paths. There was a little cemetery there that had been set aside; eventually they found the place. They left Daniel in his chair, looking at a small, carved headstone. He took his crutches from their clip and painfully stood himself up.

'Annie, I promised I would come back but I'm afraid I can't kneel and say that *Avé* as I promised, sorry; but I have found the place where you are lying.' He carefully sat himself down in the wheelchair again, took out his mouth-organ and slowly and quietly played both verses of the *Londonderry Air*.

'Rest in peace, my little Annie. I'll never forget you.' Tears coursed down his face as he held Annie's locket.

Seamus and Molly wandered round the small graveyard in the grounds of the abandoned, deserted building, reading the engravings and remembering the men and a few women, British, French and German, patients and staff, whose names they saw. They could hear the music in the distance and waited for Daniel for as long as he needed and eventually returned hand in hand; Molly pink with embarrassment and pride.

'We have a big favour to ask you, Daniel.' He looked up, he nodded to Molly. He thrust his hand into his pocket and turned Susie's stone round in his hand. 'We wanted to ask you while we are here.' She twisted her wedding ring round her finger, 'Please, will you be godfather to our child?' Molly smoothed her big belly. 'It would mean so much to us.'

The End

The Richmond Sixteen

John (Bert) Brocklesby

C. Cartwright

E.C. Cryer

Norman Gaudie

Clarence Hall

S. Hall

C.R. Jackson

William Law

Alfred Martlew

Alfred Mayers

Leonard Renton

J.W. Routledge

C. A. Senior

E.S. Spencer

Name Unknown

Richmond Castle showing cell block on the right

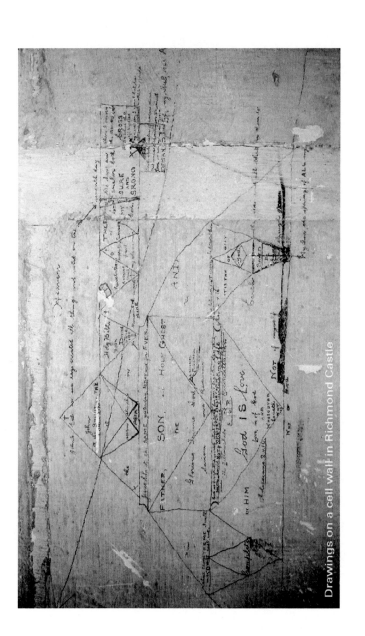

Drawings on a cell wall in Richmond Castle

Afterword

The story of Joseph is almost entirely true. The 'Richmond Sixteen' did in fact experience most of the events that Joseph experienced. The details of his story are based on the memoirs of Bert Brocklesby (unpublished but available to read at Friends House library). (The story of the Brocklesby brothers has been told in a book *We Will Not Fight* by Will Ellsworth) also *The Letters of a Prisoner* by Corder Catchpoll, *The Soul of a Skunk* by George Baker, the publications of the Peace Pledge Union, and a personal conversation with Norman Gaudie's son, Martyn.

The story of Annie is developed from the writings of Vera Brittan and the diaries of Mairi Chisholm and Elsie Knocker in *Elsie and Mairi Go to War* by Diane Atkinson; original diaries are available to be read in the London Imperial War Museum. It is also based on my own experiences working as a nurse.

The story of Daniel is based on many written by serving soldiers during WWI, too numerous to itemise, and my own imagination.

During WWI about 16,000 claimed Conscientious Objector status, many of these had to spend much of the war in prison for either refusing to register or for refusing to accept the Tribunals' decisions. Whereas none of them were actually shot, in spite of that being the sentence of many, 73 did die as a result of the ill-treatment they received at the hands of the military or of the prison authorities.

Over 3,000 serving men were convicted of Desertion and sentenced to death, of these 306 were shot, by fellow soldiers.

It is interesting to note that less than two decades later, during WWII, conscientious objectors who registered were treated entirely differently. Norman's son Martyn, at his 'Board', was given the choice between farming, teaching or The Friends Ambulance Unit and chose to go into farming and stayed in it all his life. However, absolutists who refused to register were still treated very badly.

In 1943, Winston Churchill was quoted as saying: "The rights which have been granted in this war and the last to conscientious objectors are well known and are a definite part of British policy. Anything in the nature of persecution, victimization or man-hunting is odious to the British people".

Throughout the world men and women are still being imprisoned for their conscientious beliefs and many will die at the hands of various authorities.

It is also sobering that in 2001 the World Council of Churches declared a 'Decade to Overcome Violence' and the United Nations a 'Decade to Create a Culture of Peace.'

Richmond Castle has an interactive display about the 'Richmond 16' and a dedicated Garden of Remembrance featuring sixteen groups of Yew trees, in the Cock-Pit. The Castle is in the care of English Heritage.

More information about Conscientious Objection is available from:-

> www.quaker.org.uk; (Quakers)
> www.ppu.org.uk; (Peace Pledge Union)
> www.iwm.org.uk; (Imperial War Museum)

Acknowledgements

Of the quotations in Chapter 8: the first is part of the Quaker Peace Testimony in a declaration to Charles II, 1660; the second is part of the Epistle of the Elders of Baltby, 1656; and the third from *Christian Discipline vol. 2 Church government,* 1906. The quotation in Chapter 12 is part of a letter from the Meeting of Sufferings to the House of Commons, 1915; all are reproduced with kind permission of Britain Yearly Meeting of The Religious Society of Friends (Quakers).

I would like to thank my college tutors Glen Davis and Tom Tyler who supported my interest in the subject and the help of Lorraine Cooper who worked at Richmond Castle and showed me the cells where the COs were housed.

Also David Swann and Henry Shukman, who I met in Crete and who told me to stop reading and encouraged me to put pen to paper.

The Wensleydale Writers gave encouragement and suggestions, for which many thanks.

Thanks also to Jo MacDonald for the cover design and Mike Fenwick for the cover picture; and to Kerry LeGaloudec who translated the French and German for me.

And last but not least many thanks for the support of my children and the loving encouragement of my dear Friend and companion, Henry Williams who didn't live long enough to see this in print.

About the Author

Hazel Townesend was brought up in the outskirts of South East London and after a period of living in Oxford and then the USA she returned to Oxfordshire.

A move to North Yorkshire followed where she lived, near to Richmond, for 25 years. After retiring from the Health Service she took her degree in Cultural Studies. It was while researching for a project, 'A Culture of Resistance', that she became interested in the Conscientious Objectors of WWI, who were incarcerated in Richmond Castle.

Hazel has been a Quaker for thirty years.

She has recently moved back to the Vale of The White Horse, Wantage.

She has four children and two grandchildren.

This is her first book.

www.redcappublishing.com